Trying to Hate the Player

A Sweet Romantic Comedy, Love on the Court

Tia Souders

Manufactured in the United States of America

www.tiasouders.com

First Edition : February 2019

Second Edition: February 2021

To my husband.

Your support lifts me up and keeps
me going in everything I do.

Thank you.

CHAPTER ONE

Emmett

Emmett wiped the sweat from his brow before it dripped into his eyes. With a grunt, he raised his water bottle and chugged the icy contents, draining it. Garrison, the head coach of the Pumas—the newest team in the National Basketball Association—screamed a variety of commands at them, which all came down to one thing. They needed to get their crap together.

The buzzer went off, signaling the end of their time-out. Garrison shooed them away, his face contorted in frustration.

Emmett jogged out to midcourt, thinking of the long, cool shower awaiting him at the end of the game. He needed it. He was ripe with sweat, his muscles fatigued. It had been a rough second half, and his body hadn't taken the abuse well. But before he could relax, they had a little business to take care of. They had to win.

As the rookies of the basketball world, the Pumas had something to prove. Making it to the play-offs was amazing, but going all the way to the NBA Finals would solidify their status as serious contenders.

He glanced at the scoreboard.

It wasn't looking good.

Three minutes to go, and they were down by eighteen. Dang, he wanted this.

It wasn't about the money or even the fame. It was about validation. He wanted the Pumas to be taken seriously. They'd worked their ever-loving butts off, and he craved a victory for them. All of them.

Okay, he'd be lying if he said he didn't want the NBA Championship ring or the Larry O'Brien trophy. They were coveted by any serious player. The trophy would be invaluable to the team—a symbol of all their hard work, their talent. At two feet tall, it was made of nearly sixteen pounds of sterling silver with a 24-karat-gold overlay and features a life-size basketball falling into a net. His best friend and teammate, Dean, and his new fiancée, Callie, could keep her giant Tiffany & Co. ring. Call him shallow, but Emmett wanted his diamond-encrusted championship ring and that trophy. And he intended to get them.

He took his place on the court and glanced at the stands, his eyes immediately snagging on the same spot it always did. Frowning, he realized for the first time that Jinny, Dean's little sister, was nowhere in sight. Her usual spot beside Callie sat empty. Odd. She rarely missed a game.

Even if it was unusual, why should he care? It was none of his business whether she came to their games or not.

Yeah, keep telling yourself that.

Emmett shook his head, trying to clear his thoughts. His eyes zoned in on the ball as the Celtics took it out. He defended his man, and when he shot and missed, a Puma rebounded.

He caught a pass from Dean and pivoted, but he got stuck and gave it away. Moving under the hoop, he regained possession, took a shot, and scored.

Shaking his fist in the air, Emmett hauled butt downcourt as the Celtics took control. The action slowed to a subtle dance as they passed, volleying the ball back and forth between them. Emmett defended his opponent, raising his arms and waving them in his face. When he made a poor pass, Emmett leapt in front of it and stripped the ball.

He charged downcourt, homing in on the hoop. Almost there.

He lifted his arms, jumping—airborne as he took the dunk. But something wasn't right. His left leg bowed. He was weightless as the ball left his fingertips, but the trajectory was off. The sickening *POP* echoed off his eardrum. A machete sliced through his knee. Excruciating pain shot down his leg as he fell to the ground and rolled onto his back, clutching his knee to his chest while the stabbing continued.

Fresh agony ripped through him when he heard the sharp sound of the whistle. The game stopped.

"Emmett," Coach called out. He appeared by his side, along with Gabriel Swanson, the director of strength and conditioning for the team.

Swanson knelt next to him. "Does this hurt?" He probed the muscles around Emmett's knee, eliciting a hiss. "Try and bend it."

Wincing, all Emmett could do was groan. Fire blazed through his muscles.

"Can you push on my hand?" Swanson asked, placing his palm under the sole of Emmett's shoe.

Sweat beaded on Emmett's brow. He tried to listen, moving his leg only a hair, but he had nothing left to give. Knives turned to needles, followed by a prickling sensation from his knee down.

Coach Garrison and Swanson exchanged a knowing look while Emmett's heart raced. *No, please. Don't say it.*

"What is it?" he rasped.

"Let's get you up and out of here," Swanson said, ignoring his question.

Emmett gritted his teeth as dread clogged his throat. Seconds felt like hours as reality hit. He was injured—out of the game.

His teammates huddled around him. Coach and Swanson backed off, allowing Emmett space to try to stand.

This couldn't be happening. Not to him. Not now.

He rose on one foot, his hands planted on the ground, futilely trying to place his weight on his left leg, but the muscle had turned to putty. In the blink of an eye, his worst nightmare had come true.

His insides quaked, and a hollow ache filled his chest as two of his teammates placed Emmett's arms over their shoulders, helping him stand and walk off the court. Fans cheered, but the applause stung. There was nothing to celebrate.

Emmett stared at nothing while the scoreboard counted down the time. Seconds disappeared along with Emmett's dreams. He couldn't blink, couldn't move, couldn't think. All he could focus on, all he saw, when the buzzer sounded, was the score.

They lost.

His stomach plummeted. Hope was gone, replaced by the sound of the medic's voice as he turned to Emmett, his expression somber. "I think it's a torn ACL. We need to get you to the orthopedist. I'd expect surgery."

Jinny

Today was the best day of Jinny's life. All her hard work, all the late nights, all the blood, sweat and tears had paid off. Finally.

Jinny traversed the city streets in her old beater, Betsy, a Ford that was manufactured roughly around the time she was born. But hey, who was counting? She and Betsy shared a lot of the same attributes. They were loyal, a little rough around the edges, likely to make obscene noises from time to time, and classy (despite the noise thing). She would've led with *dependable*, but that might've been pushing it a bit, considering that Betsy's health had declined.

The traffic was fairly light, despite being the weekend, for which she was grateful. It meant she'd be home in minutes. Then she and her best friend, Callie, could pop their best bottle of wine—which was probably a six-dollar bottle from the little grocer around the corner—and celebrate her accomplishments. A few nights ago, the bubbly they'd opened was to toast Callie's engagement to Jinny's brother, but tonight was all about Jinny. She and Callie were really moving up in the world, making something out of themselves.

This must be what adulting felt like.

She stopped at a red light and pinched her forearm. "Crap, that hurt." She winced, but the stinging pain meant this was real. She wasn't dreaming—like the hundreds of times before. As of today, she was officially a Sports Certified Specialist. In a few weeks, she would no longer be a starving sports therapy resident at the University of Pittsburgh. Instead, she would be the physical therapist for the Pittsburgh Pumas. She'd already gotten the call, and she could hardly believe it.

Snatching her phone out of the cup holder, she sent Callie a quick text. "You home? I have great news!"

Callie texted back, "Yup. But something happened to Emmett at the game today. Wait till I tell you."

Jinny grimaced and set her phone down as the light turned green. Like she cared about anything having to do with Emmett Hall. He was everything she detested in a man: arrogant, self-centered, entitled, a womanizer, and a player—oh, did she say arrogant?

Callie knew darn well that Jinny didn't get along with him, so why would she think she'd care?

He probably broke his man-parts on one of his many conquests. Or maybe he chipped a nail today at the game. Who knew?

Now that she thought about it, the only downside to her new position would be having to see, and, potentially, work with him. But none of that mattered. The trade-off was worth it. What mattered was her new job and the new title that would accompany her name. Jinny Kimball, *MS in Physical Therapy. Sports Certified Specialist, Team Physical Therapist for the Pumas.* It might be a mouthful, but it was music to her ears. Pure poetry.

She patted the dash of ol' Betsy as she drove. "Don't worry," she murmured. "I won't forget you. You've been good to me. I'll make sure you find a great home." A hissing sound escaped from somewhere in the bowels of the car, as if in response. Jinny ignored the smell of burning oil.

She parked outside the apartment she shared with Callie and sprinted up the stairs. When she reached their unit, she tried the knob and found it wasn't locked. She hurried inside and hung her purse on the hook by the door.

A noise came from the kitchen, so Jinny spoke loud enough for Callie to hear as she kicked off her shoes. "You'll never guess what I got today," she said in a sing-song voice.

When she received no response, she hurried into the kitchen. Their apartment was basically a box. They had a sizeable living room attached to a quaint kitchen and two bedrooms, so she didn't have to go far to find her friend.

Callie stood at the breakfast counter, pouring herself a glass of wine. When she glanced up, she smiled. "Oh, hey, there's—"

"Fabulous," Jinny said, snatching up the glass. "I was hoping we could open a bottle. Wait, you don't know yet, do you? Because I wanted to tell you myself. Please, tell me you don't know and that's not why you have the wine out."

"No." Callie shook her head, her forehead furrowing.

"What in the world are you blabbing about?" Dean exited the bathroom off the hall and headed toward her, his dark hair still damp from what she assumed was a shower.

Jinny grimaced. "Must you walk around our apartment half-naked?" she asked, eyeing his bare chest in disgust.

"Callie likes me this way." Dean winked at Callie, and Jinny groaned.

"You two are so nauseating. Tell me why you aren't at your giant penthouse apartment again?"

"It's undergoing renovations. We're making it more suited to both our tastes," he said.

"Ah, that's right. Anything to please the lady. Am I right?" Jinny smirked. Ever since they got engaged, she poked fun at them any chance she got. Though, truth be told, she couldn't have been more thrilled for them. It wasn't every day your best friend was going to become your sister-in-law.

"Actually, it's good you're here. I can share the news with you both." Jinny did a little jig. Normally, she was not the squealing, gushing, giggly type, but her news was just too good not to allow herself a little giddiness.

She set her wine down and fisted her hands by her side and closed her eyes. "I got my SCS test results back." She paused for dramatic effect but couldn't hold it in. "And I passed!"

Callie covered her mouth with her hand, then moved around the counter and drew Jinny into a hug. "That's amazing! I knew you could do it."

"All the work. It was all worth it," Jinny mumbled into Callie's shoulder.

When Callie took a step back, Dean grinned at her and rubbed a hand over the top of her head, obnoxiously tousling her hair. Normally, she would punch him for it, but she was too excited to care.

"That's amazing. Seriously. You'll be taking the PT world by storm," he said.

"Obviously."

"Well, we have news, too. It's about the game," Dean said.

"Wait. Wait." Jinny held up a finger. "I know that's super important, and I swear I want to hear all about it. But I have one more piece of good news to share first. Craig Bannon called me." Jinny grinned, knowing Dean would recognize the name. He was the sports general manager of the Pumas.

"Wait, isn't that...?" Callie asked.

"Yes, it is. In three weeks, I will officially be a physical therapist for the Pittsburgh Pumas." She jumped up and screamed, leaping at Dean and squeezing him with all the strength her wiry arms had to offer.

"That's...uh...amazing," Callie said, but she sounded less than enthused.

Jinny pulled back from Dean and frowned as she glanced to her best friend, who shifted nervously on her feet. "I mean, technically, they're giving me a chance to prove myself. I won't have a contract until the end of the year, but as long as I do an amazing job, the position is mine."

Dean chuckled. "Three weeks, huh?"

Jinny put her hands on her hips, taking in the way Callie's eyes darted around the room before landing on hers. *"Yeah.* Why are you guys acting so weird?"

Callie licked her lips. Something was up. "Um. We think we know who your first patient might be."

Jinny scrunched her nose. What were they... Then it hit her. *Him.*

"Hey, there, *Doc*," the familiar voice said.

She froze. His voice was like ice water, penetrating her

excitement.

"He just got back from the hospital," Callie explained, but Jinny barely heard her.

Anger burned hot in her veins. She clamped her mouth shut, needing to contain the nasty things threatening to spew from her lips. Slowly, ever so slowly, she turned around.

CHAPTER TWO

Jinny

A sneer curled her lips as she took him in like a platoon assessing the enemy. Emmett Hall towered over her, with his perfectly white teeth, his crop of sandy hair, and his disgustingly bright hazel eyes. The only thing different about him was the pair of crutches wedged underneath his muscled arms.

"I'm not a doctor. I'm a therapist," she said.

"Ah, that's right. To be a doctor, you have to actually

know what you're doing."

Her eyes widened, but she deflected his words with a smile. An experienced soldier never lets the enemy know when they've been hit. She slid her gaze down to the brace on his knee, like she hadn't a care in the world.

Callie came up beside her, folding her arms over her chest and glancing at Emmett. "That's what I tried to tell you. Emmett got injured at the game today."

"What's the injury?" Jinny asked, even though she already knew by the looks of him. It was one of the injuries that would require her to work with him the longest.

Emmett's gaze focused on her in challenge. "Torn ACL."

Crap

∞∞∞

Karma was a cruel mistress.

Of course, on the day Jinny got her dream job, the one person in this world she couldn't stand would become her full-time patient.

She'd be lucky if she made it past her first day.

The universe must hate her. Maybe she unwittingly ran over a cat with ol' Betsy or shoved an elderly person into traffic. Maybe this was payback for ignoring the Bird Lady in the city last week. She always gave Jinny the creeps, talking about the end of the world, but maybe Jinny should've emptied her pockets into the paper cup and given her every last dime she had, because it would've been worth it to not see Emmett on a daily basis for the next seven to nine months.

"Looks like we'll be working together." Emmett winked.

"I swear, if this wasn't a serious injury, I'd think you did this on purpose."

"Yeah. Don't flatter yourself, sweetheart."

He hobbled toward the refrigerator on his crutches, and Jinny's skin prickled as her gaze tracked his movement. When he opened the door to peer at the contents, she muttered, "Please, feel free to make yourself at home."

"Don't mind if I do." He grabbed a beer from the shelf, popped the top, and took a long pull.

She stared aghast as he nearly drained one of the craft beers she'd bought from the new microbrewery downtown. It was her last one. She had been saving it for a special occasion. Like today.

She ground her teeth so hard, it was a miracle her molars didn't turn to dust. "I hope you plan on replacing that."

Emmett lowered the bottle and swallowed loudly, then looked at the label and shrugged. "Whatever. Here, you can have the rest."

He handed her the nearly empty beer, and the muscle above her eye began to twitch in response. Gripping the cold bottle, she thought of all the ways she'd love to hurt him.

"Okay." Dean clapped his hands, a poor attempt at diffusing the tension, and shot her a warning glare. "I'll get more before I stop by tomorrow. In the meantime, maybe Emmett and I should get going."

"Great idea."

Emmett flashed her a brilliant smile. "I guess I'll be seeing you around, slim."

Jinny inhaled through her nose. Deep breaths, she told herself. *Deep. Calming. Breaths.*

Dean threw on a t-shirt and kissed Callie goodbye, then he headed out the door, with Emmett trailing behind. Once they were out of earshot, Jinny turned to Callie and squeezed her eyes closed as she tried to translate her monumental levels of annoyance into words. "How?"

"He went for a shot, and something happened. His knee just gave out."

When she opened her eyes again, Callie shrugged, and Jinny had to clench her fists in an effort not to lunge forward and shake her. How could this be happening? Why her? Why now?

"When is his surgery?" Jinny asked, her head spinning.

"He saw the orthopedist briefly today. He'll have to do

a week of pre-op therapy first, so his surgery is a week from tomorrow."

Jinny scrubbed her hands over her face and laughed. "So, he will literally be ready for PT right around my start date."

Jinny threw her hands up and took a swig of her wine. She had hoped he'd start therapy earlier. Maybe, then, there would have been a chance of his continuing therapy with someone else. But now her chances of pawning him off on a coworker were slim.

"Maybe they won't have you working with the team right away." Callie offered with a bland smile. But her expression told Jinny that even she didn't believe what she was saying.

"Fat chance. I'm certified and have a master's in science. It's not like I'm a fresh undergrad. Trust me, they'll throw me right in there. I already spoke with Bannon today. They have a couple part-time guys who work with the team at home, but they have yet to find a full-time therapist."

"What about the training and performance guy? What's his name?"

"Gabriel Swanson?" Jinny asked, and Callie nodded in response. "Nope. I mean, if they hadn't hired me, I'm sure he'd step in, but his main job is focused on training and conditioning, not working the injured list. He gets them ready, keeps them at their peak performance, and focuses on injury *prevention*. I'll do some preventive care, too, but rehabilitation will be my full-time gig. This is all me."

Callie stepped forward and patted her on the arm. "Well, you were bound to work together at some point. At least you'll have the upper hand, right? You're the therapist, calling the shots. He's kind of in a vulnerable position. He'll be relying on you."

Jinny pursed her lips and murmured her agreement. If only. With Emmett, she never felt like she had the upper hand. It was one of the gazillion reasons she avoided him whenever she could. She doubted the word *vulnerable* was even in his vocabulary.

"Regardless, we need to celebrate," Callie said, interrupting her thoughts. "You're amazing, and I'm so proud of you." She raised her glass, and Jinny followed suit. "To my best friend. To you," Callie said. "You're the smartest, most driven woman I know, and you are going to kick butt at your new job."

Jinny grinned. "And no more counting change for fast food. I'll finally make some real money."

"Yes, no more Ramen, and may Betsy be put to rest."

"Hallelujah," Jinny said, then frowned. "Wait. I like Betsy."

Callie laughed and clinked her glass to Jinny's. "Hey, wait. I have these fancy chocolates Dean bought me." She scurried off to the cupboard and returned with an ornate wooden box. When she lifted the lid, Jinny inhaled the sugary scent and her mouth watered. The tops of the chocolates were painted and swirled with beautiful designs. They looked more like mini paintings than food.

Jinny plucked one out with glee. The only thing better than fancy food was free food. Man, it would be hard getting used to actually having livable wages.

"Must be nice to have an NBA star for a fiancé," Jinny said.

"It has its perks."

Jinny snickered and popped the chocolate in her mouth.

"I don't understand why you and Emmett hate each other so much," Callie said. "When the team first formed, it seemed like you two might hit it off."

Jinny allowed the chocolate to melt in her mouth, taking time to enjoy the lush flavor before thoughts of Emmett could turn it to mud.

She thought back to last year's end-of-season barbeque at Coach Garrison's house. Emmett, much to her surprise, had flown solo. Devoid of the estrogen that usually clung to his arm, Emmett had seemed more charming and approachable, so Jinny had decided to get to know him better. He and Dean were becoming close, so it would've been nice if they all could become friends. Call her crazy, but there was even a fleeting moment that Jinny thought maybe they could be more than that.

They'd hit it off. Other than his obvious good looks, she found his ambition attractive and thought they might have a lot in common. She caught a minor glimpse of the man behind the ball and liked what she saw. For a moment, she had imagined his arrogance was all an act. Maybe he wasn't a player on and off the court. She thought he was far more than that.

When he returned, after taking a rather long time getting them drinks—which she now surmised was due to getting sidetracked by a pretty blonde—he proved her wrong. After a strained conversation about where they saw themselves in the future, she filled him in on her residency at the University of Pittsburgh. She had just received her master's in sports therapy, was putting in time as a resident at the university, and would be studying for the SCS later that year. She confided in him that she was a contender for the sports therapist position for the Pumas. If she proved herself and earned her certification, she was a shoo-in. Or so she hoped.

She remembered how he'd snorted in response. *Snorted!*

Then, killing any chance of friendship with one solid blow, he said, "Yeah, well. Some of us *earned* our spot at the top."

His words hit like a sucker punch to the gut, and her

smile faded. "Excuse me?" Surely, she'd misheard him or misconstrued the meaning behind his words.

"Well, we can't all have connections like you. I mean, a brother who plays for the NBA team you're applying to, and a father who is the athletic director of the University of Pittsburgh? Come on. Like you're not going to get that job. If the team wanted somebody with merit, they could have anyone. Surely, there are more qualified people with more experience."

She flinched. Ice filled her veins. Any interest she'd felt before was extinguished the second the words left his mouth.

"My connections will hardly be the thing to get me the job."

Emmett merely raised a brow, like he didn't believe her, and took a sip of his beer.

Heat flooded her cheeks as she clenched her fists, restraining herself from beating him with them. "I have a master's in physical therapy. Not to mention, I've been working with athletes for over a year in my residency. It'll be more than two years by the time I get my sports certification, a title that under two percent of physical therapists in the *entire country* have earned. Under two percent," she repeated. "So, no, I won't be getting that position because of my family. And you know what? You can take your assumptions and your holier than thou attitude and eat them, you a-class jerk."

Emmett's eyes flashed with an emotion she didn't recognize. Not surprising, considering she hardly knew him, but his arrogance was appalling. His gentleman act had crumbled to reveal his true character.

She brushed past him, hating how humiliated she felt. He was the one that should be embarrassed. Nevertheless, his words hit their mark. They stung. It was her reward for dropping her guard with someone like him.

What was that obnoxious saying her mother always used? If it looks like a duck, walks like a duck, and quacks like a frickin' duck, it's a duck. Prior to the barbeque, Emmett had acted like a player and a womanizing jerk, so she should've known that was exactly who he was. No amount of showboating could change that, and ever since that afternoon at the party, he had shown her nothing less.

Maybe what he said wouldn't have stung so bad if a tiny part of Jinny didn't fear it was true. Maybe his assumptions wouldn't have hurt if there were no basis to them. At the end of the day, Jinny couldn't deny who her brother and father were. There was nothing she could do about that. All she could do during college, and in the two years after, was work her tail off in the hopes that if the opportunity presented itself, then she would have truly earned it. And she had done that.

So, why did his words still haunt her?

"Do I really need to list my reasons?" Jinny asked, pushing her thoughts of that sticky summer day aside. "He doesn't like me because I call him out on his crap. I'm not one of his little concubines that follow him around like a sad-eyed puppy. *I* don't like *him* because he is cocky and way too full of himself. The man thinks he walks on water. He has a new woman on his arm every time you turn around, and he's beyond rude." She flicked her gaze toward the empty beer bottle.

Callie frowned. "I don't kno—"

"He's degrading and a jerk. He's everything I can't stand about the male sex. Everyone can see that."

Callie eyed her over the rim of her glass. "Uh-huh."

"I don't know why it's so surprising. You've been around him."

"I have. And he's not that bad. Maybe you just need to get to know him."

Jinny shook her head. "No. I don't need to get to know him. And I don't plan to. I'll be a professional. I'll help rehabilitate his knee to as good as new because I am amazing, and because I need to prove myself to Garrison. And the sooner I help Emmett heal, the sooner he'll be on his way, so I can continue to do my job without that parasite sucking the lifeblood out of me."

Callie chuckled. "Wow, okay."

Jinny flashed her a smug smile and took a sip of her

drink.

"You know," Callie said, "maybe the problem is that you two are too much alike."

"Say that again, and you're dead to me."

CHAPTER THREE

Emmett

E mmett sunk down onto his bed and leaned his crutches up against his nightstand. With a sigh, he bent forward and unstrapped the brace from his knee. Most of the pain had subsided into discomfort, but it still scared him.

He swung his legs up and under the blankets, being careful not to bend his left knee. Once he leaned back against the headboard, the tension in his back melted away.

If he remained this stiff until surgery, they might as well work on his spine, too.

He growled and turned on the television, flicking through the channels on autopilot, and stopped on the highlights reel on ESPN. Bracing himself, he watched for several minutes before they started on today's game. His likeness stared back at him. He was used to seeing himself on the big screen, but as they replayed that fateful moment in today's game, his stomach clenched tight. His palms grew damp as he leapt into the air, ball flying to the hoop, then came the sickening moment his knee gave out.

He gasped on the ground, clutching his knee in agony. Several minutes later, his teammates helped him off the court.

Emmett's heart thudded in his chest. Swallowing, he flicked the television off as the sports news commentators started speculating on his injury and what it would mean for his career.

He couldn't listen.

The Pumas wouldn't be making the final round of playoffs, and he'd injured himself. Talk about tough breaks. Though, he supposed he should be grateful. It could've been worse. This could've happened at the beginning of the season. At least they were done for the summer.

But the thought did little to penetrate his grim mood.

He'd researched ACL tears and recovery time and

consulted the orthopedist. Six months he'd be out, which meant he'd not only miss the beginning of next season, but he wouldn't be able to train and condition this summer either.

Surely, an athlete of his stature would be an exception, right? The thought was a feeble attempt at assuaging his anxiety, and he knew it. Still, he'd have the best care money could buy. That had to count for something. He could whittle that time down. Make it five months instead of six. It was imperative he get back to the game as soon as possible. He loved basketball too much not to play. He'd lived and breathed the sport since the age of two. How could he go without? More than half a year of sitting on the sidelines was a death sentence.

There was only one option. He'd heal faster than most. He'd make sure of it. All he needed to do was keep his focus.

But that was easier said than done if Jinny Kimball would be at the helm of his care. *Of all the luck...*

His thoughts flickered to her, and he replayed their confrontation in her apartment. The glint of anger in her eyes at the news that Emmett would be among her first patients was unmistakable.

He couldn't blame her for being irritated. Last summer, when he "cooled things off" at the Pumas end-of-season barbecue, he had been particularly ruthless. He'd gone to the party hoping she was there. It was the entire reason he'd gone stag. The brown-eyed beauty had caught his eye on more than one occasion, so when he sought her out and they'd clicked, he'd been pleased.

It wasn't just her petite figure or the long dark hair and chocolate eyes that held his attention. Her appeal went way beyond looks. She was freakishly smart, though she didn't flaunt it. Instead, she had a quiet intelligence he caught glimpses of through conversation. And whether it was the fact that her brother also played for the Pumas, or because Jinny was entirely difficult to impress, she wasn't instantly wooed by his NBA star status. In fact, it didn't much impress her at all. Unlike the other girls, who were always vying for his attention, she wasn't out for the title of NBA-star girlfriend. And she couldn't care less about his money. It only took twenty minutes of conversation with her to surmise she was content living off her paltry residency wages and calling her shoebox of an apartment home. Jinny Kimball, simply put, was a simple woman who enjoyed the little things in life. And he loved it.

Until he bumped into Dean at the bar and was on the receiving end of the not-so-subtle talk. Dean made it clear his sister was absolutely off-limits. And if he didn't back off, Emmett got the impression Dean would have him by the— let's just say, Emmett valued his reproductive parts. Even more, Emmett valued the team. His friendship with Dean aside, Emmett would never jeopardize their performance on the court. The Pumas had come out of the gate hard. They had taken the NBA by storm and had exceeded everyone's expectations. No way would he mess with that. Not for a woman. Not for anything. No matter how badly he wanted Jinny.

So, when he returned to her at the party, he'd ripped the bandage off fast. He said the nastiest thing he could think of to repulse her.

It worked.

Though what Emmett hadn't expected—what surprised him—was how bad it hurt to watch her walk away. He still couldn't make sense of it. Maybe because it was the first time he'd met a woman that seemed interested in him —not the captain of the high school basketball team, or the Boston College star, or the Puma. *Him.*

Now, his injury and her new position as the Pumas sports therapist would thrust them together for weeks on end. Months.

He was completely screwed.

Six months of keeping his hands off of her, despite the fact that hers would be all over him during their sessions. Months on end of refraining from kissing her soft lips. Weeks of enduring her witty retorts and biting comments, which he secretly loved. It would be six months of pure torture.

He'd better brush up on his aversion techniques. Because he'd need them.

CHAPTER FOUR

Jinny

The three weeks since receiving her official SCS certification had flown by. Yesterday, Jinny bid her residency goodbye and toured the Pumas' state-of-the-art gym and physical therapy facilities. Today would be her first day as the official team therapist.

Jinny smoothed her pale-gray slacks and silk blouse. She glanced around her office, almost in disbelief. A huge plaque with the Pumas logo hung behind her desk, but the remaining space was bare, the walls painted a neutral cream. Her gaze rested on the empty wall to her right, imagining her framed credentials in a place of honor—diplomas, master's degree, SCS certification. It was surreal. She could hardly believe she had turned her dreams into reality.

Today felt like day one of the rest of her life.

She glanced down at the schedule on her newly appointed laptop. It was almost nine a.m. and the start of working hours. The first patient on her roster was Emmett. Of course, his first day of physical therapy coincided with her first one on the job.

Talk about starting your day off on the wrong foot.

She gave herself a pep talk as she waited for him to arrive. She went over his file a billion times. She knew his medical chart like the back of her hand. His prognosis was good. Treatment would be pretty standard for ACL recovery and should proceed smoothly, with nothing out of the ordinary. So, why was her stomach all tangled in knots?

Nerves were to be expected. It was her first day, and she wanted to prove herself. She wanted to show Garrison, Bannon, Swanson, and all the team staff that she was more than qualified for the job. She'd be the only female on-staff. It was both an honor and intimidating, but she had earned her rightful place behind this desk, and she'd prove it every day on the job until they handed her that shiny contract to sign.

She just needed to get through the next forty minutes without killing her first patient. Homicide was not the first impression she wanted to make.

Someone knocked on her door, and she glanced up to see Gabriel Swanson, director of strength and conditioning, her new coworker.

"Hey." Jinny plastered a smile on her face, hiding her nerves. "Come in."

"Are you comfortable? Getting acquainted with the place?"

He was an attractive man, and according to the team site, five years her senior. With short blond hair, a strong jaw, bronzed skin, and vibrant blue eyes, he looked more suited to ride some waves at a beach, rather than work in a physical therapy office in Pittsburgh.

He smiled at her as he leaned against the doorframe to her office, completely at ease.

"Absolutely. It's a tad overwhelming, but I'm excited to be here," Jinny said.

"I'm glad to have you here, too. I was beginning to think they'd never hire a full-timer and I'd be managing both positions forever. With this season's injury list, you're right in time."

"I can imagine you were swamped," Jinny said. "And

that last game was brutal. Really did a number on a couple of guys."

"Speaking of..." Gabriel craned his neck, glancing down the hall. "I think your first appointment's here."

Emmett.

Jinny's stomach twisted. Suddenly, she felt ill-equipped to face him.

Gabriel waved toward the waiting room and cupped his hands around his mouth. "Come on back. Your new therapist awaits," he hollered, clearly familiar with the team and all its members, and unfamiliar with Jinny's loathing of this particular one.

Jinny's hands fluttered over her desk. Despite waking up at the crack of dawn to ready herself for the day, she wasn't prepared. Why did he have to invite Emmett back? She'd had a plan. She was to go out and greet him, to meet him on her own terms. After all, she might be new, but this was her turf now. He was the patient, entering *her* domain. Not to mention, she needed to check her teeth, brush her hair, reapply her lip-gloss. All very important, very professional stuff. Nothing could be off when she saw Emmett. If it was, he'd call her on it, and though she prided herself on not giving a frack about whether she looked good for a man or not, she didn't need his snide remarks. Show your enemy a chink in your armor, and they'd crack it wide open.

When Gabriel turned back to her, he flashed her a

megawatt smile.

She tried to relax. Forcing her arms to hang loosely by her side, she smiled and practiced breathing in through her nose, out through her mouth. Slow, deep, calming breaths.

She had a hunch she looked crazy.

Gabriel tapped the side of her door. "Hey, maybe we could get lunch today? Talk shop? Get to know each other since we'll be working together now?"

Jinny nodded, barely hearing him as her gaze locked on the man who appeared behind him. At nearly six foot seven, he towered over Gabriel. The sight was almost comical. He was the Hulk, and Gabriel was a meager human. If Emmett so much as leaned into him, Gabriel would topple over like a domino.

She mustered her best smile. "Sure, Gabriel, I'd love that. Lunch sounds great."

"Awesome. Noon, then? Oh, and please call me Gabe."

With that, he uttered another greeting to Emmett while Jinny murmured her agreement, and left.

Jinny stood there, alone, with Emmett hovering outside her office, fighting off the urge to run after Gabe and ask him to supervise like she was a ten-year-old in need of a chaperone.

She flexed her hands by her side. *You are a capable and talented woman. You can handle anything and anyone. You've got this.*

Finally turning her gaze to Emmett, she saw that he had dropped the crutches and wore a black DonJoy brace over his knee. When he shuffled further into her office, he did so gingerly, avoiding placing his full weight on his injured leg, which was good. For now, anyway. He'd need to be walking fully in the next week or two.

His normally vibrant hazel eyes were rimmed with shadows, hinting of poor sleep and fatigue, and his sandy hair was tousled like he'd just rolled out of bed. Without thinking, her gaze flickered over his athletic shorts and black t-shirt. The soft material clung to his muscles, sending her heart into overdrive.

He looked...lost, and for a moment, she felt a pang of sympathy as he shuffled further inside her office and turned in a half-circle. Taking in the small space, he whistled. "Man, pretty bland, isn't it?"

All sympathy vanished, replaced by a deep-seated loathing.

She gritted her teeth to prevent herself from snapping. "This is my first day. I haven't had a chance to put any personal..."

She snapped her mouth shut and shook her head. Why was she explaining herself to him? As usual, she was allowing him to goad her.

"Let me grab your file and we'll head to one of the exam rooms."

"Ah, so professional."

Jinny ignored him and moved the stack of papers on her desk, grabbing the manila file folder she had placed there earlier and snatching up her laptop.

"Already making lunch dates with your coworker?" Emmett asked as they entered the hallway.

When Jinny glanced up at him, he added. "Seems unwise, if you ask me."

"Well, I didn't ask you."

Emmett chuckled and raised his hands in defense.

"Follow me," she snarled, heading toward the first exam room on the right.

It was brightly lit, with soothing cream walls and abstract art. A state-of-the-art exam table sat in the middle of the space, and cupboards for supplies ran along one wall. Pretty typical, until you glanced to the other side of the room. A mini fridge full of beverages, a snack bar, and several leather chairs, as well as a large-screen television were arranged in an informal seating area. Nothing but the best for star athletes, she supposed. Still, the posh surroundings would take some getting used to. Replace the exam table with a bed, and it would look like a hotel room.

Jinny set the laptop and file down on the counter by the cabinets and motioned for Emmett to take a seat on the exam table. Once he was settled, she turned to him. "Let's cut to the chase. I imagine having me as your therapist is about the worst nightmare you can imagine. Likewise for me. You think I'm a career-vaulting mooch, and I think you're an arrogant jerk. So while we're inside this building, how about we keep things professional, yeah?"

Emmett shrugged, lazily taking her in. His heavy gaze made her skin prickle and her fingers twitch.

"Great. Now that we have that settled, let's get started."

She turned back to the counter and plucked the thick frames she used for reading from her front shirt pocket and put them on, skimming down his file and the orthopedist's notes. "It looks like everything went well with surgery. And when you came in, I didn't notice any abnormal swelling. Also, I see you're off crutches but still in the brace. You must have followed your R.I.C.E recommendations and elevated and iced. Did you do the recommended post-op exercises daily?"

"Sure did," he chirped.

Ignoring his smart tone, she glanced up at him, stepping toward the table with his file. Peering over her glasses, she allowed her gaze to sweep over his knee. "How are you feeling?"

"I didn't know you wore glasses."

Jinny blinked at him, caught off-guard, then narrowed her eyes. "They're for reading."

A slow smile curled Emmett's lips, and Jinny caught a

glimpse of his dimples, which framed his disgustingly perfect mouth.

"So I gathered," he said, then licked his lips. "What was the question again?"

Jinny shifted under his gaze. Why was he looking at her like that?

"I asked, HOW ARE YOU FEELING?" she said, emphasizing the words like he was hard of hearing.

"Well, I'm kind of hungry. Also, I'm a little tired today, but overall, I'm feeling pretty good. It's a Monday, and though most people hate Monday's, I—"

"Your knee." She glared at him, which only made him smile wider.

"Right. The knee. You need to be more specific, slim."

Her nostrils flared at the nickname, but she bit her tongue, waving for him to continue.

"It's fine. Great, actually. When can I get back to playing ball? I think I could shoot some hoops right now." He mimed making a shot in the air with his hands.

Jinny put the folder down on the table and removed her glasses, tucking them back into her pocket, noting the flicker of disappointment in his eyes at their absence.

"No basketball. No shooting hoops," she said, her tone firm.

Emmett rolled his eyes.

"I'm serious. Do you want to get better or not?" she

asked, sensing his impatience.

It was only week two, post-surgery. If he was already impatient, she couldn't imagine what he'd be like a few weeks from now.

"So, when?" Emmett asked.

"Let's do a little work. I want to see where you're at with flexion and extension. At the end of my evaluation today, we'll talk time frame, treatment plan, what to expect, everything."

"Dr. Bauer told me about all of it."

"Yeah, well, Dr. Bauer may be the best in his field, but he's an orthopedic *surgeon*, not a physical therapist. So let's just focus on what we're doing right now, and what I have to say at the end of it. Mmkay?" She tried to keep the attitude from her voice, but the man in front of her tested every ounce of restraint she had.

Emmett sighed.

"Let's start with flexion and extension. Lie down on your back." She patted the table.

"I knew you were a control freak, so I should've taken you to be bossy, but this is a little forward, even for you."

Jinny shot daggers at him with her eyes and gritted her teeth while he chuckled. She hated him. *So much for remaining professional.*

"More crude comments like that, and I could file sexual harassment, Mr. Hall."

If possible, he laughed even harder.

"You know you love it, *Miss Kimball*," he said, mocking her.

"Contrary to what you womanizers believe, I don't like being dehumanized and treated like an object. Shocker, I know."

"Except between the sheets, then all bets are off. Am I right?"

Jinny stiffened. "No, you are not *right*."

"Oh, come on. All you feminists act like you want to be treated with respect, like you're our equal. Women's rights and all that. Blah, blah, blah. But what you really want is a man to take the reins."

Her cheeks flushed. "You are such a total—" She bit down on her tongue until it ached, cutting off her words.

Anger bubbled inside her. And she needed to quell the building storm in order to remain professional.

Breathe.

"Lie down," she snapped, biting the inside of her cheek at his smile.

He knew what he was doing. He was trying to get under her skin, and he was winning.

She motioned to his legs. "Lay both legs flat, then bring your left knee up at an angle toward your waist. Don't push it too far. Just to where it feels on the edge of comfort."

She watched as he did as she asked. She eyed his bent

knee and took a measurement of the angle.

"Okay, good. Now, slowly lower."

She wrote his flexion down. He was close to ninety degrees already, which was great. He'd meet their goal within a week, so they'd be right on track.

"Now I want you to push your quads into the table while flexing your knee and foot. Your foot will lift slightly off the table." Jinny touched his calf as he did so. "Good, yes, just like that. Hold for a few seconds."

She paused, scanning down his leg, taking in the extension of his knee. "Fabulous."

They worked in silence for a few more minutes. It was as close to bliss as she could get in his presence until he ruined it with his mouth.

"So, is that your type?" he asked.

Jinny glanced up from his file and frowned. "What?"

"Swanson. Is he your type?"

When she stared down at him with a blank expression, he arched a brow. "*Gabe?*"

"Oh." She dismissed him with a wave of the hand and returned to writing in the file. "I don't have a type."

Emmett snickered, and she glanced up at him. Placing his file down, she crossed her arms over her chest. "What?"

"Everyone has a type."

"I don't think so."

"They do. The question is what is yours, because I know

for certain the last few losers you dated weren't it."

Jinny arched a brow. How did he always know the exact thing to say to irritate her? "Excuse me?"

"Yeah, these last few guys. Most of the men you've dated, I'm willing to bet, were just to pass the time. They were something fun to do while you prepared for your real life to start."

Jinny averted her gaze, uncomfortable with how close to the truth he was.

"And if I'm right, then we've yet to see your real type emerge. Who was the last guy? What was his name? Tim? Ted?"

"Todd." Jinny glared.

Emmett laughed, still flat on the exam table, clutching his stomach like he was a regular comedian.

"That's right. The first time I saw you with him, I thought, 'you gotta be kidding me with this dude.' His long hair, pasty skin, and budding career serving beer at the campus pizza joint. What a winner."

"Maybe I like guys who are different."

"Being an unambitious, beer-guzzling hobo doesn't make you different. Quite the contrary, actually."

She let his words deflect off her jerk forcefield.

"Maybe we should focus here. Sit up," she said, then moved toward his upper body and placed a hand on his back, helping him sit. Though she tried her best to ignore the feel of his muscled back through his shirt, she failed.

Her pulse raced, betraying her. She cleared her throat, let go of him, and subtly shook out her hand as if it burned from the touch.

"Let your legs hang freely over the table here," she instructed.

Emmett complied, but kept on talking. "Then the guy before that. I don't even know his name, he was so immemorable. That software guy from Caltech. What a nerd."

Jinny huffed. "He liked Star Wars. So do millions of others."

"Uh-huh."

"Maybe you're just jealous." She sneered and leaned in closer, taking in the scent of soap and freshly laundered clothes, which made her want to bury her face in his chest and stole a bit of her snark. "Maybe that's the real problem here."

"What if I am?" Emmett's laughter faded as his eyes shifted to her mouth.

"Wait—what?"

"What if I am jealous? I think, deep down, you want me to be."

Jinny blinked. It wasn't the response she expected. She stared at him a moment, her breath catching in her throat before she finally snapped out of the hold he had on her.

He was messing with her, but she wasn't playing his

games.

She pointed to the bottom of Emmett's leg. "Bring your ankle outward for external rotation, just a little, like this," she said, rotating his ankle. "About thirty degrees, then inward. I'm going to place my hands above your ankle for palpation, but you should be doing all the movement."

She placed her hands above his ankle, noting the warmth of his bronzed skin. A fluttery feeling rose in her stomach.

"Aren't you going to respond to what I said?" he asked.

"Aren't you going to do this flexion exercise?"

After a moment's hesitation, Emmett rotated his ankle outward, then inward, while Jinny watched his patella.

"So, going with your theory that everyone has a type," she said, ignoring his question, but still taking the bait and hating herself for it. "Then am I to assume yours is airheaded, jock-chasing bimbos?"

Emmett grinned. "Naw. See, that's where you've got me all wrong."

Jinny shook her head. "I seriously doubt it," she muttered under her breath. Then she grabbed his file and added her notes.

"Maybe I've been doing the same thing as you. Maybe I've just been waiting to date the right kind of person, at the right time."

Jinny bit the inside of her cheek, swallowing down her retort.

Could've fooled her. Last she checked, the right kind of woman wouldn't be impressed with his massive rap sheet of conquests.

∞∞∞∞

"That's all for today," Jinny said, typing into her computer.

"Wait. What?" Emmett asked, aghast.

Jinny opened her laptop and pulled up his records, then began to type out her notes. "The first session is typically shorter because it's mostly assessment and going over your course of treatment, goals, and expectations. I'll see you again tomorrow. All our other sessions will be longer, especially in the coming months."

"Speaking of the coming months. Are we going to talk about all that? When I'll be up and running again? What I'm supposed to do in the meantime?"

Jinny placed a hand on her hip. "We just finished your assessment. If you'd give me a chance, I'd love to discuss all of that with you."

"Sorry. I'm just a little impatient," he said. "I'm not good at waiting for things."

Jinny raised a brow, and, for the first time since he entered her office, she wasn't irritated.

"I noticed." She smirked and finished typing, then turned, focusing all her attention on him. "The next week will probably feel the slowest, so you need to try and be patient and not get frustrated. Remember, this is only week two, post-op. The next seven days, our main focus is going to be on continuing to control inflammation. We'll work on your range of motion, and the goal is by the end of the week to have you at 90 degrees flexion. You're already close, so that's great. You're off to a wonderful start."

She smiled, trying to ease the concern she saw in his eyes. "We'll work on achieving quad control and patellar mobilization. We'll even get you in the exercise room. We'll probably use the 4-way hip machine, as well as some other flexion exercises, and by the end of the week, I hope to have you on the bike."

Emmett clapped his hands together. "Awesome. Sounds great. I'm ready for it."

"As far as what to expect longer term, for the first three months, we'll increase your exercises and cardio, and continue working on flexion. By the end of that time, you'll hopefully progress to a light jog, and you should have full range of motion. Things will get much more intense in months three to five, with more sports-related exercises, cardio, and agility training. We'll really work on strengthening the muscle. Hopefully, by month six, you'll be able to return to team practice and by month eight or nine be able to compete."

"Whoa," Emmett held out a hand. "Hold up, little lady."

Jinny's skin pricked. "First of all, never call me that. Ever."

His face contorted, and the vein in his forehead pulsed. "Month six? You're telling me I won't even be able to train or practice with the team for six months?"

"At least."

"Uh, no. That's completely unacceptable." He crossed his arms over his chest, muscles bulging with the movement.

Tearing her eyes from his biceps, she said, "Well, I hate to break it to you, champ, but that's how this goes. You tore your ACL and had surgery. If you return to the game too early, you get reinjured and potentially do permanent damage to your knee. As it stands, successful reconstruction of the ACL is 75–97%. Your odds of a full recovery are amazing, but you can just as easily screw yourself up."

Emmett glanced away from her, staring at the wall. The muscle in his jaw worked as he took in deep pulls of air like he might be sick. "So you're telling me I don't even have a shot of playing ball for eight or nine months? Dr. Bauer said I'd be playing by six."

"Well, he was wrong. You'll be training and practicing, yes, but if you want to be smart and not a total moron, then you'll give your knee the extra time it needs. At least wait and see where we're at by the end of six months. You're making demands and assumptions at week two when we're nowhere close."

His eyes snapped back to her. "No, *you're* making demands and assumptions."

"No." She pounded her fist into the palm of her hand. "I made a *professional* assessment and recommended a course of action and treatment based off of that assessment and the extent of your injury. Big difference."

Emmett slid off the table and moved toward her.

"Your brace," she said, motioning to his bare knee, but he ignored her. He moved closer until he towered over her. Her stomach flopped, and she fought the urge to take a step back. He had nearly two feet on her.

She should've felt intimidated by the sheer force of him. Two hundred and thirty pounds of muscle stared down at her. But she wasn't a coward. She wouldn't back down. Not for a second. She ate men like him for breakfast. And she wasn't about to let him argue with her. This was her job. It was what she was born to do.

She squared her shoulders and raised a brow in challenge.

"I don't have that much time. Don't you get it?" He hesitated, and in that moment of silence, she saw something other than irritation flicker through his eyes. Something soft, vulnerable. "Nine months puts us into next season. That means I'd be out almost three months, not to mention being unable to train all summer. Three *months*," he repeated.

His eyes searched hers. What was he looking for? Sympathy? Understanding?

A small part of her broke under his gaze. She opened her mouth to speak, to give him words of comfort.

Maybe there was a soft center, a real person inside the cocky façade, after all.

But before she could say anything, disappointment swept over his features. "The Pumas may be a new team, but I'm a rookie, too. It doesn't matter that as a team we've proven ourselves. Two seasons isn't enough for a pro athlete to make himself indispensable. They could trade me. Or worse, let my contract expire, and I don't get picked back up."

Her stomach sunk. She thought of her brother and how disappointed Dean would be if he were in Emmett's shoes. He'd be stressed beyond belief, anxious, upset, and more than frustrated with his inability to do the one thing he loved most. The thought of losing it all would devastate him.

But ACL tears were common in basketball. If players listened to protocol, they'd heal nicely. Emmett would have no problem returning to the sport.

"I'm a rookie, too, so I get it," she said. "I understand wanting to prove yourself."

It was true. She understood his predicament more than he knew. She understood needing to be perfect, needing to get it right because you'd reached for the stars and finally caught one. Let it go, and they might all fade away.

"You will be as good as new at the end of this. I promise," she said. "And the Pumas won't do that to you."

Emmett scoffed. "Our situations are nothing alike."

Of course he would try to argue with her. It was Emmett, God of all things. No one compared.

"How so?" she asked, with more force than necessary.

Emmett took a step away from her, yanked his brace off the exam table, and began strapping it back on. Whatever moment of truth he had just shared with her was gone, replaced by the simmering anger in his sharp movements and abrasive tone. "Bernard King tore his ACL playing for the Knicks and was never the same. In 2000, Grant Hill injured his ankle. Same story. In 2007, Gilbert Arena's career imploded after he blew his knee out. So, excuse me if I'm a little concerned. And last I checked, you don't need to worry about getting injured in your posh little office."

Jinny straightened, but before she could get a word in, he continued, "Sorry if I'm unwilling to put my career, my entire *life*, into a resident's hands. Just two weeks ago, you were under the supervision of *real* staff at a university, helping college kids, and now you're here acting like you've done your time, when you're just some rookie that got the job because her daddy and her brother put in a good word. So excuse me for not trusting you with the most important thing in my life."

Jinny stumbled back. The blow of his words hit her in the chest. Anger zipped up her spine, red-hot. Her face flamed, and her hands clenched at her side. Any sympathy she felt for him vanished, replaced by an inferno of indignation.

How *dare* he.

It took her a moment to find her voice through her anger, but once she did, she let it rip. "Do you pride yourself on being such a jerk?"

Emmett shrugged in response, and her nostrils flared.

"Yes, my brother might play for the Pumas, and my father is athletic director of the university. I can't deny that. But that doesn't change the fact that I earned my position here. I worked my tail off getting my masters a year after my undergrad, while doing a residency. Ask anyone and they'll tell you I was the best resident these last two years"—she stepped forward and poked him in the ribs, punctuating her words—"I studied and worked while others were out partying. I put everything I had into my education and career development, and when I achieved something only two percent of PT's achieve, I proved my worth. So, I don't need to prove anything to *you*."

She gathered up his file and her laptop. She was *so* done with this appointment. It wasn't even ten a.m. and she felt like she'd worked a full day. The gall of this man was amazing. She'd tell him that, but he'd probably take it as a compliment. No, she knew he would.

She turned to him one last time. "You don't want to follow my course of treatment? Fine by me. Tell that to your coach. Tell that to Bannon and Gabe and see what they say. Could you be fully back in the game at six months? It's possible. But it's not typical, and not what I recommend to expect in this early stage. It could take you seven to eight, or the full nine months, to play competitively. I dare you to find any qualified sports PT that will tell you otherwise. I plan on doing a fan-fricking-tastic job here, but I'm also not going to wipe your sorry hind end because you want me to baby you. Nor will I stroke your ego and tell you lies. So, you don't want me treating you?" She waved her hand toward the door. "Go find someone else, big guy. You'd save me the stress and frustration of working with a sexist megalomaniac. It's your loss. Not mine."

With that, she slammed the door shut, raising her hand in the most epic mic drop ever, and stormed back to her office.

CHAPTER FIVE

Emmett

Big guy? BIG GUY?

Emmett walked to his car as quickly as he could with his bum knee and his stupid brace. He needed to get out of there.

His teeth ached from clenching them as he slid awkwardly into the driver's seat, pulling his stiff leg in behind him.

At least he'd injured his left leg, or he still wouldn't be

driving. *See? There's a bright side to everything, Hall.* He was a regular Pollyanna.

He played back Jinny's last words. Maybe he deserved a little hostility. Okay, a lot of hostility. But could she really blame him? She had to understand, didn't she? Her brother played ball. There was no way you could be close to someone who played a professional sport and not realize it was their lifeblood.

Everything that mattered the most to him was wrapped up in his career. That was the way he liked it. No distractions. No complications. Only pure focus. She had to know how much being out of commission would hurt him.

What was he saying? Of course, she knew. He'd caught a glimpse of her understanding, and it nearly crippled him. The softening in her expression. The way her supple mouth turned down at the corners and her chocolate eyes melted.

He couldn't stand her looking at him that way, because, when she did, she looked far too vulnerable, like a stiff wind could crack her wide open. In that moment, she'd looked too much like a woman he wanted to kiss. Not nearly enough like his best friends' little sister. Or like his newly appointed therapist. The last thing he needed was to get caught up in an inappropriate working relationship. It would reflect poorly on both of them, but mostly her.

Jinny could deny it all she wanted. She could hide behind her smart retorts and icy glares, but she was every bit as attracted to him as he was to her. But if they ever acted on their attraction, her career was at stake. Not his. Right or wrong, there was a double standard at play. Emmett's discretion, because he was a man *and* a professional athlete, would be overlooked, while hers would not. She'd be cast aside, written off. So he took all his pent-up anger and frustration about his injury out on her. It was a jerk move. But it got him the results he wanted.

He had zero intention of finding another therapist. He had total confidence she knew what she was doing. He had no idea if her father had been involved in getting her the position with the team, but he knew for a fact Dean hadn't pulled any strings. He had asked him. Little did Jinny know, Emmett was the one to put a good word in for her, and he didn't want to know what she'd do if she found out.

He may have only known Dean for a few years, but he'd heard him constantly blab about how amazing she was. On more than one occasion, Emmett saw Dean drag her out of her apartment because all she did was eat, sleep, work at her residency, and study for her SCS. Occasionally, she'd throw in a boyfriend or two, but the relationships were fleeting.

She'd dated several guys in the short span that he'd known her, and they were all throwaways—men to pass the time until she was ready for a real one. Jinny was at the top of her game. She deserved her position, which is why Emmett spoke with Garrison about it in the fall. Only now, he'd pay for it. He'd never imagined he'd get seriously injured and be forced to work with her regularly.

So, technically, he was partially to blame for his current situation, and it made his insistence she was "gifted" the job even more of a low blow. Regardless, the low blow worked. Just like it had last summer at the party when he'd needed to create distance between them. He'd sworn he wouldn't use it again. But when he felt her softening toward him, he needed something to keep the wedge between them, and it had done its job for a second time.

Really, when Jinny pointed out that the two of them were in similar situations, she hadn't been far off. They both had reached their dreams, and now they were in a fight to hold onto them. Except, once Jinny proved herself, she'd be fully accepted into the fold and could work as a therapist for as long as she wanted. Professional sports were more fickle than that.

His career had an expiration date. While she had a long, healthy career ahead of her, he'd be lucky to get more than five years. The average career of an NBA player was less than five years. And he may have just shortened his by a year at the least. It was a kick to the balls.

Emmett's knuckles turned white as he gripped the steering wheel. All he could do now was pray he'd proved himself enough that the Pumas would keep him.

∞∞∞

Jinny

Jinny swallowed and plunked her drink back on the bar top with a loud *clunk*. "So, I said to him, 'go find someone else, big guy. You'd save me the stress and frustration of working with a sexist megalomaniac like yourself. It's your loss. Not mine.'"

Callie grinned ear to ear. "No, you didn't."

Jinny nodded. "I did."

"How can someone with such beautiful eyes be so rude?"

Jinny took in her best friend of twenty-four years (yes, the entire span of her life) and snickered. She looked like a Barbie doll, with her hair pulled into one of those adorable high ponytails that looked like she'd spent hours perfecting, while she blinked her baby-blues dreamily. In comparison, when Jinny pulled her hair back, she looked like a middle-aged schoolmarm. Good thing she didn't care. When Jinny made an effort, it was because *she* wanted to look good. Not because she wanted to impress anyone else.

Jinny scoffed. "His eyes are not beautiful."

"Oh yes, they are."

Jinny grunted. "I've never noticed." She took a sip of her beer.

"Sure, you haven't. I'm sure you've never noticed how they're the color of finely aged whiskey, with little flecks of green in the center. I'm sure you've also never noticed how thick his hair is. Or how it's the exact shade of sand on a Carolina beach. Or wondered what it might feel like to run your hands through it. Or—"

"Enough. Please." Jinny held her hand up. "Much more and I'll barf up this beer."

"Mm-hm," Callie murmured, taking a sip of her wine.

Gosh, sometimes best friends sucked.

"Listen, the point is not what shade of puke-inducing whiskey his eyes are. The point is that he was completely out of line."

"So, what are you going to do about it?"

Jinny sighed. "I don't know. I thought about going to Gabe and seeing if he could work with him. He's certainly trained to do so, even if his main role isn't the injured list. But that'll just make me look bad, you know? I mean, I work one day. One"—Jinny held out her pointer finger for emphasis—"and I can't handle the first a-hole patient I get?"

"Right. Totally would look bad."

"Exactly. So, the way I see it, I have two options. I work with Emmett and keep a truckload of indigestion meds in my office, or I make him hate me so much that he opts to find treatment elsewhere."

"But wouldn't that look just as bad?" Callie asked.

"I thought about that, but I don't think so. He cares too much about his friendship with Dean to jeopardize that by badmouthing me. If he decided to seek his own therapist elsewhere, I'm sure he'd come up with a plausible enough excuse that it wouldn't hurt my image too much. Plus, in the meantime, I'll make all the other patients love me so much that they have nothing but glowing reviews. To everyone else, I'll be sweet little Jinny. When I walk into the room, it'll be like Santa Claus just made an appearance. I'll be the friggin' Easter Bunny dropping candy at their feet. I'll crap rainbows. But to Emmett, I'll be a rain cloud on a sunny day. I'll be the devil incarnate," she said darkly.

"Um, creepy, much?" Callie turned away from her and waved toward the bartender, catching his attention.

"I guess you've thought it all out," Callie said as the bartender appeared in front of her. "I'll take another white wine, please."

He turned to Jinny and inclined his head. "What about you, darlin'? Want another beer?" His shaggy blonde hair fell in his eyes. He flicked it away and flashed her a smile.

"Yeah. Thanks."

When he turned to get their drinks, Callie wiggled her brows. "Oh, he's cute. And he likes you. You should totally go for it."

Jinny rolled her eyes. "He doesn't like me. He was waiting on me."

"Nuh-uh. He's been eyeing you all night. And he called you darlin'. He didn't call me anything."

Jinny snorted. "Oh, okay, detective. Well, he can keep his disgusting term of endearment because I ain't his darlin'."

Jinny drained the last dregs of her beer just as the waiter placed the fresh one in front of her. She raised her brows in thanks, and he winked at her as he turned.

"Ugh. I mean, really? Come on. What is it with these men nowadays? They think they can wink at us, and we'll fall into a puddle at their feet? I don't think so."

Jinny took a healthy sip of her new beer and swallowed, wincing at the burn of the bubbles in her throat. "I mean, take Emmett for example. He calls me sweetheart. He flirts one second, throws sexual innuendos at me like candy, then insults me the next. It's all a part of their world domination game."

Callie frowned. "I'm not following."

"Yeah." Jinny nodded, getting into it, using her hands as she spoke. "You know, proving they're still on top. That they're the superior sex. Like they can just spout their degrading terms of endearment, wink at us, and wave their noodles around, and we're supposed to fall all over ourselves because we're lucky to have a man like them."

Callie coughed, choking on a sip of wine. She pounded her chest with her fist.

"You okay there, bucko?" Jinny asked.

"Noodles? I really hope you weren't referring to—"

"The point is, they think they're superior because they have an extra appendage. End of story."

Just like Emmett thought his budding career was more important than hers. Her woes were small and simple and ridiculous by comparison to his huge man-sized ones. And she couldn't possibly be capable at her job because she was lacking something between her legs.

Well, buddy, you're wrong. She mattered every bit as much as he did, and she was every bit as skilled as a man. She'd prove it, too. She'd do her job and do it well, but in the meantime, she'd be the bane of his existence. The reason he drew his curtains shut at night and locked his door. The reason he was constantly looking over his shoulder.

Okay, maybe that was taking it a little too far. Even for her. But, whatever. He wanted to goad her? She'd hit him right back. If he stayed her patient these next six to nine months, they'd be the most miserable of his life.

It was time to phase Emmett out. Operation Patient Excommunicado was underway.

CHAPTER SIX

Emmett

E mmett stood with his heels hanging off the edge of
the plastic block step and began calf raises. He
hated the way his knee felt like nothing was there
backing it up. Like it would collapse in on itself at any moment. Regardless, he gritted his teeth and did as he was
told.

He glanced at Jinny out of the corner of his eye. She
stood, one hand on her hip, chewing unusually slowly—and

loudly—on a granola bar. She looked like those ridiculous llamas at the zoo.

Her brown eyes tracked his movement, watching his knee with a hawk-like gaze. The slim black pants she wore hugged her butt with perfect precision—not that he noticed. Her skin glowed like she'd gotten loads of sleep since their first session two mornings ago, or maybe it was the way she wore her hair that made her look particularly bright-eyed.

Though her dark locks were swept back from her face, when she turned to greet someone entering the gym, a small tendril escaped. It was fitting, he mused. Nothing about Jinny Kimball could be contained.

Taylor, a Puma center, smiled at her from the elliptical and inclined his head. "Hey there, Miss J."

"Hey, Tay. How's the ankle?" she asked, turning toward him and ignoring Emmett.

Emmett forced his eyes from her backside and focused on Taylor as he continued his blasted calf raises.

"Aw, you know. Coming along," Taylor said.

"Keep at those toe scrunches and raises and the other stuff I showed you. Got me?"

Taylor grinned. "I gotcha."

When Jinny turned back to Emmett, he smirked and raised a brow. "Miss J?"

She shrugged and glanced around the room as though

it was no big deal, but she was trying too hard for it to look natural. She glanced down at her nails then wiped them on her pant leg. "Yeah. You know, it's just a nickname the guys came up with. No biggie."

"The guys?"

"Some of the guys on the team."

Emmett contained a laugh. "You've gotten to know them that well? In just a few days on the job?"

Just as the words left his mouth, Davis walked in. He threw a towel over his shoulder and eyed the treadmill, but the moment he spotted Jinny, he made a beeline for her and pulled her into a giant bear hug.

Emmett paused, shuffling his feet fully onto the block, watching the exchange with a frown.

"J, you're going to spoil me." Davis stepped back and placed his hands on his hips, grinning at her like a fool.

"Not just you."

"True. You better not fatten us up too much though," he said, rubbing his stomach. "Dang, you know I can't resist Prantl's."

"The burnt almond torte is heaven. Am I right?"

"It was gone is seconds. Hey, Friday, it's my treat. Don't eat breakfast," Davis said with a wink.

"Deal." Jinny flashed him the biggest smile Emmett had ever seen—one he definitely wasn't jealous of—as Davis sauntered onto the treadmill.

When she turned back to him, she beamed. "Take a seat on the exercise ball," she said, motioning toward it.

Once Emmett complied, she asked, "You were saying?"

A slow smirk slid over his face. He placed his hands on his hips and watched her mouth move in slow motion as she took a giant bite of a granola bar.

"Prantl's?" he asked.

It was the best bakery in the city, famous for the burnt almond torte. It was so amazing, it could drop a grown man to his knees. If Jinny took the time to stand in line and pick up pastries from them, there was a reason. She was scheming. He just had no idea what her game was.

"Yeah," she said, emphasizing the word while she chewed. A small spray of granola hit him in the face. He winced and picked a chunk of it from his eye. "I figured these guys deserved it, you know?"

Emmett hummed a noncommittal response. "What about this guy? I'm your patient, not Davis." The burning sensation in his chest was stupid. But it took effort to buy pastries for the other guys, and not him. Being jealous of a dessert was preposterous, yet he couldn't help himself.

"Actually"—Jinny raised a finger and took another massive bite—"I am working with Tay. We're strengthening his ankle after a sprain."

"Tay?" Okay, now this was getting ridiculous.

More granola hit him in the face, and Emmett

grunted. "Do you eat during all your therapy sessions?"

Jinny shrugged. "I'm a busy gal. Gotta take lunch when I can get it."

"It's ten a.m."

"I have low sugar." She huffed.

"I think it's cute," Emmett said, knowing she'd take the bait.

He watched the internal war in her head. She stopped chewing and her eyes narrowed. "What's cute?"

"The way you eat so vigorously. I mean, most women try to be all dainty about it. Small bites, small portions. But *you*," he said, "you don't care what other people think. You get all into it. Huge bites with your big chompers going a mile a minute. You don't even pause to swallow before you talk. Heck, I don't even know if you breathe. I've always thought a girl with a voracious appetite was sexy. Now, you've just proved my theory." He winked and watched with satisfaction as her gaze hardened and her face flushed.

When she stomped off to the nearest trash can and chucked the granola bar inside, he chuckled under his breath.

Emmett one. Jinny zero.

Jinny

The granola bar on Wednesday may have been a fail, but she'd seen the look on his face. Prantl's got to him. Men were ruled by their stomachs. That and the little nickname, *Miss J.* It had a nice ring to it. To think all it took was Dean calling her "J" all day yesterday at the gym, and it caught on like wildfire, just as she had hoped. Okay, maybe that wasn't *all* it took. Dean would get the last of their mom's cinnamon rolls on Christmas morning this year. The jerk.

Ever since they were kids, they'd fought over the last roll. Jinny had yet to figure out why her mother never made a double batch. It only solidified her suspicion that she secretly enjoyed their brother-sister feuds.

Regardless, the sacrifice was worth it.

She took Emmett back to an exam room. It was Friday —a whole new day. Another chance to irritate him.

They had already run through all their flexion and extension exercises for the day, as well as some minor strengthening and muscle building. His knee was still fairly acute in the third week, so they were limited. That left NMES and therapeutic massage. *Blech.*

She instructed him to sit on the exam table with his legs hanging freely over the edge. With understated confidence, Jinny adhered the three circular electrode pads above his knee and the larger one on his quad.

"You'll probably be familiar with this. I know they did some neuromuscular stimulation with you last week before you came to me, but I'm going to order it five times a week for the time being. So you'll need to come in every day. Your therapy is only three times a week, but the NMES has proven to be really effective, so on the in-between days, you'll be in and out. Some discomfort is normal, but let me know if it's too much."

"Can't bear to be away from me, huh?" Emmett asked.

Jinny rolled her eyes.

"I realize you'll do anything to get me in here every day, but you can just come out and ask. You don't need to make excus—" Emmett yelped and practically leapt off the table as Jinny turned the dial on the machine.

"Oops. Sorry." With a grin, she adjusted to the correct stimulation.

∞∞∞

Jinny swallowed the last of her apple—her breakfast —then glanced at the clock and stood. She swore Emmett liked to be her first appointment of the day because he enjoyed starting her off on the wrong foot. Little did he know, he was doing her a favor. She liked getting his appointment over with. The remainder of her Monday would be a breeze.

Jinny pulled open the drawer of her desk and removed the pack of bubble gum she bought on her way to work. She opened the package and popped a chunk in her mouth. Watermelon. Her favorite. She hadn't had this stuff in years because her mother told her it would rot her teeth out.

Today, watermelon Bazooka was her weapon of choice. Her ally in the cold war.

She unwrapped three more pieces and stuffed them in her mouth until both cheeks were full. Her jaw ached as she chewed and the sugars in the gum gave way to soft, juicy goodness. Satisfied with herself, she smoothed the front of her blue silk blouse and headed to the door.

Oops. Almost forgot weapon numero dos.

She doubled back around and snatched the perfume she brought from home. It had been a gag gift from Callie a couple years back. It was called *Bleeding Heart*, came in a red bottle in the shape of an anatomical heart, and smelled every bit as hideous as it looked.

She uncapped it and doused herself. She rubbed it into every pore until her eyes watered and her nose burned. Who needed sinus cavities?

Now she was ready.

She marched out to the waiting room to call Emmett back.

When she got there, she called his name over the wad of gum, proud of herself for only dribbling the slightest bit of drool in the process. Then she did a double-take.

A lithe blonde sat beside him. She stared up at Emmett in adoration, batting her eyelashes and touching the v-neck of his t-shirt in reverence. She had that large-eyed, sunken cheeked, starved model look. When he leaned down and whispered something into her ear, she chuckled, swatting at his arm. It was a miracle her limbs didn't snap like a twig.

Jinny had to stop herself from gagging. She wondered if he'd even heard her call his name, when he finally stood and turned.

Crossing her arms over her chest, she blew a bubble as she watched him approach, smirk in place. She inwardly fist-bumped herself when the bubble grew to be the size of her face and blocked the view of his ugly mug. It popped obnoxiously just as he came to a stop in front of her.

She sucked it back in and chewed the gum like a piece of tough steak. When he smirked, she grimaced and spun on her heel, heading straight for the fitness room.

In the hallway, they passed Jamal, the team's starting center. "What up, Miss J?"

Jinny smiled and greeted him as they passed. Then Damion exited the bathroom and inclined his head. "Miss J, my favorite person. Looking beautiful, as usual."

"Thanks, hun," she said, shooting him her sweetest smile before she turned to Emmett and let it wither and die on her lips. "It's so cute how your little sleepover bled into your therapy appointment. I'm surprised she isn't still wearing her unicorn jammies. What is she, ten?"

"She's twenty, and—"

"Let me guess," Jinny purred between chomps. "A model? An aspiring actress?"

Emmett chuckled.

"So, what number is she on your list of conquests?" Jinny asked.

"Wouldn't you like to know."

She clenched her jaw. The only reason she wanted to know was for medical and professional purposes only. Of course she didn't want to know for personal reasons. What Emmett did in his free time was his business.

She instructed him to start his first set of stretches as a fresh wave of inspiration hit. "I'll be right back," she said, then hurried to the bathroom.

She opened the cabinet across from the sink. The one she noticed the cleaning crew dipping into at the end of the day. Her eyes scanned the shelves, and she smiled as she homed in on the huge, yellow rubber gloves. *Bingo.*

She snatched them up and slid them on as she made her way back to the fitness room. Emmett sat on the bench doing toe raises. When his wandering gaze stopped at her gloves, he arched his brow.

Two of his teammates were already working out. *Per-*

fect.

"What's with the gloves?" he asked.

"It's for my protection."

"Protection?" he asked, sounding amused.

Before she could answer, Gabe walked in. He smiled at Jinny, then frowned as he drew closer and took in the gloves. His pace slowed.

"Everything okay?" he asked.

Jinny smiled. "Oh yeah, sure. You know, I just don't want to contract anything," she stage-whispered.

Gabe's eyes shifted to Emmett. "Contract anything?"

Jinny waved her hand toward him. "Apparently, he's been around town *quite* a bit lately. I saw him scratching." Jinny widened her eyes and whistled, pointing her index finger in a downward motion. "I'm sure it's nothing to be worried about, but I'm not taking any chances. You can never be too careful."

Gabe cringed and took a giant step away from Emmett, forcing Jinny to bite back a laugh.

"Be sure to bleach everything when he's done, yeah?"

"Absolutely." Jinny nodded solemnly.

Gabe sniffed the air around them. "Actually, did you spray some disinfectant already? I smell something—"

"Oh, no." Jinny batted a hand at him. "That's just this new perfume I tried out. I read an article about how the scent of dirt has therapeutic effects."

"Uh, okay," Gabe said, eyeing her like she was crazy.

It was perfect, really. She'd kill two birds with one stone—nauseate Emmett and turn off Gabe (who seemed a little more interested than she'd like) all with one go.

The corners of Emmett's mouth curled into a smile, and she couldn't help herself. She smiled back until their eyes met, then she forced a frown and barked, "Leg raises."

She felt a touch on her arm and leapt in the air, caught off guard.

"So, did you watch that movie I told you about?" Gabe asked.

She had been preoccupied with pretending she wasn't watching Emmett perform leg raises like a champ to notice him return to her side. And she definitely was *not* noting the way the muscles in his core contracted and released while he worked.

"The movie?" she asked, distracted. Then the words clicked, and she turned her attention back to Gabe. Apparently, he was not to be deterred by her scent. "Oh, yeah. I totally loved it."

He nudged her again in the arm. "I knew you'd like it."

She noted the contact. Two touches in one minute. He wanted to show her he was into her. *Abort, abort!*

"I mean, it was okay," she amended.

"You know, I think the sequel comes out Friday night. We should go see it together. We could even leave after work, grab a bite to eat, then see the late show?"

Jinny bit her lip. It wasn't that she didn't like Gabe, per se. He was handsome enough, if you liked the surfer-blond, blue-eyed thing. And he seemed pretty genuine. But she wasn't interested. Even if she were into him, dating a coworker at her brand-new job seemed unwise. But she also didn't want to turn him down in front of Emmett. Who knew what he'd make of *that*. He'd probably accuse her of professing her undying love for him.

She folded her arms over her chest. "Um. Maybe. I need to check with Callie first—I can't remember if I was supposed to meet up with her Friday night. But if I'm free..."

Spoiler alert, she wouldn't be free.

"Sounds great. And, hey, we could even double with her and Dean if you want."

Crap. She hadn't thought about that. He'd probably ask Dean when he saw him.

She opened her mouth to come up with another excuse, something to deter him, when Emmett interrupted them. "Hey, Jinny, I think it's time for me to do the standing toe raises."

"Oh, right." Jinny flashed Gabe an apologetic smile, then hooked a thumb toward where Emmett stood. "Catch you later."

She followed Emmett to the exercise ball as Gabe moved on to speak with Davis. Once they were out of earshot, Emmett turned to her. "You're welcome."

"For what?"

"Saving you from having to say yes to a boring dinner and movie date with soul surfer over there."

Jinny glared. "I happen to like Gabe. He's nice." *Liar, liar pants on fire.*

Emmett yawned.

"What? Nice means boring?" she asked in challenge.

"Hey, if you wanna go on a date with that snooze fest, don't let me stop you. Please, march right on over there, and tell him you'll go see his lame movie."

Jinny put her hands on her hips, the rubber gloves squeaking with the movement. The wad of gum in her cheek was starting to hurt her teeth.

"Fine, I will."

She wanted to spin on her heel and do it. She needed to, but she couldn't make her feet work.

When Emmett smirked, Jinny huffed and waved to the exercise ball. "Just start your calf raises, would you?"

"Nice touch with the perfume, by the way."

"I don't know what you're talking about," she said, but her lips betrayed her snark by quirking into a smile.

"You know, I kind of like it," he said, moving in close.

He dipped his head down as if breathing her in, and Jinny's pulse jumped in response.

Glancing to see if Gabe was watching, she turned back

to him and hissed, "Stop it."

He laughed as he stepped away and began the exercise. She observed while chewing her gum as loudly as she could, cracking it in between chomps. If she dislocated her jaw, it'd be worth it. She was the queen of gum snapping. She drove Dean wild when they were kids, so she had a lot of practice. She'd spent hours perfecting her technique. It was all in how you rolled the wad of gum with your tongue to get the optimum amount of air pockets. Chemical warfare had nothing on her gum-cracking capability.

After ten minutes, the vein in Emmett's forehead bulged. And, if the little muscle in his jaw was any indication, she'd succeeded in annoying him.

She smiled, vindicated.

From the other side of the room, she heard Gabe ask Taylor, "What in the world is that blasted noise?"

CHAPTER SEVEN

Jinny

J inny grinned and snuggled into the plush leather
chair, letting the supple upholstery cocoon her. It was
her favorite piece of furniture in the apartment. She
and Callie had bought it at a thrift shop their sophomore
year in college. It had been their first purchase for their first
apartment upon leaving the dorms. It held good memories.
When Callie married Dean and moved into his place, she'd
have to fight her for it.

Jinny put the finishing touches on the roster for the annual Kimball Family Olympics. This year, the coveted Kimball trophy was hers. All hers. Dean was going down.

She rubbed her hands together and chuckled to herself with glee.

Every year for the Fourth of July, the Kimball's hosted a barbeque for family and only the closest of friends. While the old geezers grilled and smoked an assortment of meats and set out the potluck dishes on a huge table, only the fiercest competitors prepared to compete in the games.

From sack racing to bobbing for apples to the Tic-Tac challenge, no one knew what the day's actual list of events would be. No one except her mother, who had taken the role of randomly choosing that year's races. The secrecy kept anyone from gaining an advantage by prepping ahead of time. Usually, she and Dean tried to bribe her mom a month before, but she was like a Navy SEAL. She'd never crack.

Regardless, Jinny had been sneaking in some extra exercise at work, focusing on her flexibility, dexterity, and hand-eye coordination—all necessary attributes for competing.

Each year, every contestant vied for the same thing: first dibs on food at the buffet and, most importantly, the title of Kimball Ninja Warrior and the family trophy. To date, none of the non-Kimball contestants had ever won the title. Before Dean and Jinny had been old enough to compete, their father often won, followed closely by their Uncle Sal. But for the last ten years, Jinny and Dean had dominated, with Dean on a winning streak. Three years in a row, he'd claimed the title. Last year was due to a technicality. But not this year. If she had anything to do with it, his winning streak was over. This was the year of Jinny.

She smiled to herself. It had a nice ring to it. *The year of Jinny.*

She stretched like a cat, curling her legs underneath her as she balanced her laptop. She took a bite of her chocolate chip muffin, then reached beside her to the end table and gripped her steaming cup of coffee, completely content in the moment. It was Sunday, which meant no work and, most importantly, no Emmett. Pastries for breakfast, a cup of her favorite Kona brew, and a little pre-planning for her Fourth of July attack. Life was good.

Callie padded out of her bedroom and did a double-take when she saw Jinny. "You're up early." Her eyes slid over the laptop, and she must've noted the vicious gleam in Jinny's eye because she smirked and said, "You're prepping for the Olympics, aren't you?"

"What gave me away?"

"The fact that it's the weekend and you're up before nine a.m. Plus, the smiling was a dead giveaway."

Jinny pumped a fist in the air. "Just practicing a little

positive visualization for when I smoke your fiancé in the sack race this year. I might work on my acceptance speech now." She tapped her chin. "I think I'll start it with, *bow down lowly subjects and make way for the rightful victor*," she said with a flourish of her arm.

Callie laughed. "You are so unhinged. I've never won that stupid thing, and I'm just fine."

"That's pathetic. I wouldn't be bragging about that if I were you."

"Don't you think you guys get a little too into it?"

Jinny blinked at her like she was stupid.

"Just last night Dean was talking about some new technique he came up with for Junk in the Ba-Dunk-a-Dunk," Callie said.

Jinny's eyes widened. "He was, was he?" She hummed and narrowed her eyes, deep in thought. This was the kind of intel she needed. "What does he have up his sleeve?"

"He swore me to secrecy."

"You're the worst best friend ever," Jinny muttered.

Callie smacked a palm to her forehead. "You two of you are hopeless. It's a miracle I love both of you."

"But me more than him. Am I right?" Jinny angled her body toward Callie, assessing her. "Your problem is you're an underachiever when it comes to physical competition."

At Callie's icy glare, Jinny corrected. "What I mean is, you don't have the Kimball drive to win like Dean and I do.

It's been ingrained generation after generation. Winning is the only word in our vocabulary. It's the only thing that matters to us. But, you... You weren't raised by wolves like we were."

Callie poured herself a cup of coffee. "Funny. I don't remember your mother being this competitive."

"She hides it behind her impressive cooking and sweet smile. But there was a time when she was a real ball buster."

Callie grinned and took a sip of her coffee. "You're crazy. You know that?"

"I do." Jinny smiled sweetly and set her laptop aside.

Callie made her way into the living room and took a seat on the couch. "So, how's it going with Emmett? Any progress on making him hate PT life?"

Jinny pursed her lips, mulling over her question. "He's definitely hating me more. Dangling the not-so-proverbial pastries under his nose and yanking them away is really getting to him. And I think he hates the way everybody calls me Miss J and seems so friendly with me." Jinny smirked. "Most of all, I think he is starting to resent Gabe."

"Gabe? You mean, Gabriel Swanson?"

Jinny nodded.

"Why's that?"

"He may or may not have been flirting with me at work the other day. *And* he asked me out. Right in front of Emmett."

Callie's expression brightened. "Oh, that's perfect."

"It is, isn't it? I could tell Emmett hated it. It was really eating at his craw. Normally, I would despise such blatant flirtation from a coworker, but he seems nice enough. And Emmett's irritation somehow makes Gabe's California-good-looks even more appealing."

"*Nooo*," Callie said. Her voice held an edge of irritation. "I meant it was perfect for *you* that Gabe is into you."

Jinny scrunched her nose. "Why?"

"Who knows? Maybe you two will hit it off for real. It's about time you seriously dated someone."

Callie smiled at Jinny over the rim of her mug, and Jinny didn't like the dreamy look on her face.

It was no secret Callie had hated Jinny's last couple of boyfriends. It reminded her of the conversation she had with Emmett about her dating nothing but losers, and she felt her hackles rise before she could stop them.

"Why do I need a serious boyfriend? The last thing I need is a man. I landed my dream job, and pretty soon the Kimball trophy will be in a place of honor in my home"—Jinny motioned toward the shelf across the room, which was empty in preparation for her epic win—"What else could I need?"

Callie groaned. "Oh, my gosh. You're going to put that ugly thing there? Everyone will see it when they walk in the front door."

"Exactly." Jinny beamed, despite Callie's wide-eyed mortification.

"Anyway, my point is, you could at least bring him as your date to my wedding."

"Hmm. Maybe." It might not be a bad idea, considering half the people in attendance would be from the team.

Callie and Dean had opted for an intimate venue since Callie's parents were killed in a car crash seven years ago and she had almost no family. Seeing as how Gabe was familiar with half the guest list, he'd fit right in.

"Just think about it," Callie said, then paused.

Without warning, she scooched closer to Jinny and reached out to take Jinny's hand into her own as moisture filled her eyes. For a second, Jinny stiffened—until she noted Callie's smile and the pink glow to her cheeks.

"Will you be my maid of honor?" Callie asked.

Jinny grinned and smacked Callie on the arm. "Of course, you dummy. Like I thought you'd choose anyone else. I'm the best option. Obviously." She rolled her eyes and Callie laughed.

"This should be some wedding," Callie said.

Jinny removed the electrodes from Emmett's legs, a

little rougher than necessary, yanking out several hairs in the process.

"Ouch." He rubbed the four angry-red circles forming on the skin over his muscular thigh.

"Oh, sorry. Did I take them off too quick?" She blinked up at him innocently.

He smirked. "That's okay. Now it's time for the best part of my day."

Jinny groaned. "One man's pleasure is another woman's pain," she said, voice dripping with sarcasm.

Giving Emmett manual therapy had to be the worst part of her job. Still, if she had to do it, she'd make it the most amazing leg rub of his life. Make him leave wanting more, so nothing the rest of his adult life could ever compare to the time when he was gifted a massage from Jinny Kimball.

Emmett scoffed, breaking through her thoughts. "Please, like this isn't the best part of *your* day. So many women would pay to be in your position—would kill for it. What lady wouldn't die for the opportunity to put their hands on NBA super-star Emmett Halls' game-winning muscles?"

"Hold on." Jinny held up a hand and fake gagged. "I think I might have just puked a little." Then she headed to the counter where she kept her special blend of essential oils and almond oil for massage.

"What must it be like, being so full of yourself that you have actual bullcrap seeping from your eyes?" she asked.

Emmett shrugged. "Just being honest."

She returned to his side and eyed his leg with resentment. It was impressive. If you liked muscles.

"The question is how many women before me have actually touched your leg. I'm willing to bet the number is monumental. I should probably have my gloves out for this."

Emmett chuckled. "I noticed you haven't been wearing them this week."

Jinny gave the bottle of oil an angry shake and squirted some onto his leg. Then she began to rub the muscles of his quad in the answering silence.

Where the heck was Gabe?

She'd asked him to stop by ten minutes ago. Just like she had done all the other times. Three massages under her belt and she had yet to be in the room alone with Emmett for any of them. She could only imagine the snide remarks he'd make if she didn't have a buffer. It had absolutely nothing to do with needing a distraction from the way her skin burned as she worked. Or how her stomach squeezed when he leaned back on the table, causing the hard lines of his washboard abs to strain against his t-shirt. Gross.

She pressed her fingertips into his quads and applied steady pressure as she drug her hands down the length of his muscle toward the knee, then back again.

More unnerving than the scent of cedarwood, or whatever heavenly—er, ghastly—cologne he wore, was his gaze. It burned straight into the side of her face as she worked.

She tried to ignore it. Really, she did. But in a moment of weakness, she glanced up and caught his eye. Something dark and dangerous flickered through the hazel and honey. Flushing, she looked away. Clearly, he had some kind of voodoo going on. Well, she, for one, would not fall victim. She was not another one of his bimbos. She was Jinny Kimball, sports certified specialist and physical therapist for the Pittsburgh Pumas. She was a professional. And she was *not* thinking about his chiseled jaw or his pouty lips.

Before she could register what was happening, Emmett leaned up and gripped her wrist. She froze. Her heart threatened to pound from her chest.

When she heard the knock on the door, she jumped, and he released her.

She said a prayer of thanks to all that was holy as she hollered for him to come in, and Gabe stepped inside.

"Hey, you wanted to—"

"Yeah. Uh...er...I..." Jinny trailed off.

Dang it. With all her scheming, and all her rubbing Emmett's sinewy muscles, she forgot what excuse she was supposed to use.

"I just wanted to see if you were free for coffee later."

Gabe's face lit up. His blue eyes were the exact opposite of Emmett's warm amber. It was like looking at a bleak sky versus staring into the blazing sun. With one, you got burned.

She wiped the thought away and smiled as Gabe took another step closer.

"Yeah, I have an appointment in five minutes, but come see me after. I should have time then."

Jinny nodded. *Great.* Thus far, she had avoided making any overt gestures to imply her interest in Gabe. Until now. Smooth move, *Miss J.*

Gabe placed his hands on his hips and smiled, but Jinny no longer cared about her impending coffee date— was it a date?—because all that mattered was that Gabe wasn't leaving yet.

She refused to meet Emmett's eye. Instead, she kept massaging, her gaze vacillating between her hands and Gabe, despite Emmett's gaze burning a hole right through her.

"Actually, I was going to ask if you were free this weekend. A friend of mine has a boat and was going to take it out on Saturday," Gabe said.

"Oh, gosh. I'd love to," she lied. "But my family has this thing every year. It's kind of like a Fourth of July celebration and family reunion all in one. But there are games and stuff. It's kind of a big deal, actually."

She smiled, grateful for the excuse. *Thank you, Kimball Olympics.*

Gabe's smile fell, but she gave him credit; he only faltered for a minute before the glistening hope returned to his eye. "Rain check?"

She ran her fingers down the front of Emmett's calf, then back up the length of his leg, trying to think of the proper response when Emmett moaned. Like, a deep-in-your-gut ecstasy moan.

Her head whipped in his direction, as did Gabe's. And she swore she saw a flash of a smile on Emmett's face before it vanished and he continued his groaning and moaning.

What the—

She glanced over at Gabe, at a loss for words, slightly horrified.

Gabe swallowed, then loosened the collar of his dress shirt. "What do you put in that stuff?" He nodded toward her homemade oils.

Jinny blinked over at the bottle. "Just some peppermint, eucalyptus, frankincense, and—"

Emmett mewed.

All she could do was turn and stare as the noise escaped his parted lips.

She bit the inside of her cheek, stifling a laugh. She was two seconds away from losing it when Gabe exhaled and backed slowly out the door.

Once he'd disappeared down the hall, Jinny removed her hands from Emmett's leg and forced a scowl. "Very funny."

She moved to the counter and grabbed a paper towel to wipe the oil from her hands.

"What?" Emmett blinked innocently.

"You know what."

With a smug smile, he straightened. "If I promise to behave, will you continue?"

"No. I think you've had all you can handle." Jinny grabbed his chart and made a couple notes.

"So, is this how the next six to nine months are going to be, then?" he asked.

"I don't know what you're referring to." Jinny put the file down and stared at him.

"At massage time, you're going to call him in here?"

"I did no such thing."

Emmett arched a brow at her.

"I wanted coffee," she muttered.

"Sure, you did."

Jinny lifted her chin in defiance.

"Oh, come on. You want coffee with him like you want an enema. I can see it all over your face. Soul surfer might be into you, but he is the last thing you want. He's just too blind to see it. Poor guy. It's sad, really."

Jinny pursed her lips, keeping her mouth shut as she

burned him with her gaze. But stern gazes were hard to hold when his dimples winked at her behind a radiant smile. Invisible fingers drew her toward him. One wrong move and she might crack.

"Admit it," he insisted.

"Are you this annoyingly persistent with everything in your life?"

"Is there any other way to be? Persistence is for winners. The opposite of persistence is quitting, and I'm no loser, Jinny." He cocked his head. "So, what'll it be? Are you going to admit I'm right?"

She crossed her arms over her chest, her gaze unwavering in their silent game of chicken. Only, she hadn't accounted for how good he was at a standoff. His expression turned to stone. He didn't even so much as move his chest to breathe. She wouldn't be surprised if, under his ribs, his heart stopped beating just to win this game. He was inhuman, a freak of nature.

After a moment of silence, she threw her hands up. He would never let it drop until she admitted it. "Fine! You're right. I didn't want coffee. I just didn't want to be alone in the room with you. Not because I'm attracted to you, of course. It's more like I need a witness to protect me from false accusations of harassment in the workplace."

She sagged under his triumphant gaze. "Happy?"

Emmett chuckled. "Very."

CHAPTER EIGHT

Emmett

The Pittsburgh Pirates entered the bottom of the ninth. It was a beautiful day. Blue skies above and sunny, temperate weather. The city lay beyond the stadium, a backdrop to the pandemonium inside as the Pirates made a comeback to tie the score.

It was a good game, but Emmett found it nearly impossible to focus. He had yet to broach the subject of the Fourth of July weekend, despite that being the reason he bought the special VIP seats and invited Dean along.

He glanced at his friend out of the corner of his eye. Dean plucked his phone from his pocket and texted his fiancée—for the millionth time that night—with a dopey grin on his face.

"Everything okay?" Emmett asked.

"What?" Dean glanced over at him. "Oh, yeah. Sorry. Callie just...it's nothing."

Dean's eyes gleamed, his skin glowed, and he had an utterly distracted look on his face, the look of being madly in love.

The lucky jerk.

"So..." Dean scratched the back of his neck. "One of the reasons I came out with you tonight was because I need to ask you something. I don't know if there's some special way I'm supposed to do this, but—"

"Dude," Emmett gasped and widened his eyes in mock horror. "I can't believe you would do this to Callie. No, I won't marry you," he yelled, loud enough for the people around them to hear.

Several sets of questioning eyes turned on them, and Dean smirked. "You idiot. I want to know if you'll be my best man."

"Of course. Who else is there? I mean, I did practically help you land your fiancée."

Dean cocked his head. "You're seriously taking credit?"

"I'm pretty sure it was my idea for you to fake a relationship with her."

"That's not how I remember it."

"Getting dementia already?" He smacked Dean on the arm. "Callie's got a long road ahead of her."

Dean laughed. "Well, I just wanted to run it by you first because Jinny's the maid of honor, and I can't have you two killing each other before you walk down the aisle."

Emmett visualized walking down the aisle next to Jinny while she clung to his arm. The image made him smile. Most women loved weddings, and though he didn't see Jinny as being the sappy type, it was her brother and best friend getting married. She was bound to be emotional and nostalgic—the perfect combo to swoop in and—

"What's that look on your face?" Dean asked.

"What look?"

He peered at Emmett closer. "You look like you're trying to take a massive dump."

"What?"

Dean shook his head.

If he made that face when he thought of Jinny, no wonder she was repulsed by him.

Emmett glanced away from Dean, lest he see the yearning in his expression. He wasn't supposed to want his best friend's little sister so badly. Dean would kill him if he knew the direction of his thoughts.

Emmett would rather take a dagger to the eye than cue Dean in to the fact his heart raced at the thought of dancing with Jinny at the wedding. Feeling his side brush against hers as he escorted her toward the altar. Placing his hand on the small of her back.

He shouldn't be picturing her painted lips, or the way she'd look in her bridesmaid's dress as it hugged her curves.

Emmett cleared his throat and pushed the image aside. "What did Jinny say about it? Being in the wedding with me?"

Laughter danced in Dean's eyes. "Callie chickened out. I don't think she told her yet."

Emmett nodded. He expected as much. When she did find out, the news would go over about as well as a mother being told she'd have to sell her firstborn child.

With a resigned sigh, Emmett leaned back and raked a hand through his hair. Over the past two weeks in therapy, Jinny had proved as stubborn and feisty as a mule. She'd done everything to get under his skin. What she didn't realize was that the more she tried, the more he wanted her. With every ridiculous thing she did to push him away, to annoy him, she only endeared herself to him more. He had no idea what her plan was. Annoy him to death? Try and get him to seek treatment elsewhere? Curb his attraction to her? Well, the joke was on her because none of it was working.

She was so unlike anyone he had ever met. It wasn't just her dark hair—the color of cocoa and smelling of cookies and vanilla—or her warm brown eyes that turned molten when she was angry. It wasn't the little crease of concentration on her brow as she worked, or the way she took her job seriously, despite her antics. Or the fact that the feel of her strong hands at work, in juxtaposition to her baby-soft skin, turned him inside out. Those were all things that he liked about her, but they weren't the things that made him wish he could be a man worth having. It was how much she loved her job. Her passion. The way she didn't fall all over herself to impress him. She didn't tell him every-thing he wanted to hear. Instead, she called him out on his crap. She mocked him and pushed all his buttons.

Jinny pretended for no one. She was herself no matter what, and if that wasn't the single most attractive thing in a woman, Emmett didn't know what was.

He was caught—hook, line, and sinker.

He needed to stay away from her. There may as well be a blinking caution sign in his head, warning him away. But Emmett was never one for treading lightly, always throw-ing forethought to the wind.

"I heard Swanson might have a thing for her," Dean said, interrupting his thoughts and bringing him back to the present. "You know anything about that?"

"I think maybe they went for coffee."

Dean stared at him like he was waiting for more.

"I wouldn't be too worried about it," Emmett added. "I've seen her talking to him. She's not into him."

Dean grunted. "Well, when you're in there, you're my eyes and ears, man. We need to squash that. Gabe's okay, but he's not good enough for my sister."

"Is anyone?"

"If I'm honest, no." Dean shook his head. "But I don't want her with anyone associated with the team. If things went south, I'd have to kill them. I'm pretty sure homicide is against the NBA code of ethics."

Emmett snorted. The blinking caution sign grew so bright it nearly blinded him. He had to lift a hand to shield his corneas. Everything inside him told him to let the conversation die, watch the game in companionable silence, and then go home.

He valued his life, didn't he? He valued his friendship, the team. Basketball was his lifeblood. So, why in the world was he opening his mouth to speak?

"So, got any plans this weekend?" He eyed Dean from his peripheral, hoping he'd miss his deliberate tone.

"As a matter of fact, I do. You?"

"Nah." Emmett shook his head. "Usually, I'd fly home to Philly, but my dad and my brothers always play ball on the Fourth." And every other time they get together, for that matter. "I can't do that this year. I'm not sure what's worse.

The thought of having to sit on the sidelines and watch my old man play or sitting the bench come September." He exhaled.

Maybe the trajectory of the conversation was prefabricated, but what he was saying was true. "The last thing I want to do is go and be reminded of how I'm down and out. My little brother, Jon, is halfway to the NBA. He has recruiters breathing down his neck already, and he's only in his junior year at Duke. Wouldn't it be ironic if they recruited him as my replacement?"

"Not gonna happen, dude. You're not going anywhere," Dean said.

"Don't get me wrong. I'm happy for him. I remember when the Pumas came calling. Best day of my life. I'm just not sure I'm up to hearing about it, ya know? Right now..." Emmett lifted his shoulders and let them fall.

"I get it." Dean hesitated. His gaze shifted off into the distance, not seeming to focus on anything. "You should come to my parent's place," he said finally, and Emmett just about dropped to his knees in prayer.

"Yeah?"

Dean nodded, turning his gaze on him. "There's always tons of food. All my extended family comes. We barbeque, and everyone brings something to share. Plus, we play games. It's kind of this whole big thing. Be warned though, if you come, Jinny will be in rare form. She gets extra hyped for it, and she doesn't like unexpected competition."

Unable to stop his spreading grin, Emmett basked in the small victory of the invite.

"I'd love to come. Thanks, man."

He had no idea what Jinny in rare form was like, but he couldn't wait to find out.

$$\infty \infty \infty$$

Jinny

Jinny woke with an extra pep to her step. Today was her version of Christmas. The one day she waited for all year long. The day she reclaimed her title. Today was the Kimball Olympics.

She took her time showering, noting the perfect temperature of the water. The body wash she used smelled like victory, and the sound of the spray pelting the shower door sounded like applause.

She dried off and changed into her most comfortable pair of spandex workout capris, a sports bra, and a razorback tank. She topped it off with ankle socks and her best pair of running shoes. The best workout clothes money could buy, designed to heighten performance and allow maximum movement and flexibility—the textiles of champions.

Yanking her hair up into a messy ponytail, she left it as-is, swiped on some lip gloss with SPF in it, then headed out to the kitchen to grab some breakfast before going to her parent's house. No point in wearing makeup that would just melt off the second she started racing around in the heat. Fresh-faced and bright-eyed was the way to go.

Callie was already at the breakfast counter, munching on granola and fruit. Jinny offered her a smile, grabbing her travel mug out of the cupboard. She filled it and took a sip. The nutty aroma and bold flavor instantly lifted her spirits. Not that they needed lifting. Vindication was stronger than any cup of coffee could ever be. Especially when you'd waited three long years for it.

Today was the day she would claim her rightful place on the Kimball throne.

She smeared a cinnamon raisin bagel with cream cheese and filled her water bottle from the tap.

"You look ready to go," Callie noted.

Jinny inhaled deeply, absorbing oxygen into her lungs and soaking up the sunshine streaming through the window. "It's a beautiful day, isn't it?"

"Mm-hm."

"Is that what you're wearing?" Jinny asked, motioning to Callie's strappy sandals, jean shorts, and silky, cap-sleeved shirt. "You'll never be able to run in those shoes.

And that shirt." Jinny grimaced. "You'll be sweating all over the place."

Callie glanced down at her ensemble. "I don't plan on trying that hard. Besides, I wanted to look cute for Dean."

Jinny groaned and rolled her eyes. "You are everything wrong with the female race." She ripped a chunk of bagel off with her teeth and chewed. The sweet bread and tangy cream cheese filled her mouth, a glorious combination. She swallowed and licked her lips.

"But that's okay," Jinny said "You'll be one less body in the way. Not that you were competition before."

"Oh, thanks." Callie rolled her eyes, but Jinny knew her well enough to know the insult had bounced right off.

"Ready?" Jinny asked over her shoulder, already headed for the door.

"Someone's eager."

"It's never too early to scope out the competition."

Jinny blabbed on, in between bites of bagel, as they stepped out onto the sidewalk and headed for her car. She paused in front of Betsy, tapping her hand on the roof. The blue paint was chipping and dotted with rust.

"You know," Jinny said, eyeing Callie over the roof of her car. "If you're going to be a Kimball soon, we really need to work on your competitive drive. It's unnatural." With that, she sunk into the driver's seat and turned her key in the ignition.

Betsy started right up. Jinny hooted, pumping her fist in the air. "See! Today is my day. Even Betsy knows. The coffee's hot, the bagels are fresh, the sun is shining, and I am prepared to crush some Kimball butt. Even Beater Betsy's roaring and ready to go, eager to get started. Well, ol' girl, here we go." She patted the peeling steering wheel. "This day couldn't get any better if it tried."

By the time they arrived at her parent's house, it was after ten o'clock in the morning. The Kimball Olympics were set to start at eleven-thirty, followed by a late lunch at two o'clock (of which the victor got first dibs), and after everyone had eaten their fill, they held the victor's ceremony. This was when the rightful owner of the Kimball Ninja Warrior trophy received their honor and was crowned the winner—in this case, when *she* was proclaimed victor.

After that, the rest of the evening was a crapshoot. Usually Uncle Bill got drunk and started grabbing Aunt Mindy's butt, then her father started dancing to eighties music, giving his best rendition of the running man, and Uncle Sal relived his glory days. If they were lucky, her mother amped up the karaoke before fireworks, and then everyone went home in food-induced comas.

She practically floated out of the car and into the house. She entered the kitchen, where her mother was prepping the macaroni salad and fruit tray for lunch. Dean was already there. His dark hair was rumpled, and he wore a ratty old t-shirt and gym shorts. He looked like he'd rolled out of bed at five a.m. and hightailed it there, just so he could beat her. A sorry intimidation tactic. But she was no longer sixteen. His mind games didn't work on her. His early arrival meant nothing. There was something to be said for being well rested.

Dean stuck his foot out as she passed, but she expertly skipped over it, countering with an elbow jab to the ribs.

When her mother turned at the *oomph* of Dean's breath catching in his lungs, Jinny smiled sweetly. She was the picture of innocence. "Hi, Mom."

"Oh hi, dear."

Callie followed behind, slightly out of breath, carting the giant roaster full of cheesy potatoes. "Where would you like me to put this, Mrs. Kimball?"

Mrs. Kimball drew Callie into a hug. "Those smell delicious. We'll just plug them in right here," she said, patting the counter. Then she shot Jinny a look that asked why she didn't ever contribute to the meal.

Jinny put her hands out in a gesture that was half-shrug, half-question. What did her mom expect? She wasn't there for the food; she was there to compete.

Yeesh. Did her mother think Michael Phelps had time to make fat-laden potatoes the morning of a race? She swore that sometimes the woman who'd birthed her liked

Callie better than her own children.

"Well, I guess I'll go outside and stretch," Jinny announced.

She headed for the door, but her gait slowed as she spotted a shiny silver Audi pull up and park on the side of the road. It looked familiar, but she couldn't place it.

Alarm bells blared in her head. She squinted, but at this distance, she couldn't make out the driver. The windows were far too dark for her to see inside.

"Who's that?" Jinny asked, peering out the door.

The driver stepped out. He wore dark aviators and a navy-blue Pumas cap pulled down low over his eyes. She took a moment to appreciate his shapely derriere as he closed his door. *Well, hello, Mr. Nice Booty.* When he turned around, her eyes swept back up to his face, and she froze.

Shock blasted through her, and a prickling sensation ascended her spine as she took in the sharp jaw and tan skin, the hint of sandy sideburns below his cap. She'd recognize him anywhere. The broad shoulders and muscular chest below the clingy Under Armour shirt were dead giveaways, as well as his familiar swagger.

Her eyes widened. It was Emmett-friggin'-Hall.

CHAPTER NINE

Jinny

"You what?" Jinny screeched, her voice shrill enough to shatter mirrors.

Dean winced and stuck a finger in his ear.

Good, his hearing would be off for the competition.

He spread his arms in front of her like he had done nothing wrong. Like he was innocent in all this, when everyone could plainly see the blood on his hands.

"He didn't have anywhere to go, and I didn't want him to be alone, so I asked if he wanted to come," he said.

Pah! Like *that* was a defense.

Jinny's hands fisted by her side and she nearly lunged at her brother. "Of course he didn't have anywhere to go. No one can stand to be around him for more than five minutes."

She seethed as her mother gasped behind her. "Jinny Ray Kimball."

Jinny groaned at the sound of her full name.

"I can't believe you would be so unwelcoming." Her mother scowled then stormed out to the front yard to greet him.

Once she was gone, Jinny turned her icy glare back to Dean's full-bore. Now he had no one to save him.

"We never invite outsiders," she hissed.

Dean shrugged. "What was I supposed to do? He has four brothers, and it's a tradition for them all to play ball with their dad every Fourth. His younger brother, Jon, is about to get an offer and is all hyped up about going pro. You should've seen the look on his face when he was talking about how he'd have to sit and watch. I'd go stir crazy if I were in his shoes."

"Of course he did." Jinny rolled her eyes so hard it was a miracle they didn't fall from their sockets. "He probably even had a little glimmer of a tear in his eye. I bet he just made that whole thing up to get an invite."

Now that she said it, her theory seemed rather valid. Hadn't she mentioned her weekend plans to Gabe in front of Emmett?

The sound of her mother's voice pulled her from her thoughts. Jinny didn't need to look to know her mother was fawning all over him. She could hear it from there. Her warmth for the enemy was sickening.

"Seriously? You're that mad?" Dean flicked his gaze to Callie for support.

Callie shrugged. "You know how much you guys look forward to this every year. And she and Emmett don't exactly get along."

Jinny flashed him a smug smile as if to say *even your fiancée agrees with me.*

Dean straightened, his expression tight. He was clearly offended Callie had backed Jinny up. "Whatever. He's my friend, and I'll invite him if I want. I think you're being a child."

Jinny crossed her arms over her chest and turned to face the door.

Never turn your back on the enemy. She preferred to have Emmett right where she could see him.

Her mother waved him inside. He practically walked on air as he joined them in the kitchen, like he was part of the family.

Jinny's jaw clenched as he made his rounds, greeting everyone in sight. He even said hello to her Aunt Penny out the kitchen window. Everyone except her.

He had yet to acknowledge her presence as Dean engaged him in some ridiculous conversation about a new machine they got at the gym.

She straightened, snatching her water bottle off the counter, and took an angry drink. Emmett's lips twitched as Dean spoke with him, and she could tell he was repressing a smile. He was trying to get under her skin. Like she cared if he said hello. She was glad he finally took the hint and pretended she didn't exist.

Where had she gone wrong? The day had been perfect. She woke up at just the right time, wore the right clothes, ate the right breakfast. The weather was perfect. Her favorite song came on the radio on the way there. Even Betsy had been at the top of her game. How could this—of all things—be happening?

Today was her day to shine, and Emmett was like a giant rain cloud blocking her rays from reaching the ground, darkening everything in his path.

Dean said something and tipped his head in her direction, causing Emmett to laugh.

Oh no they didn't. They weren't going to talk about her like she wasn't there. But she hadn't heard what they said. As she focused on their conversation, she realized, to her horror, that Dean was explaining the Kimball Olympics to him. LIKE HE MIGHT *PLAY*.

Over her dead body.

She leapt forward to stop them but was slightly off with her trajectory. The side of her body crashed into Emmett, but he didn't even budge. He just stood there, a giant, stupid wall of muscle. He may as well have been made of concrete.

Everyone turned to stare at her while Emmett's right hand shot out as she wobbled, steadying her so she didn't fall. She tried to ignore the way his touch singed her skin and instead focused on shooting death rays from her eyeballs.

"He's not a Kimball. He can't play," she said.

Dean glared at her. "Callie's not a Kimball, and she plays."

"Nuh-uh. Technically, she *is* going to be a Kimball."

"Yeah, but she's been playing for years." Dean pointed out.

Out of the corner of her eye, she noticed her mother lingering by the front door, readying herself to come back inside. If Jinny didn't hurry, her mother's scorn would crush her efforts to disqualify Emmett from play.

"He's injured." Jinny motioned to Emmett's bum leg. It was a low blow, but the truth hurt.

Emmett merely grinned his infuriating smile, dimples on full display. God, she hated them—always scream-ing, *look at me, look at me*, like they were something special.

"Good thing I have this really amazing therapist. She's actually at the party. I'm sure she'll keep me in check," Emmett said at the same moment her mother approached them.

"Jinny, you didn't tell me you were treating Emmett, but I guess I should've known."

"Yes, it's lovely," Jinny said in a bland voice. "He's a pic-ture perfect patient." *From Hades.*

Emmett smirked and leaned back against the counter as her father appeared from around the corner, offering him a beer.

"Dad, it's eleven o'clock," Jinny protested.

"It's five o'clock somewhere. Am I right, Hall?" he said.

"Yes, sir."

Sir? SIR?!

Her father shot her a look as if to say, *See, he's a keeper.* There was nothing he loved more than respect for author-ity. It was probably why she was his least favorite.

Jinny grunted. She was losing.

Ignoring her, Dean turned to their mother. "Emmett can compete. Right, Mom?"

Her mother paused a moment, then nodded. "Yeah. Sure. I don't see why not."

"Thanks. You're the best." Dean flashed her a triumphant smile.

Her mind reeled, grasping for a reason for her mother to take her side. "Mom, let's be real for a moment. How is Emmett supposed to do a sack race with a torn ACL? As his therapist, I cannot sign off on this kind of activity. I'm only thinking of his well-being. We all should." She let her words hang in the air, placing a hand over her heart in a solemn oath.

"We'll choose a different event instead," her mother said.

What? "Different event? Um, no. You can't switch things up like that. You—"

Jinny bit her tongue at her father's warning glare. Behind him, Dean looked way too happy and her mother scowled.

Everyone had come unhinged. She was the only sane one in the house.

She had no idea what Emmett had said to her mother in the two minutes they had chatted outside or what kind of mind games he was playing with her father, but clearly, they were brainwashed. She blamed it on the dimples. They were hypnotic.

With a huff, Jinny watched as her father handed Emmett a beer.

Jinny's mother lifted the fruit tray in offering. "Hungry?"

Jinny gaped at her. Since when did her mother allow them to eat the prepped food before mealtime? If Jinny had tried that, she'd get a finger lobbed off.

With a smug grin, Emmett reached over, grabbed a handful of cantaloupe chunks, and crammed them in his mouth. Her mother smiled like he was the prodigal son returned. When she told him to make himself at home and scurried outside to greet Uncle Ed, Jinny turned on him.

"You're an animal," Jinny said. "Go ahead. Fill up on carbs and booze. By all means, please dehydrate your muscles before we compete. Maybe they'll atrophy and you'll get an arm cramp during Pick the Pickle."

Emmett took a long drag on his beer, washing down the cantaloupe.

Jinny grimaced. "That's disgusting."

"Nice to see you, too." Emmett grinned. "Tell me, how was your coffee with Snooze Fest."

Jinny narrowed her eyes at him. "Wouldn't you like to know."

She took a step toward him, like a lion stalking its prey. "You know, it's bad enough I have to see you Monday through Friday; you just had to come and ruin my weekend, too?"

"Puh-lease." He plucked a strawberry off the tray and popped it into his mouth.

She watched him chew, transfixed by his mouth for

a moment and the way his jaw worked—*he had really nice mandibles.*

What in the world was she thinking?

She yanked her gaze away as he swallowed.

"Seeing me is the highlight of your day. All the moments in between are filler," he said.

"More like the fiery pits of hell," she muttered.

"Um, maybe we should..." Callie trailed off.

Out of the corner of Jinny's eye, she noticed Callie tug on Dean's arm and pull him from the kitchen. Jinny had forgotten they were there. She had been too busy with her staring contest with Emmett to care.

Now that she thought about it, Dean inviting Emmett made perfect sense. Obviously he sensed he would lose this year, and he'd invited him along as a distraction. It was all tactic. The sneaky jerk.

Well, Big Bro was about to be disappointed because he'd just fueled her fire.

Emmett leaned back against the counter, beer in hand, like he hadn't a care in the world. When he finally removed his aviators, his eyes were trained directly on her. Their vibrant hazel punched her in the gut. Suddenly, she wished she had done more with her appearance than a sloppy pony and lip gloss. But, come on. This was an athletic competition. Not a beauty pageant. Dean could die a slow death for even making her think twice about it.

"Afraid you'll lose?" Emmett asked.

"*Psh*, not likely. I'm just afraid you'll further injure your sorry butt, and then I'll be stuck with you till the day I die."

"Don't you think it's a little too soon for a marriage proposal?"

"Funny."

Emmett set his beer on the counter, his expression placid. Lifting his sunglasses to his mouth, he puffed a breath of hot air onto them and wiped the smudges from the lenses with the hem of his shirt, revealing a sliver of his toned torso.

Jinny swallowed, wrenching her eyes away from the triangle of skin. He was playing games with her head, trying to distract her.

Well, not today, Hall.

"Call it what you want. I see fear in your eyes," he said.

"Ha. That's just me forcing down the vomit from the back of my throat."

"Care for a little wager?" Emmett asked as he perched the sunglasses on the top of his ball cap. His boyish appearance was disgustingly appealing.

"Fine." Jinny crossed her arms and tipped her chin. "What are the terms?"

"If you win the Kimball Olympics, I'll leave. I won't even stay for so much as a burger. And if I win..." He trailed off, pursing his lips.

He was toying with her. Jinny could see it in his eyes. He already knew what the stakes would be, but he wanted to drag this out.

Jinny arched a brow, letting him know she wasn't playing his game.

"If I win," Emmett said slowly, taking a step toward her.

Her breathing hitched.

Now, who was the prey?

"You have to kiss me," he murmured.

CHAPTER TEN

Jinny

Round 1

J inny rolled her head on her neck, working out the kinks. All of the contestants lined up, facing off in front of a massive row of folding tables. The first event had yet to be announced, and the tables were no giveaway—a lot of the games required the use of a level surface.

Her mother explained the rules while Jinny only half-listened. She'd heard them a million times, knew them all by heart. Everyone was ranked per event, with the person at the bottom being dropped from the competition. With each new game, their scores were recalculated. Whoever finished with the most points after round ten was the winner. Even someone as thick-headed as Emmett could understand the rules.

Jinny waited as her mother announced the first game. Coinhole. It followed the same concept as cornhole, except instead of tossing bean bags into the hole on a large board, you had to bounce a quarter onto a tiny board with a small opening.

It was much harder than cornhole. With no practice, it was practically impossible to score well.

Jinny dared a glance at Emmett across from her and gave him a pitying smile. He had removed his sunglasses, so she could see the flecks of green in his eyes.

"Nice knowin' ya, Hall." She gave him a little wave, but he said nothing.

Instead, he raised a brow and lifted his ball cap, turning it backward and resituating it on his head.

Jinny flexed her fingers. She refused to lose focus just because he looked kinda cute with his hat turned backward.

What was it with men and baseball caps that was so appealing?

"Don't go getting all distracted staring at me, slim. Wouldn't want you to miss the starting call because you're too busy ogling."

Jinny offered a tight smile. "Actually, I was just thinking I should thank you. You did me a favor. Your giant body's blocking the sun from my eyes."

"So, you admit to checking out my body."

"That's not what I—" She snapped her mouth shut. "Nice try goading me, but it won't work."

"I should feel violated."

She rolled her eyes, ignoring him. She needed to focus.

She flexed her fingers. Coinhole was all about the flick of the wrist, the bounce of the quarter toward the mini-board.

She did some shoulder rolls and cracked her knuckles, ignoring the way Emmett leaned over the table as the boards were laid out in front of them, fingers twitching at the ready.

Her mother held the whistle between her teeth and raised her arm. The second she blew the whistle, Jinny snatched her quarter from the table and began.

Round 4

Jinny clapped her hands. Bring it on.

She was two for four, with Dean taking one and Emmett taking one. Callie had already been eliminated, which led to her being teased mercilessly. Even their seventy-eight-year-old Uncle Ed with his walker managed to last longer.

A bubble of excitement filled Jinny's chest, but she worked to suppress it. She was off to a good start, but she had a long way to go. If she got too cocky, things could fall apart.

"Next competition," her mother announced, "is Nut Stack."

Emmett chuckled. "Not to be confused with—"

"Really mature," Jinny snapped.

"The objective of the game is to stack as many iron nuts as you can on top of your plastic cup. You have one minute," her mother explained. "If your tower topples, you have to start from the beginning."

"Easy," Emmett cooed.

Jinny gritted her teeth. Did he have to comment on everything?

"But there's a catch," her mother added. "You have to use chopsticks."

Jinny filled with joy as she watched Emmett's smile fade.

"Where's your confidence now, Hall?" She snickered. "You know, if you want to bail out now, I wouldn't blame you. It wouldn't make you any less of a man." She cocked her head. "Well, not really."

Emmett's lips twitched. "You'd like that, wouldn't you? That way, there's no chance of me winning."

"Am I that obvious?" Jinny feigned innocence then rolled her eyes. Glancing over at Dean to ensure he was out of earshot, she leaned over the table and hissed, "Who knows what I'd catch if I had to lock lips with you."

"Or there's another reason you're afraid I'll win."

"What? Like having to endure all afternoon watching you schmooze my family?"

Emmett shook his head and shrugged, a smarmy grin on his face.

He was trying to act all nonchalant, but he wasn't fooling her. She wouldn't bite. She didn't need to know.

She crossed her arms over her chest as her mother tucked her whistle between her teeth. Whatever Emmett hadn't said was irrelevant.

"Fine," Jinny all but barked. She had to know! "What is that you think I'm so afraid of?"

Emmett met her gaze. "You're scared you might like it."

The whistle blew, catching Jinny off guard, but that must've been his plan all along because Emmett immediately jumped into action. The cheater.

He already had two nuts stacked by the time Jinny even picked up her chopsticks. With her pulse racing, she worked, trying to will herself to calm down. She was still in this.

Round 7

Dean 2; Emmett 3; Jinny 2.

It was her worst nightmare. How could she be losing? And not just losing. But losing to *him*?

Because Emmett played dirty. That's why.

The nut trick had thrown her off her game. His win in Nut Stack put a chink in her confidence, which led to her defeat at apple bobbing—an event she always prided herself on dominating.

The work the man could do with his teeth and mouth was astounding. He'd smoked everyone. Jinny broke out into a sweat just thinking about it.

But all was not lost. There was plenty of time to catch up and take home the trophy. So when Callie brought out the tissue boxes, Jinny smiled.

Junk in the Ba-Dunk-a-Dunk. No one shook their booty like Jinny. No one.

Wait. Hadn't Callie mentioned something about Dean practicing for this particular event?

Jinny's gaze darted to Dean, and she sneered as they each received an empty tissue box. Promptly strapping hers around her waist, she waited as they received their instructions.

Each contestant had eight ping pong balls inside the tissue box that they had to shake out of the opening *without* the use of their hands, forced to rely on their hips and butt.

Good thing she did all those squats. Her glutes were prime.

An image of Emmett getting out of his car that morning flickered across her thoughts. What had she called him? Mr. Nice Booty?

She glanced at him, and he winked at her.

Ugh. It was like he could read her mind. So he had a nice butt. So, what?

She spread her legs, readying herself to pop her booty like Beyoncé in a music video. She'd drop it down. Drop it low. These balls didn't stand a chance.

The whistle blew and Jinny began shimmying.

She told herself not to look, to focus only on her own ping-pong balls, her own tissue box. *Eyes in your lane, Kimball,* she told herself.

But her eyes were traitorous. She glanced beside her to

see Emmett had already released four of his. What the—

Inspiration hit. Emmett wasn't the only one who could shake his rump.

Jinny bounded in front of Emmett, looking like a dancing hippo. She planted herself smack dab in front of him, and shook, shimmied, bounced—did everything in her arsenal to release those balls and distract the undistractible, the uber focused, Emmett.

Sweat beaded her brow and her breathing grew heavy. Her lungs burned.

When she risked a glance back at him, she noted the dead stare and slack-jawed expression. He had all but stopped shaking his hips.

"Ahahaha," she laughed, but the sound snapped Emmett from his trance.

She fell silent as he reentered the game with renewed vigor. But it was too late. Jinny had released all but one of her balls, and when the last one popped out, she jumped in the air, hooting in victory and pumping her fist like she'd just won the Super Bowl.

She passed Emmett, stretching her legs out as she strutted, taking a victory lap around him and giving the crowd a round of high fives as Emmett watched on, lips curling at the corners.

He shook his head, trying to suppress his grin, and her stomach clenched in response.

When she finally stilled and stood beside him, slightly out of breath, he murmured, "Well played, Miss J. Well played."

CHAPTER ELEVEN

Emmett

Round 10

He should've stayed away from her. He knew this, and yet here he was, at a Kimball party, competing against her for a prize he had no right to claim.

A kiss was off-limits.

Yet he'd do just about anything to win.

He had to give himself credit. He had even half convinced himself that he was capable of staying away.

Prior to arriving at the Kimball's, he told himself he'd spend the day hanging with Dean and watching Jinny from a distance. No problem. It might be a little like self-torture, but he was a big man. He could handle it.

Then he showed up and saw her with her tight little workout clothes on, looking so young and adorable with her snippy comments and her blazing eyes. The bet had just slipped out of his mouth.

He knew how much her job meant to her. The last thing he wanted to do was jeopardize it. And his own situation was precarious enough as it was.

Then there was Dean. He would kill Emmett if he saw the way his gaze tracked Jinny's every move. The way he watched her hips sway as she gloated after a win or how he fantasized pressing his mouth over those heart-shaped lips.

It didn't matter how wrong he knew it all was. The moment he saw Jinny in the Kimball's kitchen, all his reasons for keeping her at a distance faded away.

Maybe it didn't matter though. He had done a fine job of making her hate him. Maybe he'd pushed her so far away that she'd never let him in.

He stepped up to the table with the plates. He had to admit, as goofy as this whole Kimball Olympics thing was, it was the most fun he'd had in a while. He was almost sorry for it to end. Mostly because he loved watching Jinny's face light up when she won.

Jinny took her place next to him. The air between them snapped with tension.

The makeshift scoreboard—a giant dry-erase board—read Dean 2, Emmett 3, Jinny 3, and their Uncle Sal had shocked them all with a round eight win. It didn't matter though, Sal had been effectively eliminated. Even if he won the final event, he had no chance of winning now.

It was down to Dean, Emmett, and Jinny. If Dean won, he would cause a three-way tie and force them into overtime.

Emmett noted the way Jinny glanced down at the flour-filled plate in front of her, then peeked at him out of the corner of her eye. He could practically feel her nerves.

His stomach tied in knots as he watched her.

With sun-pinkened cheeks and tendrils of hair that had escaped her ponytail, she looked effortlessly beautiful. Natural. Real. Like the proverbial girl next door everyone wanted, but no one was good enough to touch, least of all him.

He turned his attention back to his plate as the event was explained. Technique for this one was obvious. Buried somewhere in the plate of flour was a lifesaver. All they had to do was retrieve it with their mouth—no hands.

He readied himself, knowing the best way would be to hold his breath, dive in deep, and use his face to mash the excess flour off the plate, then grip the lifesaver with his front teeth. The key was being uninhibited, unafraid to get flour in your eyes, up your nose, and in your mouth.

Callie sidled up next to Jinny. He tried not to listen, but couldn't help himself. It's like his brain was a radio that only tuned in to Jinny's frequency. Everything else was static.

Callie was giving her a pep talk. "You got this," she said. "One more, and this is all yours. But we're not putting the trophy on the shelf in our apartment."

"We totally are," Jinny whispered, focused.

Emmett hid his smile, amused that Callie chose to help Jinny instead of Dean. When he met her eye, Callie shrugged.

"What? Us girls have to stick together."

Emmett nodded, but as Callie stepped away and Mrs. Kimball raised her hand, he noticed Jinny swallowing. Her hands shook slightly as she gripped them behind her back and bit her lip.

Winning this ridiculous competition meant something to her. Something bigger than Emmett knew. And, whatever it was, he suddenly didn't want to take that away from her.

He stared at her furrowed brow, the crease between

her eyes, as he contemplated what to do. Maybe he didn't care about winning this competition, but he cared about the bet they'd made. He was used to getting what he wanted. Winning meant he got a kiss. And he wanted to kiss her more than he wanted to breathe.

When the whistle blew, he dived face-first into the flour. His execution was perfect as he pushed half of it off right out the gate and found the lifesaver with his lips. Just as he opened his mouth to nip it with his teeth, he heard Jinny beside him, coughing. He lifted his face just enough to see her—face caked in flour, like a ghost with two blinking eyes—hacking flour from her lungs.

Their eyes locked and she dived back down, wheezing as she did. She'd rather aspirate than lose.

Emmett clenched the lifesaver between his teeth and paused, biting down so hard he cracked it.

Crap.

He knew what he had to do.

He dropped the candy back to his plate and continued to root in the thick white dust. When a whistle blew, the winner was declared.

When he stood back up, the sight of Jinny raising her arms in victory tugged at his heart.

She beamed, completely giddy with excitement. She didn't even bother to wipe the flour from her face as she did a cartwheel of victory, landed in a half split, and pointed at him. "Beat you!"

Moving to Dean, she poked him in the chest, gloating. "And you. And you, and you." She hooted, pointing into the Kimball crowd.

Finally making a full circle with her rounds, she reached for the towels Callie was holding out at the same time Emmett did. Their hands met for a brief moment, long enough for electricity to spike his veins, adding to the twisting of his stomach.

He wiped his face with the damp towel. When he finished, he glanced back up to a half-clean version of Jinny.

Her snide grin was unmistakable as she fluttered her fingers in a wave. "Bye, Felicia."

Dean sidled up next to him as he watched her go back into the house. "You were a fierce opponent, Hall." Dean clapped him on the back. "I blame you for the next year of gloating I have to endure, but especially for the next twenty-four hours."

Emmett shrugged, toying with the towel in his hands.

"Wait..." Dean narrowed his eyes in the silence. "You didn't throw it, did you?"

Emmett's head snapped up. "What?"

"No one loves winning more than you. And you won the apple bobbing. It's similar..."

"I'm pretty sure no one is more competitive than Jinny."

"If you threw it just so she could win, I'd have to question your motives." Dean shook a finger at him.

Emmett ran a hand through his hair and took a step back. His heart raced as he protested. "Like I would let her win. That would be stupid. Why would I do that?"

Dean stared at him a moment, brows drawn low, before he broke into a smile and whipped him with his towel. "Nah, I'm just messing with you, man." He doubled over in laughter. "You should've seen your face."

Emmett exhaled in relief. "I kind of value my life."

"Come on, I know you better than that. Like you'd go after my baby sister." He clapped him on the back. "You know she's off-limits."

$\infty \infty \infty$

He knew the terms of the bet. He knew Jinny expected for him to leave, to run away with his tail tucked between his legs. She had graciously reminded him so an hour ago. But Mrs. Kimball had insisted he stay and eat, ignoring his protests that he had somewhere else to be.

Hey, he'd tried. A little.

He watched while Jinny, the victor, sashayed around the buffet, with her medal around her neck, as she got first dibs on the food, taking half of her mother's famous brownies out of spite. The plate sat in front of her, piled high with the fudgy dessert.

Emmett sat at the table across from hers, finishing the massive plate of food Mrs. Kimball had placed in front of him, while Jinny stared daggers at him. It didn't take long for Mrs. Kimball to notice he didn't have any dessert.

She pointed at his plate and perked up. "Oh, you must have something sweet. Hold on a minute. You know, I'm famous for my brownies."

Mrs. Kimball made a beeline straight for Jinny's hoard. As she tried to steal one from the top, Jinny covered them with her arms, shielding them like Gollum from The Lord of The Rings with his *precious*.

After a moment of dancing around her, Mrs. Kimball swatted her arms away and went in for the kill as Jinny jerked to deflect her shots. Stealing a brownie from a hole in her defenses, Mrs. Kimball smiled.

"Traitor!" Jinny yelled.

"Here ya go, dear," Mrs. Kimball said, handing it to him.

She sat down, oblivious to the staring contest he and her daughter were embroiled in.

Emmett arched a brow as he brought the brownie to his mouth and took a bite, moaning with pleasure and closing his eyes. But maybe he pushed it too far. Because when he opened them again, Jinny was gone.

CHAPTER TWELVE

Jinny

She skulked off, carrying her mountain of brownies, her hand hurting from the sheer weight of the plate.

She set it down on the kitchen counter with a loud thunk and crammed a brownie in her mouth while she stared out the window at Emmett, muttering to herself about take-backs, traitors, and lack of respect. Whoever said blood is thicker than water clearly didn't know Emmett

Hall. Or her mother.

"Traitors, all of them," she seethed as she waved a brownie in front of the window.

Maybe she could get a new family for Christmas. Yup. That was going straight to the top of her wish list. She wondered if Amazon Prime delivered new family members. If so, that two-day shipping wouldn't be fast enough.

Dean and Callie took a seat across from Emmett.

She huffed in annoyance as she watched. Looks like she'd be adding *new BFF* to the list, too.

Chomp, chomp, chomp. Her teeth gnashed at the massive brownie in her mouth, imagining it was Emmett's skull her jaw was crushing. If the Kimball Olympics had a brownie eating competition, she would've demolished it.

She watched with wide eyes as her father approached Emmett next, two beers in hand, and offered him one.

NO. Don't you take it.

Condensation dripped from the bottle in the afternoon heat. If it weren't for the chocolate in her mouth, Jinny'd be drooling at the sight of the cold beverage. She had yet to have one. She'd been too consumed with hydrating for the competition. Consumed with winning—which she'd done. Yet, here she was, hiding out in the kitchen because Emmett didn't know how to honor a bet.

Her eyes zoned in on the icy brew. *Don't even...*

Her father laughed at something Emmett said, and

before she knew it, Emmett smiled and accepted the bottle.

Jinny grunted and crammed another brownie in her mouth. Of course he took it. Sore loser. The Kimball Olympics was probably the first time in his life he ever lost anything. Especially to a woman. His giant-sized ego must be torn to shreds.

The thought made her smile. Several crumbs fell from her lips.

Maybe she should cut him some slack. The shock to his system must've given him temporary dementia. Clearly, he didn't know how bets worked. If you won, you got what you wanted. If you lost, you didn't. Honoring your side of the bargain wasn't optional. At least not if you were a *real* man.

Plowing another hunk of dessert into her mouth, she glanced down to the half-empty plate and grumbled to herself, cheeks full.

Why was he still here? And was this her plan—to eat a bazillion empty calories as revenge?

Someone tapped her shoulder, and she froze in her closet, stress-eating. In slow motion, she lifted her gaze back to the window. Emmett's seat at the picnic table was empty, and he was nowhere in sight.

She glanced up at the ceiling, expecting confetti and balloons to fall from the sky and rain down on her. Anytime now "Girl on Fire" by Alicia Keys would start playing.

Emmett had honored the bet. Victory was hers.

But instead of glee filling her blackened heart, her stomach twisted.

Must be the brownies. A bad batch. Emmett probably poisoned them when her back was turned.

There was another tap on her shoulder, followed by the clearing of someone's throat, jolting her from her thoughts.

She had forgotten about the person behind her, and she instantly knew who it was. She could smell him, even if she couldn't see him.

His cologne hit her like a freight train. The glorious scent of cedarwood, earth, and spice, with a hint of sweat. She took a deep breath, pinching her eyes closed and breathing it in. Then she glanced behind her as she stifled a gag. How nauseating.

She was fully aware of her cheeks stuffed to the helm with brownie—practically bursting. The chocolate had turned to paste in her mouth. She couldn't swallow if she tried.

With as much dignity as she could muster, she spit the glop of food into the garbage disposal, washing it down with tap water.

"Finished with your dessert?" he asked.

Jinny turned around and smiled. *Please, don't let there be chocolate in her teeth.*

"Of course. I just didn't want you to have any. But seeing as how the woman I used to call my mother stole one from me anyway..." She trailed off, turning her gaze away.

He didn't deserve her undivided attention. He got enough of it throughout the week.

Emmett moved in, stepping close and forcing her to back up until the edge of the counter pressed into her lower back. She had nowhere else to go.

He reached for her arms. "Jinny, listen—"

"Hey." Dean's voice cut him off, and Emmett's hands dropped to his sides so fast Jinny thought she'd imagined it.

She glanced toward her brother. His frown said it all. She hadn't imagined it, and Emmett had been too close for his comfort.

"Are you ready?" Dean asked, looking at her.

Jinny's eyes lit up. The trophy. "Of course."

"Let's go, then," he said.

Once they made their way outside, they stood in front of their closest friends and family as Dean gave up the trophy. He handed it over to her, denouncing his title as the Kimball Ninja Warrior.

Jinny took it, eyes brimming with tears as she hugged the golden statue to her chest. She and Dean had created the trophy when they were ten, and it had aged well over the years. It looked like some deranged form of the Academy Awards statue, with a bald Barbie duct-taped to one of Dean's old basketball trophies from middle school. Super-glued to the sides were two giant wings and a cluster of silk flowers, all spray painted a gaudy metallic gold. It was the most hideous, yet beautiful sight she had ever seen.

"I'd like to thank my brother for being a fierce competitor," Jinny said, "who in the end submitted defeat. Better luck next year, buddy." She flashed him a pitying look. "And for Emmett Hall for being second best. Hopefully, this taught you that there are winners and losers in life, and I, Jinny Kimball, will never be the loser."

Her family chuckled good-naturedly as she raised the trophy in the air then kissed it. Once the crowd parted—a little too quickly, in her opinion—she took her trophy back into the house. She'd place it in her old bedroom until it was time to leave. She didn't trust Dean not to swipe it and run.

Setting it down on her old desk, she turned and jumped at the shadowy figure looming in the doorway. "Gah!" She placed a hand over her racing heart. "Why are you always sneaking up on me?"

Emmett stood in the threshold of her room, looking like a giant in the small space. He shoved his hands in the pockets of his black gym shorts, allowing his gaze to drift over her belongings.

"So...this is Jinny Kimball's lair."

Jinny snorted. "My lair?"

"You know, you can learn a lot about a person from their teenage bedroom."

"Is that so?" She crossed her arms over her chest, trying to quell the fluttering in her stomach.

Emmett stepped over to a shelf and lifted a framed photo of Jinny and Callie from junior high.

"Please, make yourself at home."

He set the photo back and moved closer to her bed, pausing as he smiled at the posters on her wall. "Brad Pitt? Really?" he asked, arching a brow. "Let me guess, *A River Runs Through It*? *Legends of the Fall*? Or was it *The Curious Case of Benjamin Button* that got you all googly-eyed?

Jinny scoffed. "*Fight Club.*"

Emmett laughed like she'd told a hilarious joke. She didn't see what was so funny.

He turned around, and she wondered what it looked like through his eyes. The creamy walls with posters of movie stars and bands. The old jewelry box on her dresser. The faded photos stuck to nearly every surface. Mainly ones of her and Callie growing up through various phases of life. Her frilly pink bedspread and old CD collection.

"I didn't know you played ball," Emmett said, picking up one of the trophies off her desk.

"There are a lot of things you don't know about me."

Jinny grinned when his eyes latched onto hers and he said nothing. That shut him up.

"Anyway, what are you doing up here?" she asked, picking at the peeling paint on the edge of her footboard.

She didn't like him in her space. There was only one of him, yet the room filled with his presence. It was like he was everywhere.

"I just came to say goodbye."

Her gaze lifted to his. "You're leaving?" she asked. "Er... I mean, good. You're leaving."

Emmett cocked his head, then took a step forward. "If I didn't know any better, I'd say you didn't want me to leave."

"That's ridiculous." She toed the nap of the throw rug under her feet.

"Is it?" Emmett stalked forward, closing the distance between them.

"I named my stakes, didn't I?"

"You did," Emmett confirmed, but his words contradicted the knowing grin on his face. "But, I wonder..."

He paused in front of her and widened his eyes. "You tried to throw the contest. That whole coughing thing with the flour was all an act. Maybe you wanted me to win? You secretly wanted me to beat you so that you'd have an excuse to kiss me."

Jinny gaped. Never mind her heart beating rapid-fire in her chest. The man was delusional.

"I would never throw the Kimball Olympics. I was

choking. I practically perished rooting through the flour just so that I could beat you. I snorted more powder up my blowhole than a crack addict. I'm lucky I'm still alive."

She leaned forward and poked a finger into the concrete of his chest. "In fact, I may still drop dead at any moment from flour inhalation. All because I wanted to win. Because I wanted you to leave."

She crossed her arms over her chest, but Emmett stepped closer, ignoring her body language that told him to back off. The warmth of his body soaked into her skin, warming her from the inside out.

"Well, it's a good thing I'm here now, then," he whispered. His gaze dipped to her lips, distracting her.

"What? Why?"

"So I can give you mouth-to-mouth and revive you. You know, when you drop dead from all the inhaled flour."

"You're super hilarious." Her voice shook, betraying her.

When Emmett laughed, she pushed at his chest, but she had all the strength of a toddler. "Seriously, I'm glad my loathing of you is amusing."

"I don't think you hate me as much as you say you do."

"Of course you'd say that." Jinny rolled her eyes, but her throat bobbed.

"You know what they say. There's a fine line between love and hate."

"From where I stand, the line is looking pretty thick. It might as well be the Berlin wall."

Emmett grinned, dipping his head closer. "Ah, but the Berlin wall came tumbling down."

"If you don't step away, at any moment, I could puke all those brownies I ate all over you."

The warmth of his breath cascaded over her mouth. "I'll take my chances."

He reached a hand out to her, cupping her cheek, and her breath snagged in her throat. "I think you want me to kiss you," he murmured.

She tried to scoff, but the noise that escaped her throat was a feeble squeak. "What makes you so sure?"

"This." He slid his hand down the curve of her jaw to her neck, pressing a finger gently over her racing pulse. "And this," he said, gripping her trembling hand in his.

The synapses in her brain fired, but the messages crossed. He was going to kiss her. And a part of her—the part inexplicably leaning into him, staring up at him from under her lashes—wanted him to.

He leaned even closer, a breath away. "And this," he whispered, and then his lips were on hers.

Jinny's breath caught. Her heart leapt in her throat as he brushed his mouth over hers softly, slowly. He raised a hand to her cheek, brushing his knuckles against her skin, down her neck, until he rested his palm on her clavicle. The contact ignited a raging fire inside her chest.

"Where the heck did they go?"

Jinny heard the sound of Dean's voice, but her brain had stalled.

"I think I saw Jinny head to her room," Callie said, and it sounded as though she was right outside the door. In one swift second, Emmett's lips vanished from hers.

She stood, blinking, one hand clinging to the bedpost while the other held nothing but air. Her brain reeled as the sound of footfalls jolted through the fog.

Trying to catch her breath, she inhaled when Dean and Callie appeared in the doorway. She tried to suppress the blush rising to her cheeks. Across the room from her, Emmett admired the trophy she had placed on her desk.

Callie's eyes widened, a knowing look on her face, as she caught sight of Jinny. Luckily, Dean was a bit more oblivious. He stared between them then broke into a smirk as he took in the direction of Emmett's gaze. "Admiring our handiwork, are you?"

"It sure is something," Emmett said, staring at the trophy.

Jinny met Callie's eyes, silently communicating, *we'll talk later.*

"Anyway," Emmett said, turning to Dean. "I just came up here to confirm my Monday appointment with Jinny before I left."

"Man, you don't have to go so soon. Did Jinny force you out?" he asked, shooting a glare in her direction.

Jinny raised her hands but promptly dropped them when she realized she was still shaking.

Emmett gave Dean some lousy excuse she couldn't hear through the buzzing in her head and asked if they'd walk him out. Grateful for the moment alone to compose herself, Jinny flopped back on her bed but kept her eye on the doorway.

Her gaze caught Emmett's one last time as he retreated from her room. She expected to see his knowing smirk, to tell her he knew how much the kiss affected her. To tell her that he won. Instead, his lips pressed into a tight line, and his eyes blazed the color of warm brandy. This was far from over.

When he disappeared from sight, she wrenched the pillow off her bed and pressed it over her face, suppressing a scream.

How in the world was she supposed to face him on Monday after *that*?

After five minutes of splashing cool tap water on her face and wrists, Jinny weaved her way through the partygoers to find Callie sipping a wine cooler while her mother talked wedding dresses. Apparently, she was helping Callie alter her mother's dress to make it uniquely hers.

Jinny stood behind her mother, trying her hardest to follow the conversation. Something about lace and silk and taking in the skirt to make a mermaid tail. She had no idea why they were talking about mystical sea creatures. In her altered state—she'd call it *post kiss*—her brain had short-circuited.

She was only mildly freaking out as she wrung her hands, pacing behind her mother. She didn't want this ooey-gooey warm feeling inside when she thought of Emmett. Things were perfectly fine before they'd kissed. She was happy hating him.

His voice eclipsed her thoughts. *You know what they say. There's a fine line between love and hate.*

No. He was wrong.

So what if he was a good-looking guy? Just because she admitted he was attractive didn't mean she had feelings for him. And, okay, maybe there were times when she enjoyed their verbal sparring. Some may even call it flirting. But not her. It meant nothing.

She did not have feelings for him. Just like she did not want him to kiss her.

Right.

Callie glanced back and forth between Jinny and her

mother. Finally, her mother took notice and glanced behind her.

Jinny stiffened. Her mother's scrutiny was often brutal. She'd see right through her.

"Did you run that nice young man off already?" Her mother's gaze flickered through the yard, taking quick inventory.

"You're dead to me, you know that?"

Her mother stood and chuckled, then patted her on the shoulder. "Oh, honey. You're too funny. You were the same way as a child. When you liked someone, instead of writing them love notes or drawing their name on your notebook, you'd torture them. Chased them around the playground and threw rocks at them. I always thought it was kind of cute. But, then, I always thought you'd grow out of it, too."

Jinny gaped. Before she could insist she had zero feelings for Emmett Hall, other than pure unadulterated hatred, her mother walked away.

"Did my mom just hit me with an epic burn?"

"Pretty much." Callie grinned.

Lunging toward her best friend, Jinny gripped Callie's arm and pulled her away from the table, out of earshot of any nosy family members—of which there were plenty.

"He kissed me," she hissed.

"I knew it! Oh my gosh. Tell me all about it. How was

he? I bet he's a good kisser. He has those really full, luscious lips."

"Ew." Jinny straightened and pulled back. "Aren't you engaged to my brother?"

"Doesn't mean I'm blind."

Jinny huffed. "What am I going to do?"

"What do you mean?"

"It was everything I thought a kiss with Emmett *wouldn't* be." Jinny paced in front of Callie. She needed some way to expel the nerves clustered at the base of her spine and the pit of her stomach.

"I'm not following."

"It was soft and gentle. It was like...kissing a dang butterfly's wings. It was the kind of kiss that makes your stomach swoop and your breath catch. The kind of kiss you want to lean into, to grasp with both hands and hold onto. The kind of kiss you give to someone you've wanted to kiss for a long time. Not the kind of kiss you give to prove a point."

Callie gasped and pressed a palm to her mouth, her eyes glittering with amusement.

Jinny grunted. "That's not helping!"

"Sorry."

"And now I hate him even more because I won't be able to *unkiss* him. I can't just go back to BK."

Callie scrunched her face. "BK?"

"Before Kiss. Haven't you been listening?"

Callie chuckled, but covered it with a cough at Jinny's glare. "Okay, just calm down. So, you kissed. What's the big deal? Maybe it's a good thing. Now you can put your differences aside and actually get along. Physical therapy can go smoother because you don't have to totally hate each other's guts. Maybe it'll be more bearable now."

Jinny shook her head and placed her hands on Callie's shoulders. "Oh, you poor, sweet, naive thing. You know nothing about the art of war. Emmett threw down a landmine in there"—she nodded toward the second story window —"and I stepped right on it. I fell right into his trap, and *pblewww.*" Jinny mimed an explosion with her hands. "He knew I was affected. This was all some sort of mind game for him, and now I have to face him on Monday with him having the upper hand."

"Why are you making this into a competition?"

"Hey, he started it. The moment he said I was a sucky PT, he declared war."

"He never said you were a sucky therapist."

"No, but he implied it. He said I only got the job because of my father and Dean, *and* he questioned my abilities. The moment he did that, it was game-on to both prove him wrong and make him hate me so he'd move on. I wouldn't be surprised if this were some kind of trick."

"Um…"

"The way I see it, I have two options." Jinny skulked to the table where Callie had been sitting and grabbed her fruity drink. Tipping her head back, she swallowed half of it in one go. "I can either address the kiss, which feels a little like admitting defeat, or I can ignore it. Pretend it never happened, like I was totally unaffected."

Callie groaned. "Oh my gosh, you guys are hopeless."

Jinny ignored her. She'd go to work on Monday and be the ultimate professional. She'd show him he had zero hold on her. What happened up in her bedroom would be the first and last time he ever got a piece of her.

The kiss had been a mistake. He and his perfect mouth could find another woman to torture. She was done.

CHAPTER THIRTEEN

Emmett

Emmett leaned one arm against the floor-to-ceiling windows of his apartment overlooking the city. He stared at the view without seeing it. Any minute now, the pop and boom of fireworks would explode above him in the indigo sky. The same fireworks that would burst among the stars in the Kimball's backyard.

Would Jinny be watching? Would she glance up to the sky and think of him?

He pressed his forehead against the cool glass and squeezed his eyes shut. He was a fool. One minute he was pushing her away, and the next he pulled her in.

He never should've followed her up to her room. But she had been so sweet, so innocent, with her fresh face and pink cheeks from the afternoon in the sun.

He knew the minute he took those stairs that it wouldn't end without him making a move.

He wished he could say he regretted it, but he didn't. Not one bit. Whatever penance he had to pay for kissing his best friend's sister, he'd gladly pay. Because nothing compared to the feel of her mouth pressed against his. The only things he regretted were the things pushing them apart— the wedges between them. He was responsible in part for putting them there. But what was he to do?

If it were just Dean, he'd talk to him man-to-man. He'd explain his intentions. That Jinny wasn't just another one of his girls. With her, he wouldn't just be passing the time until someone worth knowing came along. She wasn't a fleeting thing. She was *the* thing. Dean wouldn't like it, but in time, he'd see his true intentions.

But Dean wasn't the only concern. Jinny had a job to do. How would it look for her if, weeks after getting the gig as team therapist, she were caught making out with one of her patients? She needed to prove herself to the organization, and he understood that probably more than anyone else.

He could only pray he'd made himself valuable enough to the team. And if the Pumas kept him, he'd have to prove himself all over again next season. He'd need to show them that he could rebound after his injury and make a comeback. The last thing he should be doing is pursuing a relationship that might be controversial, especially while he was under the microscope. Garrison and Bannon would be watching his progress, his recovery. They'd want reports. How would it look if they discovered he was dating his physical therapist instead of taking his treatment seriously?

Neither of them needed a relationship right now. Neither of them needed the distraction. What they both needed was to focus on their careers. To prove themselves worthy of the positions they'd been given. Otherwise, they were jeopardizing a lot more than their hearts. But something about her made him want to throw it all out the window.

Maybe caution was overrated. Because when the distraction was Jinny Kimball, staying away was easier said than done.

Monday morning, he arrived at his session like usual. He sat in the waiting room on the edge of his seat. When Jinny appeared, his stomach twisted. She wore fitted pale-gray pants and a white blouse, paired with a stony expression. Her hair hung in loose waves, framing her face, and she must've been reading his chart before she came out to get him because her thick frames sat on the end of her nose.

He stood and followed, telling himself to keep it professional. He needed to keep his focus on his recovery, on getting back to playing ball.

She took him straight back to the fitness room, pausing just inside the doors. Hugging his chart to her chest, she glanced over at him. "So, week four post-op. That means some changes in routine. We'll still be working on a normal gait cycle, but we'll get you on the treadmill this week. And we'll do some hamstring curls."

So, she wasn't going to address the kiss. Okay.

He tried to listen as she droned on about his treatment, but he found it difficult to focus as his eyes homed in on her lips.

Maybe he didn't want to ignore what happened. Maybe he wanted to address it.

"Jinny, we need to—"

"Have you still been doing all your at-home stretches and exercises?" she asked, like he hadn't spoken.

He sighed. "Yeah. I've been doing everything like you

said."

"Good." She glanced down at his chart. "In the next two weeks, we'll even get you using some sports chords and add a little bit of weight."

Keep it professional.

"Weights. Right. But don't you think we ought to talk about what happened?" The fact that she was intent on ignoring what had happened between them made him want to address it.

She smiled, but it didn't reach her eyes. "You'll even get to do some modified lunges. Let's start with some stretching, shall we?"

Emmett pursed his lips, staring at her a moment before taking a seat on the bench in front of her. He followed her instructions, going through the motions, doing the stretches, but his heart wasn't in it.

He should be happy she didn't want to talk about it. Maybe she'd forgotten already. He seriously doubted it, but it would be best for both of them to put the kiss behind them and move on. Going back to sparring with her and irritating her was a lot safer than dwelling on how that kiss had been hot enough to light the room on fire.

Thirty minutes later, he was walking on the treadmill, focusing on his gait, and feeling a bit like a child. Frustration picked at him, spiking his blood. His leisurely pace was lightyears away from the intense sprints he did when training. His muscles yearned to feel the slap of pavement beneath his feet. His palms ached for the smooth leather of a ball, and he craved the sound of the net swishing when he scored.

He glanced down at Jinny, watching her with narrowed eyes, trying to read her thoughts as she made notations in his chart. A small crease formed between her brow as she bit the end of her pen then made another note. When she glanced up at him, her big brown eyes sent shockwaves straight through him.

She held his gaze only for a moment. Her mouth opened as if to say something when none other than Gabe popped into the fitness room.

Emmett slid his eyes over to the intruder, and his expression hardened. He'd never had a problem with Swanson before. He had no idea why he irritated him so much now. *Oh, wait. Yes, he did.* The guy was desperate for Jinny. It made him sick.

To make matters worse, every time Emmett was in session, Gabe happened to appear. He'd find any excuse to talk to her, and, every time he did, he found some small way to touch her. How many times had he asked her out during Emmett's sessions alone? Talk about being indiscreet.

Gabe made a beeline for Jinny, his Crest Whitestrips smile glinting under the fluorescent light. The muscles in Emmett's legs coiled as Gabe reached out and touched

Jinny's lower back.

Emmett clenched his fists. It was all he could do not to jump down from the treadmill and break the offending fingers. Luckily, she saved him the effort as she smoothly stepped out from under Gabe's touch.

"Did you get the memo about the trip?" Gabe asked her.

"Yeah," Jinny nodded, and Emmett could tell by the way she glanced away from him and moved her gaze around the room she didn't want to talk about it.

Emmett's feet hit the belt harder, his pace increasing. Jinny glanced up at him, her eyes sliding to his knee and back again, flashing him a warning to take it easy.

Finally catching on, Gabe turned and acknowledged Emmett. "Hall, I'm glad you're here. I wanted to talk to you about Vegas, actually."

Emmett blinked the anger from his vision before Gabe's words registered. *The trip. Vegas.* Of course.

He'd completely forgotten. This year, every team in the NBA was going to Vegas for the MGM Resorts Summer League. Tournaments didn't stop just because you were injured.

"You can either go with the team as scheduled and watch, or you can stay here if you prefer. As the team therapists, Jinny and I will be going, but we can find someone else qualified to work with you for the week if you choose to stay behind."

The corner of Emmett's lip curled. It wasn't lost on him the way Gabe referred to him and Jinny as a unit. The guy was pathetic, and if Emmett didn't know any better, he would think Gabe viewed him as a threat. Anyone else would've encouraged him to go and travel with the team as a show of support, if nothing else.

Emmett's gaze drifted to Jinny. She clenched her pen and his file so hard, her knuckles turned white. Too bad Gabe didn't stand a chance with her.

"I'm good to go, man," Emmett said, smiling. "I want to support my team. Besides, I don't want another PT. The best works with the best. Right?"

Jinny stared up at him, her brown eyes bright, surprised by the praise.

Gabe pursed his lips and nodded, then reached out to Jinny again, touching her arm.

Emmett gritted his teeth to stop the threatening growl.

"If this is your first time in Vegas, I'd be glad to show you around. The great thing about the tournament is that it's a week long, so there will be plenty of downtime between games and work." His eyes twinkled as he pulled away and walked backward out of the room. "But, anyway, we have plenty of time to talk about it."

Once he left, the only sound between them was the

whirring of the treadmill.

"So, now I'm the best?" Jinny said, turning on him. "Did you mean it? Or was that all a load of bull because you didn't want me hanging out with Gabe in Vegas?"

Emmett grinned and his heart pinched. "Both."

Jinny grunted and crossed her arms over her chest.

"You're good, Jinny, okay?" When she met his gaze again, his heart soared. "Better than good." He stopped the treadmill then stepped down. "I don't need to be six months along in my treatment to see you know what you're doing. You have half the team wrapped around your finger already, and you've only been on the staff for a few weeks."

She grinned. "They like me better than you."

"Of course they like you better than me." He ran his eyes down the length of her body. "Have you looked in the mirror?"

He took a step closer. When she didn't move away, he reached a hand up to her hair, watching with rapt interest as the silky strands slipped through his fingers. She shivered, a totally different reaction to his touch than to Gabe's.

"Are we going to keep skirting around what happened?" he asked.

Idiot. Even though everything told him to let it go, he couldn't.

Jinny's gaze dipped to his mouth then away again. She

stared past him, avoiding his eyes. "I don't know what you're talking about," she said, her voice flat.

"Don't toy with me." He dipped his head in an effort to meet her eye. When she didn't comply, he leaned down further, whispering into her ear. "The kiss, Jinny."

Color flooded her cheeks, but she shrugged. "It was just a kiss. There's nothing to say."

Emmett clenched his jaw, staring down at her. He moved his hand to the side of her face. If he just leaned forward another couple inches and swept his lips over hers, he knew she'd change her mind. She was playing with him.

He slid his hand down her cheek to her throat, and she gasped. The beat of her racing pulse hammered into his palm. The air around them snapped, thick with tension. "Somehow, I don't believe you."

"The kiss was a mistake, Emmett."

He chuckled, a humorless sound, but he took a step back. "A mistake you enjoyed."

"The only part I enjoyed was the end."

He smirked. "The lady doth protest too much."

Jinny's brown eyes darkened. "It shouldn't have happened, and it won't happen again."

"That sounds like a challenge."

Jinny placed both palms on his chest and pushed him back. "Don't flatter yourself, Romeo. I'm not one of your toys. I'm not so easily duped into believing you have some kind of valiant intentions."

Emmett grinned. "Who said anything about valiant?"

"Oh, don't try and be cute." She sneered, which only made him want to reach out and draw her into his arms even more.

"So, you think I'm cute."

Jinny's cheeks reddened. "Listen, you can take your perfect lips, your almond eyes, your compliments, and all your flirtations, and you can use them on somebody else. Because I'm not interested. Got it?"

Emmett's brows furrowed. "Funny how Gabe comes on to you, and all you do is evade his advances. But when *I* come onto you, all I hear are protests. Maybe someone's scared."

"The only thing I'm scared of is contracting something from that kiss."

Emmett laughed, a booming sound in the empty fitness room, to which Jinny scowled in response.

"Nice try, but I'm not buying it," he said.

She exhaled, an angry sound, so he continued. He reached a hand up and pinched her cheek. "You're so cute when you're all riled up."

She batted his hand away, which only made him laugh harder. "You're disgusting."

"I didn't hear you complaining when you were kissing me back."

"That was purely a reactionary reflex."

"Sure, it was."

Emmett leaned against the front of the treadmill, enjoying her irritation. There was nothing better than the flush of her cheeks and the glint of anger that darkened her eyes to near onyx. "Seems to me like you're working awful hard to suppress your attraction to me."

"The only thing I'm suppressing is my gag reflex," she said, then gestured back to the treadmill. "Now, can we get on with today's treatment? Or do you not care about playing basketball again?"

He raised his hands in surrender and headed back to the treadmill. She had a point.

"So, Vegas, huh?" he said, stepping onto the belt. "You know what they say..."

Jinny rolled her eyes. "Don't say it."

"What happens in Vegas, stays in Vegas, baby."

CHAPTER FOURTEEN

Jinny

J inny huffed as she entered her office. Her jaw ached from clenching it, and she had to wonder how much pressure her teeth could take before they'd pop. Chances were, during the course of the next six months, she'd find out.

She made a note to review her new dental coverage.

Stomping over to the wall beside her desk, adorned in her diplomas, awards, and certificates, she tore the framed photo of the Pumas team down. Then she ripped open her desk drawer and removed a Sharpie.

Her eyes zeroed in on Emmett. His smug smile stared back at her, dimples popping, a cocky gleam in his eye. With the dexterity and skill of Van Gogh, she drew devil horns and a tail on him, then stepped back and smiled at her handiwork.

Nice. The pressure in her chest eased, allowing her a smile as she hung the framed photo back on the wall.

Much better.

∞∞∞∞

Friday finally came.

To her relief, Jinny entered the Mexican restaurant, her stomach growling. It was a miracle she'd made it to the weekend. It meant two whole days without seeing *him.* Two days without his full lips taunting her. Without his dimples making an appearance in her dreams. Two days of Emmett-free bliss.

Jinny spotted Callie and Dean almost immediately. They sat at a table in the back of the restaurant. Being the third wheel on a Friday night wasn't exactly at the top of her list of fun things to do. Then again, she may as well get used to it. Once the Pumas' season started, it would be virtually impossible to meet someone. Work days, along with game nights, would occupy most of her time, which also meant a ton of travel. Where the Pumas went, she'd go. For a sports fan like herself, it was a dream. But on the relationship front, it wouldn't exactly be conducive to finding and keeping a man.

Hello, singledom, care if I settle in and stay a while?

She made her way to their table and took a seat across from them. "What's up?" she muttered as she reached for a tortilla chip.

Callie flashed her a smile. Her fingers were intertwined with Dean's, and she glanced up at him with so much adoration in her eyes, it made the back of Jinny's throat ache. She didn't want a relationship. Absolutely not. She was too busy. There was no space in her life at the moment for all the cuddling and kissing and hand holding and flowers and… *Ugh*. It all sounded so time-consuming and… regular. Yes, that was it. Time-consuming and regular. How mundane.

She swallowed, her throat tight. "Please, tell me you got queso dip," she said just as the waitress placed a bowl of gooey, white cheese dip in front of them. "I love you," she said. "Both of you. I'm so hungry, I could eat this with a spoon."

She crammed a chip in her mouth. A giant dribble of cheese dripped down her chin. Heaven couldn't possibly taste better.

"Cute. So dainty," a voice said from behind her.

She froze, the chip half in her mouth, the cheese congealing on her skin. *No-no-no-no-no. Not tonight.*

She slowly chewed the chip and grabbed her napkin, wiping the cheese from her mouth. "Please, someone tell me I imagined that voice behind me."

"There's no way your imagination can conjure anything that sounds as good as this," the voice said.

Jinny squeezed her eyes shut and heard the shuffling of feet and scraping of the chair next to her. When she blinked them open, she was greeted with Emmett's smug mug.

Jinny stiffened. "Excuse me for a moment while I murder my brother and soon-to-be sister-in-law."

She yanked on Dean's arm as she stood and all but sprinted toward the back entrance of the restaurant. Callie followed close behind them.

Dean shoved his hands in his pockets, and Callie averted her gaze. At least they both had the sense to look guilty.

"I take back everything I said about loving you two a second ago." Jinny alternated glares between them. "I wanted a nice dinner. Why is *he* here?"

Dean sighed. "We leave for Vegas this weekend, and you insist on driving because you let your ridiculous phobia control you."

"The fear of flying is far from ridiculous," she snapped.

"Have you looked up directions on your phone? It will take you nearly thirty-three hours to get there by car."

Jinny rolled her eyes and crossed her arms. "No. I haven't. I have to be there in a few days, but I'm just guessing my magical transportation machine will get me there on time." She clenched her fists. "Of course I looked it up!"

"You can't drive that whole way on your own," Dean said.

"He's right, Jinny. It's a long way to go in one weekend by yourself. You need someone to go with you so you can switch off driving. Plus, you haven't gotten a new car yet."

Jinny glanced to their table, to where Emmett was consuming the queso at record speed. She'd be lucky to get any by the time she finished hashing this out. From the looks of it, he had the appetite of a whale.

She flashed Dean a tight smile. "Looks like you'll just have to drive with me."

Dean's eyes widened and he took a small step forward. "No. You know I get carsick on long trips. There's no way I'll make it that far without puking my guts out or being completely knocked out on motion-sickness meds—I'd be no help driving."

"Welp," Jinny said, clapping her hands. "Looks like that's settled, then. I'll be driving myself. But that still doesn't address which one of you is dead to me. Who invited the enemy to dinner and why? This has yet to be explained."

She stared at them. They wore identical looks of guilt.

Then it hit her.

NO. No *way*. They couldn't possibly think...

Her eyes widened, and her heart threatened to beat from her chest. "Please tell me you didn't ask him to ride with me." Her frantic gaze darted to Callie. "You're my best friend. I know you wouldn't do that to me."

"It might be good for you," she said, wincing. "You guys will have all that time to work through your differences and stop fighting." Even Callie's tone conveyed how full of crap she was. Yet there she was, suggesting Jinny spend the weekend enclosed in a confined space with the devil incarnate.

Differences? They didn't have *differences*. They had mutual hate, lack of respect, and war.

They'd kill each other. Eat each other alive after the first few minutes.

"Do I look like a child to you?" Jinny asked, brows raised, her tone deceivingly calm.

Dean eyed her, a glimmer of fear in his eyes.

Good! He should be scared.

"No?" he answered like it was a trick question.

"And do I look like some kind of addict that needs an

intervention? Did I just turn ninety and not realize it?"

"No, but—"

"Then what in the world makes you think I need a chaperone on a road trip? I'm perfectly capable of getting myself from point A to point B. I'm an independent, single woman. I'm not helpless."

Dean frowned and glanced behind her, no doubt at Emmett stuffing his face full of *her* cheese dip.

His shoulders drooped. "Okay, maybe you're right. But you have to admit, it's really far to drive by yourself in one weekend."

Jinny nodded. She could be reasonable. She could admit he had a point. "It is. But that's why I'm already packed. When I get home, I'm going to take a cat nap and then head out tonight. I'll sleep at a rest stop or get a hotel for the night, then get up early and be back on the road. I'll probably drive through the night Saturday, but I'll take a ton of breaks and sleep. I'll shoot a couple energy drinks, and I'll be fine. Now, can we dismiss him, please?"

Callie frowned. "There are so many bad stories about things happening to women alone at rest stops."

Dean nodded. "Yeah, sorry. I know this is the twenty-first century and *blah blah blah*, but the fact of the matter is stuff happens. I don't feel comfortable with it. Emmett's going with you."

"He is not."

"Is too. Push it, and I'll tell Mom."

Jinny glared at him. "What are we, three?"

He shrugged.

"So, let me get this straight. You can't be carsick for thirty-three hours, but *I* can be? You do realize I'm getting hives just thinking about being stuck in a vehicle with him. We won't last. Only one of us will come out alive."

Oh, gawd. So, this is what it came down to. Plummet to a fiery death from the sky or endure a three-day journey with a man who seemed born for the sole purpose of irritating her.

It was a tough choice.

She imagined strapping herself into the seat of an airplane. The torch of the engines as they took off, nosing into the sky and clouds, the force pushing her into her seat. Then they'd level out and hover weightlessly, like a bird. Except a plane wasn't a bird. It was a giant hunk of metal, full of people. They'd be sitting ducks, just asking to be shot down.

"You know I won't fly," Jinny practically cried.

"I admit, when I was talking to Emmett and he volunteered to ride with you, I had my doubts, but—"

"Whoa!" Jinny held out her hand to stop him. "Slow down. It sounded like you just said this was Emmett's idea."

Dean shrugged. "I wanted someone to go with you, and he volunteered."

"Unbelievable," Jinny said.

She turned, hands anchored to her hips, staring laser beams at the side of Emmett's face. As if he could feel the heat of her gaze, he met her eye and winked.

Jinny frowned. Emmett probably concocted this whole thing because he thought she couldn't handle being in a car with him for that long. After that kiss, he was so convinced she had the hots for him. What, did he think she wouldn't be able to resist him if they were stuck together? That she'd fall for him on the open road like some kind of cheesy chick-flick? Heck, no. She had news for him. If he wanted to make the drive with her, fine. She'd show him just how easy to resist he was.

"Okay, fine," Jinny said.

She heard Dean and Callie exhale. No doubt, they were both astounded and relieved she'd conceded so quickly.

When she sauntered back to the table, they scurried after her.

"So, *Dean*," Jinny said. "Since you're such a caring brother and all, I assume you're paying for my dinner?"

"Sure, whatever you want," he said.

"Great." She waved the waitress down and nodded toward the people sitting at the bar and those surrounding them. "We'll take a pitcher of margaritas for the table and a round on the house for everyone. And don't be stingy. Definitely use top shelf, your best booze."

She smiled sweetly at her brother. "Thanks, sweetie."

CHAPTER FIFTEEN

Jinny

J inny grumbled as she made her way outside and plopped her suitcase down next to her car. Riding with Emmett to Vegas had seemed favorable when she had been irritated with Dean and determined to make a point. But now, she dreaded it. And it had nothing to do with the way her stomach swirled with anticipation when she saw him already waiting for her outside her car.

His punctuality was a minor positive to his many,

many flaws.

"Grab your bag and let's go," she said, avoiding his eye.

She fought back a yawn. After the righteous indignation had faded, she'd regretted her decision to agree to ride with him, which led to a craptastic nap. She tossed and turned, consumed with thoughts of enduring thousands of miles alone together. Now she was tired and crabby, and they hadn't even left the parking lot of her apartment.

"Uh, no," Emmett said.

She glanced over and noticed his defiant stance, along with the distasteful way he eyed her trusty-rusty pal.

"Uh, yeah," Jinny said. "If I have to endure this trip with you, we're doing it on *my* terms and taking *my* car."

Emmett snickered. "You call that thing a car?"

"If you recall, this wasn't my idea. So, the choice is yours. You can ride with me in this, or you can book yourself a cushy first-class flight to Vegas on a coffin-in-the-sky and leave me to drive in peace."

Emmett narrowed his eyes. The muscle in his jaw ticked as she stared, unwavering. She would not concede. No way was she riding the whole way in his car. His car, his rules. And she was not letting him call the shots. The second she relented and stepped foot inside his domain, it would be like stepping into the lion's den.

The irritation in Emmett's eyes cleared and he smiled. "Okay. We'll do it your way. Your car it is."

Jinny flashed him a victorious smile.

He rounded to the back of his Mercedes, and the trunk magically opened. Whether it was with telekinesis or a remote, she had no idea. With Betsy, she had to jam her key into a rusted lock and give it a thump first.

He reached inside and retrieved a giant duffle bag before the trunk slowly closed again, like magic.

Jinny huffed and unlocked her trunk. She bumped it with her hip, gave it a hard thump with her fist, and—*voila*—it popped open. Er...it was supposed to pop open, anyway.

She jammed her hip against it again, turning her key. *Come on!*

Emmett stopped next to her, fighting a smile. "Need some help?"

Jinny grunted as she curled her fingers under the lid of the trunk and yanked with all her might, grunting with the exertion.

"Sometimes, she just...gets...a little...stuck..." She gave it one last hip-bump, and it popped open, the force of it knocking her off-balance. She stumbled back as Emmett dropped his bag inside. Then he yanked her suitcase off the pavement, before she could grab it herself, and plunked it down beside his, not bothering to be careful.

"Easy there," Jinny warned, catching her balance. "She's not as young as she used to be."

Emmett snorted. "Really. I never would've guessed."

Jinny rounded the car and got in, with Emmett following suit. Once they were settled, she pulled out onto the road and switched the radio on. The staticky sound of the only station she got blared through the speakers.

"How about you drive two hours, and then I'll drive a few more before we stop for the night," Emmett suggested, tugging on his seatbelt as if testing its efficacy.

Jinny opened her mouth to argue, but a wave of fatigue swept over her. She had really needed a good night's sleep.

Sighing, she said, "Fine. But I pick the hotel. We're not staying at the Four Seasons or whatever stuffy, ritzy place you're used to."

"Deal. See? Look how nicely we're getting along."

Jinny glanced over at him, a smile tugging the corner of her mouth. "Don't push it, Hall. You and I both know it's only a matter of time before we'll be going at it." The words spilled out of her mouth before she could mop them back up. But boy did she wish she had an industrial-sized Swiffer.

Going at it? Nice choice of words, Hemmingway.

Emmett's gaze flicked to her. Flames engulfed her cheeks.

She refused to look at him. She didn't need to see his face to know that slow, trademark smile had consumed him. "Was that a Freudian slip?"

"Ha-ha. You wish."

He opened his mouth to reply, but her arm shot out and she quickly muffled his words with her fingers. "Just. Don't," she said as they pressed over his lips.

He vibrated with laughter as she removed her hand. She made a show of grimacing as she wiped her fingers on his t-shirt, even as her heart fluttered in her chest.

She took the ramp onto the interstate. Betsy was a small space to begin with, but with Emmett in the seat beside her, it felt like a Matchbox car. His presence loomed. The musky scent of his aftershave surrounded her. Every move, every sound that escaped his lips, had her hyper-aware of his presence.

Jinny had never let her fear of flying inhibit her. She was a good driver and a contented passenger. If she wasn't driving, she could easily spend days in a car finding things to occupy herself with—a snack, a nap, a magazine, the radio. Emmett, on the other hand, hadn't stopped fidgeting. In only twenty minutes, he had adjusted the volume knob on the radio, rolled his window up, then down, and played with his phone. At the moment, he was occupying himself with angling his body toward her and drumming the fingers of his left hand on the center console.

Without warning, she flattened his left hand with her right. "Must you make so much noise? Why don't you take a nap?"

He shook his head. "I'm busy."

"Doing what? Annoying me?"

"Trying to figure out the silent ways of Jinny Kimball."

"Here's a tip. Don't."

Emmett grinned, then glanced around the confines of the car, pausing on the droopy material of the ceiling and the missing buttons on her dash. He pointed at the gaping hole next to the defrost button. "Hope that one wasn't important."

"It's just the button for my hazards. I don't need it."

Emmett guffawed. "In this thing? I beg to differ."

He glanced around him some more, touching nearly every surface like a man from Mars, taking everything in. He likely realized the lever to recline his seat was broken and that the fabric of his seat was ripped, the stuffing inside poking through.

"You know, I know you don't have the salary of an NBA player, but I would've thought they paid you pretty decent for being the team therapist."

"They do. But I only got my first paycheck this past week, and I'd like to save a little more before I go blowing it on a new car. Besides, Betsy is perfectly able to meet all my needs. Cars are a waste of money."

Emmett raised a brow. "Betsy? She has a name?"

Jinny nodded.

Emmett whistled. "Car is a strong word. But it has four tires, I'll give you that."

Four bald tires, Jinny mused. Of course, she kept that information to herself.

"Let me guess..." She glanced at him as she switched lanes. "After you got your first paycheck, you went out and blew it on something extravagant. I bet you're the type that thinks saving money is a waste. Why make it if you're never going to spend it. Am I right?"

Emmett stretched his arms then placed his hands behind his head. "Wrong," he said, surprising her. "I had a decent car. It had all its buttons and didn't need staples to keep the ceiling material from flopping in my eyes. So, I kept that. I didn't get a new car until this year, and though my apartment does have a nice view, it's small. The only reason I bought it *was* for the view, in fact. I save most of what I earn."

"Even though you could easily buy twenty fancy cars and not break the bank? All that money, and you don't blow it?" He was arrogant and a showboat. No way he didn't blow it on expensive things to feed his ego.

He shrugged. "I made the team, knowing the odds. I'm great at what I do," he said, his lips curling. "But most of us don't have a lengthy career. Chances are I'll play a handful of years, ten if I'm lucky, and then I'm out. What's the point in blowing all my money so that I'm broke afterward? What does that accomplish? I have everything I need to make me happy."

She stared at him in openmouthed shock. Even Dean was more extravagant than Emmett. If she'd heard this from someone else, she wouldn't have believed it. But she could see the sincerity in his expression.

"So many guys do that—celebrities, athletes, musicians—and it just irritates me," he said. "It's like, you were blessed with this amazing opportunity and given more than you'd ever need or want, and now you're trying to say you're broke? What about the rest of America? The world, for that matter. No one wants to hear them crying over money. It's the most obnoxious thing."

"So, what was the first thing you did when you got paid."

"As soon as I signed my contract, I paid off the mortgage on my father's house."

Jinny swallowed and stared out at the road. "You paid off your dad's house?"

Out of the corner of her eye, she noticed the way he nodded then stared out the window. "He deserved it. He worked hard raising five boys by himself. It couldn't have been easy. I owe him a lot more than what my wallet could ever give him."

Gosh, why was that so unbelievably...sweet and kind and...

"The next thing I did was hire a financial advisor to come up with an investment plan," he added.

"Impressive."

Emmett tipped his chin toward her. "How much did that admission just cost you?"

Jinny laughed. "I can give a compliment when it's due."

Emmett hummed in response. "Lately, I worry that I knew, deep down, I'd only get two years. Like a part of me had some sick sense that I'd get injured as a rookie and be out."

Jinny shifted in her seat. She could handle jovial Emmett, sarcastic Emmett, and even flirtatious Emmett, but this vulnerable version of him—that was only showing itself inside the walls of her car—it was dangerous.

"That's crazy. You don't really think that, do you?" she asked.

Emmett said nothing. He stared at the road before answering. "Not really. But I can't say I don't worry that it's true. About every single day, I worry I'll get traded, wind up sitting the bench, and dropping off the NBA's radar altogether."

"Good thing you have the best sports therapist to ever walk the earth."

Emmett snorted. "And you thought I had a big ego."

"Maybe both of us *deserve* our egos."

"Is that a roundabout way of saying I'm a good ball

player?" he asked, his tone teasing.

"You know you are," she mumbled under her breath. "Anyway, we're both good at what we do. Why not own it?"

"Touché."

∞∞∞

After their conversation, Emmett began fidgeting again. He flicked open the center console, where he found her old Pitt ID, which he examined far too closely for her liking.

He pulled out a hairband. "How many of these things do you have?" he asked, flicking it back into the console. "I think I saw two on the floor, and there's one in your cup holder, one in the door..." His voice trailed off. "Do you shed them?"

"They get lost easily," Jinny said in defense. She plucked one out of the spare change flap and braced the steering wheel with her knees as she pulled her hair up. She turned to him with a smug smile.

He smiled and shook his head, then opened her glove box, where he pulled out a couple old ticket stubs and a handful of crumpled paper. Behind those odds and ends, she glimpsed her spare tampons.

She felt her face flush, and she reached across him,

snapping the glove box shut before he could pull them out and ask some ridiculous question regarding her choice of feminine products.

"Must you be so nosy?" she asked, but he ignored her, staring at the ticket stubs with wide eyes.

Which ones were they? She racked her brain.

"*One Direction*?" He held the stubs out, aghast.

Jinny tipped her chin up in defiance. "Don't judge. They have some good songs."

"Who are you, and what have you done with Jinny Kimball?"

"Ha-ha. Funny. What? I can't like a boy band?"

"Sure, you can. I suppose. It's just that they sing all these cheesy love songs, and I'm just wondering where the girl who loves horror movies and action flicks went? The one who'd rather eat tar than watch a rom-com."

She screwed up her face. "Trust me. She's alive and well and getting sick of this conversation."

He laughed. "Fine."

He lapsed into silence, but not before the crinkling of paper filled the car. Jinny glanced over to where he had smoothed out the notebook paper he'd found in her glove box. With a jolt of shock, she lunged toward it. "Give me that!"

"What? Why?" He glanced over at her, holding the paper as far away from her reach as possible.

How long were his blasted arms?

She made another lunge for it, but he yanked it away at the last minute as the car swerved and ran over the rumble strips. Behind her, a car honked.

Emmett laughed, infuriating her. He had one hand on the wheel, while his other continued to hold the paper out of reach. "Maybe you should keep your hands and eyes on the road."

Jinny placed both hands back on the wheel. It would be just her luck to go to her death with him beside her. "That's private," she said, glancing from him to the road.

"You're not making me want to look at it any less."

"It's just...notes from my latest gynecology appointment."

He pulled a face that was almost comical. He held it away from his body, staring at it dubiously. "They have notes for that?" Then his eyes narrowed.

Sweat beaded on her brow.

"My name is on it," he said, glancing back to her. His brow furrowed while she tightened her hands on the wheel, her knuckles turning white.

Maybe if she acted calm and cool, he wouldn't notice. Her mouth thinned as she pressed her lips closed.

"Hmm...what is it that you don't want me to see. Let's read it, shall we?"

Emmett finished smoothing out the paper on his hip.

At this point, Jinny didn't even make a play for it. It was too late. He'd already set his sights on it, and taking it from him now would only make him more intrigued. With her luck, he'd assume it was some sort of love note. Besides, all she had done was a little research. Any good therapist would've gone to those lengths to assuage the concerns of a particularly troubled patient.

Only Emmett hadn't been particularly troubled, had he? Not beyond the scope of reason. But still…

"Kyle Lowry suffered from a torn ACL in college and went on to excel in the NBA. Most would never know he tore his ACL, and he shows no signs of slowing down. Al Harrington tore his ACL after four years in the league. After reconstructive surgery, he returned to the game even stronger than before his injury. He delivers consistent numbers and has played fourteen seasons and is now thirty-two years old. David West was taken off the court in a wheelchair, following his tear. Despite gruesome reports of his severe injury, he returned to the game a year later." Emmett paused in his reading, silent as he glanced over at her.

She refused to meet his eye.

"Jamal Crawford, Jason Smith, Baron Davis… There must be fifteen guys listed on this thing. All torn ACL's, all fully recovered, some having rebounded even stronger."

Jinny cleared her throat. "I was going to give it to you, but then I…" Her voice trailed off. Why hadn't she given it to him?

"When did you write this up?"

She hesitated. Did she tell him the truth?

With a sigh, she said, "Shortly after that first appointment. You were upset and worried about your chances, about being traded and—"

"I know everything I said. And I was rude to you."

Jinny nodded, saying nothing. Her throat went tight. Suddenly, she couldn't speak.

"And despite the things I said, you went home and researched these success stories for me. Why?" He peered over at her.

She met his eye for only a second before glancing away again. She lifted one shoulder then let it fall. "I wanted to give you hope, inspiration, comfort." She screwed up her face. "I don't know."

Gosh, why was she so bad at this? Sharing feelings and being...open...only seemed to be difficult with him. Why?

"Because you like me." His smug voice sent a twinge through her chest.

"No, definitely not."

"Yup. You do. Just admit it."

"Never."

"I was rude to you, yet you still went on to find something to comfort me. But then you chickened out and didn't give it to me because you were afraid I'd see right through it."

She gasped, turning to him. "I was being a good therapist."

"Uh-huh."

Emmett leaned against the passenger-side door and crossed his arms over his chest, looking supremely proud of himself. With any luck, the door would fly open and he'd go tumbling out.

"So, did you do this for Taylor and his twisted ankle?" he asked.

Jinny scoffed. "It was a twisted ankle! Big difference between an ankle sprain and a torn ACL."

"Okay, whatever you say."

"Stop it."

"Stop what?" he asked.

"That. That grin you have on your face. Like you know what you're talking about when you so clearly do not."

"Okay, fine. I'll stop smiling." He mashed his lips closed.

"I can still see your dimples."

His mouth curled slightly at the corners, and his dimples deepened.

Jinny turned her attention back to the road, fighting the full-body flush she had going. She had nothing to be embarrassed about. Emmett was wrong. She would've made that list for anyone. So what if she spent her free time Googling and writing notes. That was prior to the Fourth of July kiss, to him barging in on her family festivities. Since then, she no longer wanted to console him.

After a moment, he said, "I just want you to know how touched I am that you care. The feeling's mutual."

She risked a glance at him out of the corner of her eye. Biting her lip, she drove in silence.

CHAPTER SIXTEEN

Jinny

J inny chewed the gummy bears she bought at the rest stop and stared out the window as Emmett took the wheel. He guided them back onto the highway, and Jinny shifted in her seat, trying to get comfortable.

The air was thick. Tension lingered, ready to snap, growing since Emmett's discovery of her inspirational notes.

Intent on ignoring it, Jinny cranked the radio, but only

static pumped out of the ancient speakers. With a sigh, she flicked it back off and crammed another gummy bear in her mouth.

"If you couldn't be a sports therapist for the Pumas, or a physical therapist at all, what would you do?" Emmett glanced at her.

It was a serious question, one she had asked herself a million times before, but had no real answer for it.

For a moment, she wished she had feigned sleep. The longer she spent with him in this car, the more uncomfortable she became, and not the snappy, you're-irritating-me-to-death discomfort. Instead, it was like the plucking of guitar strings below her ribs, a slow strumming of something inside her that she didn't want to feel.

"I don't know," she answered.

"Come on. You must've thought about it," he persisted.

She had. The truth was if she couldn't work in sports therapy, she'd be nothing. It was always her plan, always her dream, and without it, she had no idea who she was. "I'd do nothing. Probably be a hobo or something."

"That's not an answer."

She turned to him. "No, I'm serious. I have no idea. There was never a backup plan for me. I went from the childhood fantasy of being an actress, or whatever little kids want to be, to sports therapist. My family was always very sports-centric. We're competitive. It's what we do. From the time I was little, I was groomed to love it. I knew I'd never go pro though. That just wasn't for me. I was decent when I played in high school, but not gifted. Somewhere along the line, I learned of sports physical therapy, and there was no going back."

"We're a lot alike, you and I."

"We're nothing alike."

He shook his head. "There are differences in my background, but like you, basketball was everything to me. I couldn't imagine doing anything else but playing ball. The only difference for me is that I know it'll end eventually. I could just retire once it does. I've invested well enough. I've made more money already than some will in their lifetime, but...I think I'd like to coach."

"Yeah?" Jinny asked, taking him in.

"Yeah," he answered.

"Did we just have a normal conversation?"

He laughed as Jinny snuggled down in her seat, biting back a smile.

"Chocolate or vanilla?" Jinny asked.

Emmett scoffed. "Vanilla."

"You're inhuman."

∞∞∞

"The most important question of them all," Jinny said. "In *Stranger Things*—please don't tell me you haven't watched it. If not, you can get out of my car right now."

"I've watched it."

"Whew, okay. Who should Nancy end up with? Steve Harrington or Jonathan Byers?"

"Is that even a real question?"

Jinny held her breath, waiting for his answer.

"Harrington."

She sighed. "Yes! I mean, I get how they made Jonathan all sad and the underdog and all, but...come on. Especially when Steve comes back and helps the kids."

"Did you really take me for the Jonathan type?"

Jinny quirked her lips. "No. You're definitely a Steve."

"Thank you."

∞∞∞

"So, what's the real reason you volunteered to drive with me?" Jinny asked.

"Isn't it obvious?"

"I have my theories and suspicions. All of them end

with you throwing my body in the ditch or a dark alley or leaving me waving helplessly on the side of the road."

Emmett shook his head and chuckled. "I volunteered because your car is so nice."

She punched him in the arm.

"Ow. Okay." He raised a hand and grew quiet.

For a moment, Jinny thought he was going to say something serious. Then he grinned and said, "Because I knew at some point over the next thirty-odd hours, you'd wind up kissing me."

She smacked him again.

Emmett

"Greatest fear?" Emmett asked, and Jinny eyed him like he was stupid.

"Flying, duh."

"That's it? Flying?"

"I chose to forgo a flight that would've taken four hours in favor of driving for thirty hours in a car with *you*. That's how afraid of flying I am."

"Point made."

"What about you? I can't wait to hear it. It's spiders,

isn't it?"

When Emmett said nothing, she cooed. "Oh, it is! I love it. Big-bad Emmett Hall is afraid of a wee little spider." She pitched forward, clutching her stomach with glee.

"Nope. Not it."

She straightened, her laughter fading. "Then what?"

"Germs."

Jinny cocked her head, looking unimpressed. "Germs? No."

"Yes. Definitely germs."

She narrowed her eyes at him.

"Look, I'm serious. The real reason I agreed so quickly to not stopping for the night is because, unless it's a hotel I've meticulously checked out, I can't do it."

She raised a brow.

"I swear. If we had stopped, I would've taken the hotel towels, because at least they bleach them, and lined the top of my bed with them. I would've either froze or used the hoodie I packed as a blanket."

Laughter bubbled in her chest. "You're serious?"

"Dead serious."

She shook her head, seemingly in disbelief.

"I'm not ashamed to say that I call ahead and ensure that I have a room with fresh blankets. Ones that have been actually washed between guests. I pay extra for it."

"How do you know they actually do it? Maybe they just

say they do."

"I'm banking on the fact there are still honest people in the world. That, and clearly this is your first NBA trip because the staff bends over backward to ensure we're happy."

Jinny rolled her eyes. "Of course, since you're practically royalty and all."

"Practically."

"What about all the women? Don't you worry about their germs?"

"First of all, most of the women I hang out with are fleeting dates, nothing more. Taking out different women is an excuse not to be alone, while also not having to get serious."

Jinny tucked her legs underneath her. "So let me get his straight. You're saying you don't actually hook up with most of those women?"

"That's what I'm saying."

"What about the blonde at your PT appointment that morning?"

"I took her to breakfast prior to my appointment." And he may or may not have brought her along in an attempt to make Jinny jealous, but she didn't need to know that.

"Okay, so, if what you're saying is true, and you're really not the player you seem to be, then why not anyone serious? Why not just find someone you actually like?"

Because he'd already found her.

He rubbed a hand over the ache in his neck. "Have you seen my choices?"

"I'm not 100% following, but if you're referring to the vapid mass of silicone and plastic that tends to nip at your heels, then yes. But I thought you liked that kind of thing?"

Emmett shook his head. "A lot of the guys don't care. They'll use the women that follow them around and don't think twice. They use their celebrity as a tool to get what they want. But most of those women are only after our money, or the title that comes with dating an NBA athlete. I'm not trying to say that all the women that try to get with us are bad or that none of them care, but, in my experience, it's not worth the time it takes to find out which ones can be serious and which ones can't." He shrugged. "I've gotten burned once or twice when I thought she was actually into *me* and not the kind of lifestyle I could offer. So, I give them what they want by taking them out a couple times, letting them snap their selfies, and that's the end of it. None of them are too brokenhearted, which is saying a lot."

"That's..." Jinny trailed off, glancing at him out of the corner of her eye.

"Cold-hearted? Maybe."

"I was going to say...kind of depressing."

Emmett swallowed. Great. The last thing he wanted was for Jinny to feel sorry for him. Pity definitely wasn't what he was going for. "It's fine."

"Do you want to find someone, though?"

Emmett took the ramp for a rest stop. When he parked and turned the ignition off, he turned to her. "Remember during our session, when I told you that you were just dating all those losers to bide your time until you were ready for the right man to come along?"

She nodded.

"That's what I'm doing, waiting for the right woman to come along," he said softly, letting his words hover in the air between them.

CHAPTER SEVENTEEN

Jinny

The last couple of hours were stifling, and not just because it was in the upper eighties outside and her air conditioning only wheezed the occasional puff of cool air. The heat had more to do with the man next to her.

Over the course of the last thirty hours, he had single-handedly smashed every preconceived notion she had of him. He tore them to shreds, obliterated them with ridiculously endearing anecdotes about his family, his perspective on life, or random things about himself she would never have guessed in a million years.

He was basically every woman's fantasy come to life.

He wasn't the arrogant jerk she'd thought he was. He wasn't self-centered or a player. Quite the opposite.

His favorite holiday was Thanksgiving because it wasn't commercialized and had nothing to do with presents. Although, he loved buying presents. The bigger surprise the gift was, the better. He read at least a couple pages from a book every single night before he went to bed or he couldn't fall asleep. Oreos were his downfall, and, as a kid, his most treasured possession was a stuffed dog named Wuff-Wuff.

These little bits of him, these pieces that turned him from the man she loathed into the one sitting beside her —sound asleep with a boyish expression on his face—were like mini grenades, creating chinks in her armor. Very few people surprised Jinny, but Emmett was managing it quite well.

She came to a red light and stopped, glancing over at him. The soft sound of his breathing filled the car. His mouth was slightly parted, his lashes dark against the top of his ridiculously perfect cheekbones. The thick layer of stubble covering his jaw was so enticing she had to grip the wheel to stop herself from reaching out and running a finger over it.

He was proof that appearances didn't tell the whole story. Proof that perception could shape misconception. And she had no idea what to do with this information.

A part of her was scared of what would happen once they arrived in Vegas. In five more hours, they'd waltz into the MGM hotel, and then what? Would their temporary truce fall apart? Would they go back to goading each other and getting under each other's skin? Would she go back to hating him? Did she want to?

She needed time to wrap her head around her conflicted feelings, to decipher them and analyze them to pieces until she knew exactly what she should do. But with each passing mile, time slipped further from her grasp. They'd reach their destination and no longer be stuck together in this small space. Any moment, Emmett would wake and turn those hazel eyes on her and she'd be no more capable of translating the Morse code in her brain than she was in this moment.

She swallowed as she turned back to the road. The light turned green and she accelerated.

An hour later, Emmett stirred beside her. The first remnants of morning sun shined through the windshield, making him squint as he blinked his eyes open. Her stomach flopped to the floor by the gas pedal as he turned his gaze to her.

He yawned and stretched, bringing his arms high above his head and arching his back. The muscles in his arms flickered and flexed with the movement, and when her gaze dropped to his torso, catching sight of a sliver of tanned, rippled abs, her stomach clenched. She swallowed and turned her gaze away so fast it was a miracle she didn't get whiplash.

He rubbed his eyes with his curled fists, while Jinny winced and reached to the back of her neck with one hand, massaging the pinched muscles.

"Oh, man. I'm sorry," he said. "We should've switched a while back, but I was out. Why don't you find a place to stop, and I can drive?"

He mistook her discomfort and the crick in her neck as fatigue from driving. How cute.

She wondered what he would say if he knew the truth. *Oh, no. I'm fine. Really. I just got a strain from staring too hard at your abs, then I pulled a muscle in an effort to make it look like I wasn't staring. No biggie. Carry on with your stretching.*

When she said nothing, he glanced out the window. "Where are we? It's hot as Hades in here."

"Somewhere in Arizona," she said, shrugging.

Emmett nodded as if this made sense.

"The air doesn't work very well. Sorry." She grimaced and felt his gaze boring into the side of her face, but she couldn't look at him. She couldn't be faced with his eyes and his dimples, not while her brain was in overdrive. She needed to prepare herself first, put the invisible force field back up to stifle her attraction.

"Want to grab some breakfast? I could use about a truckload of coffee."

Jinny nodded a little too eagerly and bit her lip. Getting out of the car sounded like a good idea at the moment.

"Why aren't you looking at me?" he asked.

Jinny huffed. "I'm driving."

She noticed his eyes narrow. "You're being weird. Why are you being weird?"

"I'm not being weird," she said, her voice cracking.

"Hmm," he hummed.

Something rumbled and Jinny felt the car shimmy beneath her. She frowned, glancing down at her dash.

"What was that?" Emmett asked, glancing behind them, as if expecting to see a body on the road.

Jinny opened her mouth to reply but was interrupted by a loud grinding noise followed by a series of popping. She jumped in her seat as the car started to slow on its own accord.

Uh-oh.

She glanced around at their surroundings, which were sparse, to say the least. They had left a small town about ten miles back and were currently on a stretch of highway in what appeared to be the middle of nowhere. This was the place cars went to die. Cars like her beloved Betsy. As if to punctuate her thoughts, a plume of smoke puffed from the hood, and they slowed to a complete halt.

She pounded the steering wheel. "No!" she wailed.

Oh, come on. Betsy, don't do this to me now! Couldn't you breakdown when, oh, I don't know, I was completely alone? I would've gladly risked being picked up by a creepy trucker with a claw hand if it meant not having to be stranded in the middle of nowhere with Emmett right now. Not when I feel so weird inside.

"Huh," Emmett said like he had expected this all along. "I'll get out and take a look, but I have a feeling we're not getting back on the road any time soon."

He got out of the car, closing his door behind him with an ominous thud, leaving her in the tomb of her car with nothing but his scent.

He tapped on the hood, waiting for her to open it. A few minutes later, he returned and placed his arms on the roof of the car, leaning down to the passenger side window. "You want the bad news or the good news first?"

She glanced at his sweat-dampened sideburns and his mussed-up hair and swallowed. "Good news," she said. She needed it.

"Well, we have plenty of time for breakfast."

"*What?* That's the good news?"

He shrugged. "The bad news is there are no restaurants in sight and your engine's shot."

He said it like it was no big deal.

"How far back was the town?" he asked.

"Ten miles, maybe? Not too far," she said, desperate.

He nodded and placed his hands on the roof of her car. "The other bad news," he said, glancing around at the open expanse of nothing, "is that, even if we're lucky enough to find a shop back there, I doubt anywhere will be open on a Sunday."

"So, what are we supposed to do?" she asked, incredulous.

Emmett fished in the pocket of his gym shorts and pulled out a pack of gum. He unwrapped a piece with a slow, easy calm that made Jinny want to strangle him. He brought the stick of gum up to his mouth and curled it onto his tongue.

Her stomach clenched.

When he noticed her watching him, he held the pack out. "Want some?"

No, she didn't want some. *Gah!* She took back everything nice she'd thought about him minutes before. He was the most infuriatingly cruel man on the face of the planet.

Jinny got out of the car and slammed her door shut. She placed a loving hand on the roof of her car and gave ol' Betsy a pat. *This might be farewell, but it's not goodbye.*

She grabbed her suitcase from the trunk, tossed Emmett his bag, and began walking before she realized something she had missed, something she had forgotten. She turned back around to him. Apparently, Emmett hadn't forgotten.

Of course, he didn't forget! It's his knee.

"We can't walk ten-plus miles," she said, stating the obvious. "Not with your knee."

Emmett ambled toward the edge of the road and took a seat on a giant boulder. "Looks like we're going to have to hitch a ride into town."

Jinny huffed and dropped her bag on the pavement, and made her way toward him. She plopped down onto the dry earth, not even attempting to sit on the tiny edge of rock left over after Emmett's giant body hogged it all.

Several minutes ticked by with excruciating slowness, and the only thing to pass by them on the road was a tumbleweed. Meanwhile, Jinny's thoughts grew more panicked by the moment. She tried calling Dean, but in this desolate place, she didn't even have so much as one bar on her phone. The call refused to go through no matter how many times she tried. Regardless, she knew the Pumas' flight didn't get in until that evening, anyway.

"How many times are you going to try that?" Emmett asked, eyeing her from his perch on the rock, where he commenced doing his daily stretches.

"Until it works," Jinny said between clenched teeth. She told herself to relax, to calm down. She had been stuck with Emmett in the car this entire time. What was the difference now?

Because now she was truly stuck. Because now her feelings had deepened. She had caught a glimpse of what it would be like to be with Emmett, and it made her want things she shouldn't.

Next to her, Emmett grunted, and she turned in time to see him removing his t-shirt.

Her eyes widened, and she hopped up from her perch on the ground. "Whoa, hold up!"

Her gaze flickered over his washboard abs, toned chest, and sculpted biceps. He was a living, breathing Ken doll. A masterpiece. He may as well have been chiseled out of marble, except he was all tanned skin and firm muscle.

She shielded her eyes with her hands like she was staring into the sun. "What do you think you're doing?"

"It's a million degrees out here."

She huffed. "You don't see me taking off my shirt."

"Please, don't let me stop you," he said, waving her on, obviously amused.

She shot him a glare and was rewarded with the sight of Emmett leaning back on the rock, muscles glistening in the hot sun.

Holy—

She couldn't just stand there and stare at him.

She turned and started walking down the side of the road. "What are you doing?" he called after her.

"Walking to town. I'll get a ride and come back for you," she said.

A moment later, Emmett's hand curled around her bicep, searing her skin. His touch was hotter than a blazing inferno. He turned her around, and she had to fight the urge to cover her eyes. He was almost too perfect to look at.

"You are not going alone. Either both of us go or neither," he said.

"You can't."

He shrugged and crossed his arms.

Someone seriously needed to tell him not to do that without a shirt on. Every muscle flickered with the movement, drawing her eye across his chest. Her cheeks flushed, and she forced her gaze back to the road with longing.

"You know, you have no one to blame for this but yourself."

Jinny whipped around to him. "What?"

He shrugged. "If you would've let us take my car like I wanted, we wouldn't be stuck in the middle of nowhere. We'd be sitting on smooth leather upholstery, being blasted by ice-cold air right about now."

Jinny narrowed her eyes, her hackles rising. "It's your fault. You're the one that insulted Betsy," she said, waving toward her pathetic-looking car. "You put a dent in her confidence and jinxed us."

"You do know you're talking about a car, right?"

"I know what I'm talking about," she snapped. *Well, hello, anger and irritation. Welcome home.*

Jinny settled into her frustration, nestling in the warmth of its comforting presence. Being annoyed with Emmett was so much easier than the ambiguity of the feelings she felt for him. Anger she could handle.

Emmett lifted his hands and turned, making his way back to the rock as Jinny glared holes in the broad shoulders that narrowed to a trim waist.

She kicked at a clump of grass and dirt then skulked after him.

CHAPTER EIGHTEEN

Emmett

Maybe he was being unfair. He knew what she was feeling because he felt it, too. Yet he persisted. When he should push her the other way, he continued to try and pull her closer. Sometime during the two-thousand miles they'd traveled together, something between them shifted. He had wanted Jinny prior to the road trip, but that was nothing compared to the bring-him-to his-knees, bone-deep yearning he felt for her now.

Truth was, he didn't mind being stuck in the middle of nowhere with her, even if it was nearly ninety degrees at only ten in the morning. But she was desperate to get away from him.

Why, when they had gotten along so well? There could only be one explanation. Her feelings had changed, had turned into something real.

He was playing with fire. He shouldn't want to be with her. Everything he'd shared during the drive had been true. Despite his occasional cockiness, he was never self-indulgent. He lived in a posh, but not an overly flashy apartment. He paid his father's mortgage off and waited a year after he signed with the Pumas to buy a nice car. He didn't splurge on lavish, frivolous luxuries like some of the athletes he knew. No private jets or diamonds or a Rolex that could feed a small village for a year. But just this once, he wanted to indulge.

So, when he unzipped his duffel bag and began playing cards, ignoring her, he knew what he was doing. He leaned his back against the giant boulder, with Jinny on his other side, her arms crossed as she seethed at nothing—or everything—he wasn't sure which.

He held the cards in his hands, drawing from the top of the deck and flicking them onto the dirt in front of him in a lazy game of solitaire. After a few minutes of tense silence, she shifted, glaring at him from around the rock. "Do you always carry cards with you?"

Emmett grinned. He knew she would crack and break the silence, irritated he had something to pass the time, while she didn't. "When I travel for games, I always bring a deck. Keeps me busy when I can't sleep in the hotel or when I'm bored."

She grumbled, then turned back to her seething.

Emmett continued his game, not really even looking at the numbers, just flicking the cards to the ground, knowing it was only a matter of time before she spoke up again. *Three, two, one...*

"Do you have to be so loud over there?" she asked.

Emmett chuckled. "I'm sorry. I didn't know cards made so much noise."

"It's the flicking."

He said nothing. A moment later, she stood and moved in front of him, glaring down at him. "What are you even playing, anyway?"

"Solitaire."

She crossed her arms over her chest. "I think we should have a session while we wait."

Emmett raised a brow. He hadn't expected that. "Now?"

"It's as good a time as any. We've got nothing to do and your knee is probably stiff from the car ride."

Emmett lifted himself to his feet so he towered over

her. "I don't really feel like it."

"Well, I'm your therapist," she said. "And I think we should."

"I already did some stretches."

"We can do more."

Emmett shook his head. "It's too hot."

She pointed to his bare chest. "You're half-naked. How hot can you possibly be?"

"Look, I'm hungry, it's a million degrees out here, and I'm sweating like I just ran a marathon. I don't want to work right now. If you insist, we'll work later tonight, once we've cooled off, gotten some rest, and I can focus."

"You," she said, stepping forward and poking him in the chest. "Don't get to call the shots."

He clasped her wrist, holding her hand against him. She gasped, and her eyes met his before she clamped her mouth shut. The skin-to-skin contact scorched almost as much as her hot gaze. A flash of desire ran through her deep brown eyes before she could squelch it.

His heart pounded against his ribs as he dipped his head and softly pressed his lips to hers. She stiffened, no doubt fighting to hold on to her anger. Then he felt it dissolve, and she reached up, raking her hands through his hair.

He parted her mouth with his and deepened the kiss. Her resounding groan sent him into a tailspin. If kissing were a competition, he was losing, because she was completely demolishing him with her lips, the warmth of her breath, and her hair that smelled of vanilla.

Time faded. The earth stood still.

The first time he kissed Jinny had been amazing. But this kiss—it was the kind of kiss that curled your toes, shot sparks into your stomach, made your insides blaze, and scattered any form of coherent thought.

He trailed his hands down her back to where her t-shirt clung to her sweat-dampened skin. He tugged her even closer, kissing her like it might be his last. Like it might be the only thing he'd have to sustain him for the rest of his life. Every single feeling he'd repressed came crashing to the surface.

Her breath hitched as he pulled away and trailed his lips to her jaw. Brushing his mouth over hers once more, he kissed her until she panted for air. Until a roaring sound broke through the steady rhythm of his pulse, and Jinny pushed him away.

The air wheezed from his lungs as she stepped back toward the road, waving her hands in the air. He blinked and shook his head before he was able to clear his sight enough to notice the semi-truck making its way toward them.

She hollered and jumped, then waved again, like she was desperate for it to stop and whisk them away. But he wanted nothing more than to stay in this moment forever. He would've let the truck pass. He would've spent all day, all night, right there in that moment with her, as long as it meant he got to feel her mouth pressed against his.

The truck's engine blared as it powered down despite his silent prayer for it to pass them by. She was too persistent. Jinny had flagged the guy down like her life depended on it. Like she hadn't just had the best kiss of her life. Like she hadn't just wrung him inside-out.

$\infty\infty\infty$

The truck dropped them off at the next town over, which consisted of a couple diners and gas stations. They grabbed breakfast in silence, then Emmett went to chat with some patrons he'd noticed upon entering, while Jinny cleaned up in the restroom.

He waited for her by the door. When she came out, she paused in front of him, her gaze wary.

"I got us a ride," he said.

"With who?"

"Jerry over there is headed to just outside Vegas." Emmett nodded toward a middle-aged man handing the waitress some cash at the counter. "He said he'd take us the rest of the way in exchange for a couple autographs and tshirts."

"Oh." She met Emmett's eye like she wanted to say something, but instead, she headed toward the table where they'd had their breakfast and grabbed her suitcase.

They sat wedged together in the front seat of Jerry's truck. He was a talker. Carrying the conversation for both of them, he droned on about his travels, the world of trucking, and everything under the sun.

The cab smelled of fried onion and bubblegum, a nauseating combination that left Emmett, once again, longing for the beating sun and the boulder by the side of the road. At least there, he had Jinny to himself. At least there he would've been able to talk to her, to pick her brain and see what she was thinking, without a third party being a witness.

He watched her from the corner of his eye. She stared out the window, chewing her lip, seemingly deep in thought.

What he wouldn't give to be inside her head.

CHAPTER NINETEEN

Jinny

The truck rumbled away from the curb, wafting a puff of gray exhaust in its wake. After several hours of the truck driver's incessant blabbing, Jinny was once again face-to-face with Emmett. She didn't trust herself. Now that they were alone again, all she wanted to do was jump him.

She turned to him and noticed some indecipherable emotion brewing in his honey eyes. Part of her wanted to be bold, reckless even. She wanted to reach out, grab his hand, and address what had happened between them over the last three days.

Instead, she offered him a weak smile. "We're here."

When he said nothing, she continued, "So, I know we seemed to have a truce going—"

"Go out with me."

"What?" Her skin pricked as she waited for him to confirm that her ears weren't playing tricks on her.

"Just because we're not stuck in a car with each other doesn't mean that whatever this is needs to end," he said.

"I don't know."

It was one kiss. Okay, two, technically. But what did a couple of kisses mean? So they got along on the car ride, did that really mean there was something between them? Maybe they had both just been acting like adults—something they probably should've done a long time ago.

"Come on." He stared her down. "You can't stand there and honestly deny that you felt something over the last three days. I know you did."

Jinny stammered. "It was just a kiss."

"Uh-uh. I don't buy it. Just admit that a part of you is curious if you and I could have something real."

"We're attracted to each other, but—"

"It's more than that."

"What in the world are you doing stepping out of a

semi?" Dean's voice sliced through Jinny's thoughts.

She jerked her head toward the sound to see him coming toward them. "Er, hi," she mumbled.

Stellar timing. Emmett leaves her reeling right as Dean shows up.

Emmett didn't want to just be friends. Maybe it should've been obvious before now, but she'd thought he was just playing with her.

"So, anyone want to explain why the trucker dropped you off?" Dean asked again.

"Oh, yeah." Jinny smacked her head. "My car died."

"Death is a good term for it," Emmett agreed.

"Still glad you drove?" Dean asked her.

She stole a glance at Emmett. "Uh, yeah, I am," she said meaningfully.

At Emmett's heavy gaze and the furrow in Dean's brow, she corrected. "Better than plummeting from the sky to my death."

Emmett flashed her a private smile before he clapped Dean on the back. "Well, I'm going to head up to my room and catch some z's. You two have fun."

"Catch you later?" Dean asked.

"Sure."

With one last lingering look at Jinny, he turned and left.

Jinny faced her brother, pushing her nerves aside and

hoping he didn't read the disappointment in her eyes. "So, how was your flight?"

∞∞∞

She tried not to watch Emmett walk away, she really did, but she couldn't help herself.

Her gaze followed him through the lobby, where a hoard of staff from the hotel, meant to cater to the Pumas every whim, scurried among the team members as they trickled inside.

"Earth to Jinny." Dean snapped a finger in front of her face.

She blinked and tried for a smile, but it fell flat.

She did not want to follow Emmett inside. She did not want to know what he planned on doing for the rest of his evening. Definitely not.

"Um, sorry. Did you all just get here?"

"Yeah. About fifteen minutes ago. They're carting our stuff up to our rooms now." He nudged her arm. "Hey, you wanna go to dinner or something? I'm starving."

"You don't want to eat with the team?"

Dean grimaced. "I just spent four hours with them on a private plane. I've had enough fart-filled air for a lifetime. I need to expel the methane from my lungs."

"Ew. TMI."

Dean shrugged. "You asked."

"No, I asked what your teammates were doing and if they'd miss you, not for details on their gas levels."

"If you would've flown with us, you could've witnessed it for yourself. Then I wouldn't have to fill you in."

"Well, thank heavens for that."

"I'm not sure where the guys are going, probably some-place wild, but what's it matter? I'm going to take my *wittle* sister out," he said as he stepped forward and vigorously rubbed his hand over Jinny's head, mussing her hair.

Jinny smacked his arm.

Someplace wild? Her thoughts shifted annoyingly to Emmett. Would he join them?

Even if he did, she totally didn't care. It didn't matter to her if he went out with the team and met a woman. They probably flocked to them, but it wasn't of any concern to her. What Emmett did in his spare time was his busi-ness. He could meet a woman, take her out, take her home. Whatever.

"I don't know. I'm pretty tired," Jinny said, lamely.

"You're in Vegas for the first time, and you just en-dured more than three days in a car with your mortal enemy. It was probably DEFCON 1 in there. I want the de-tails of your trip down. You can't just go up to your room and go to bed."

Who said anything about going to bed? Hanging in the lobby to see if Emmett went out with the guys and find out where they were going sounded like as good a plan as any.

But, of course, she wasn't going to do that.

She wasn't some lovesick loser.

"Fine. I'll go to dinner with you, but don't expect me to enjoy it." She pointed at him. "And I'm ordering the most expensive thing on the menu." She paused. "And a bottle of wine."

Dean laughed. "Noted."

∞∞∞

Jinny glanced at her phone one last time. Why did they need to be in Vegas—2,200 miles from her best friend? And why in the world wasn't Callie answering her phone? What could she possibly be doing? These days, her life consisted of work, Dean, and clipping ideas out of bridal magazines for "the big day," with the occasional meal in between.

So much for being there when Jinny needed her most.

This was probably the first time since high school that Jinny could recall needing Callie's advice in regard to a man. The ol' BFF was really dropping the ball.

She needed to tell her about the kiss on the side of the

road. How the car ride there had made her question everything. She needed to hash out the significance of their temporary, or maybe not-so-temporary, truce.

The twisting in her gut told her she desperately needed to expunge the conflict churning inside her. The gnawing ache might kill her if she didn't confide in someone about how she was feeling, never mind actually coming up with a game plan for how to cope.

"Uh-huh, sure," Jinny murmured in response to something Dean said. She checked to make sure her ringer was turned on then set her phone back down.

"And then I told Callie, 'If you don't let me wear Bermuda shorts for the ceremony, it's off,' " Dean said.

"Oh, yeah?"

"Yeah. And she told me in no uncertain terms where I could shove my shorts and gave me the ring back."

"Wait. What?" Jinny's eyes widened as she caught the tail-end of what Dean had been saying.

"About time I got your attention."

Jinny scowled. "Did she really give the ring back?"

"Over Bermuda shorts? Were you even listening to anything I was saying?"

"Um...a little." Jinny rubbed the back of her neck.

"What gives?" Dean asked as he pushed his empty plate away. "I've eaten all my food, and you've barely touched yours. You've been distracted all night."

"Have not."

Dean arched a brow. "I just told you that I hired a stripper for the reception, that I insisted on wearing shorts to my wedding, and that Callie gave me her ring back. You barely blinked."

Busted.

"Hey, it's not my fault. I warned you before we came out that I was tired, but you insisted."

Dean leaned back in his chair, studying her. "No. That's not it. If anything, you look wired. And don't think I haven't noticed you checking your phone every two seconds."

"Well, if your *fiancée* would answer, I wouldn't need to check it every two seconds."

"So, you're distracted and desperate to get a hold of Callie, which means...you have some sort of crisis. Am I right?"

Jinny pinched her mouth shut. Crap. What could she say? *Oh, I just think I might have a thing for your best friend and teammate—who's also my patient. Oh, and did I forget to mention we kissed? Twice. And now it's all I can think about.* Sure, that'd go over well.

He must've sensed her reluctance because he waved the waitress over and ordered her a chocolate lava cake.

They sat in silence until her cake was delivered, doused in hot fudge, melty vanilla ice cream, and whipped cream.

Jinny dug her spoon in and took a giant bite of heaven. When Dean made for it with his dirty dinner fork—*ew*—she pulled the plate out of reach. "No way. If you wanted some, you should've ordered two, Mr. Stingy."

"I'm the stingy one? And you didn't even eat your dinner."

"Okay, Mom."

"Fine." Dean set his fork down and crossed his arms over his chest. "Now that you have chocolate, spill it."

Jinny grimaced.

"Don't give me that look," he said. "I'm your brother. You should be able to talk to me about anything. We're not thirteen anymore."

"Some of us aren't," Jinny muttered under her breath.

Dean inclined his head, waiting.

Ugh. What choice did she have?

"Fine. But you can't get all preachy." She pointed her fork at him.

He drew an invisible *X* over his chest. "I promise not to judge."

She took another bite of cake in silence. She couldn't believe she was about to do this—to confide in Dean. Her desperation must've hit an all-time high.

"It's about a guy," she blurted.

Dean blanched. "Okay."

Jinny felt a stab of sympathy. He was really trying. Poor

guy.

"I kind of...might have feelings for someone?" She squinted. Even she couldn't believe what she was saying.

Dean turned completely puce before his expression changed and his eyes darkened.

"See!" Jinny stabbed her cake. "You're doing it."

"Doing what? I said nothing," Dean said, defensively.

"First you looked like you might be sick, and then your eyes did that thing they do"— she waved her fork in the air —"that angry, dark-blue thing. You're going all big brother on me. It's written all over your face."

"Would you prefer it if I closed my eyes?"

"Yes, actually."

He shot her a dirty look. And she answered him by blinking her eyes exaggeratedly.

He groaned and squeezed his eyes shut. "Where is my fiancée when we need her?"

"You're telling me."

"I'm waiting. My judging eyes are closed."

Jinny hesitated. In high school, whenever a guy showed interest in her, Dean had made his presence known. She remembered the time Tommy Fazone had finally worked up the courage to ask Jinny out. It had been a relationship she had nurtured for the better part of her sophomore year. Finally, he got the guts and asked her to Spring Fest, a local event with live entertainment and food.

She had worked dang hard for that date. Then he'd canceled the day before.

Turned out, Dean had caught wind of Tommy's feelings and gave him the third degree. Scared him so bad that Tommy wrote Jinny off as a liability. It wasn't until Dean went off to college that she was finally free to date without fear of his intervention.

So, as she stared him down, even with his eyes closed, she knew saying anything to him would be a mistake. But he wouldn't stop bugging her until she did. Besides, how long could she keep this a secret? He'd sense something was up the second he saw Jinny and Emmett were no longer at each other's throats.

"What if..." She paused and bit her lip. *Here goes nothing.* "What if I liked someone from work?"

There. The words were out.

Dean's eyes shot open. She pointed at him. "Hey—"

"Who?" He frowned. "If you like someone from work, that would mean it's..." He trailed off before his eyes brightened. A knowing grin curled his lips.

Did he know who it was?

He pursed his lips. "So, are you asking me what I think about you pursuing something with this colleague?"

Jinny pushed a piece of a cake around on her plate. "Maybe."

"It's not ideal because it could be super awkward if

it doesn't work out. But, actually, if you think about it, it makes a lot of sense."

Hold on while I pick my jaw up off the ground. "It does?"

"Think about it. You're basically one of us now. I mean, your summer schedule is more laid back, but during the in-season, you have to travel with the team, keep office hours, *and* go to all our games. You practically have to be married to your work. It's not the easiest for maintaining a solid relationship with someone who works a nine-to-five. But if you found someone with the same exact schedule. Someone who understood the sport, who loved it, who loved the work... Well, that would be pretty great for you."

It was true. Jinny hadn't really thought about it before, but everything Dean said made total sense. All along, she had looked at a relationship with Emmett as being a liability. Working relationships were generally frowned upon, but her job took sacrifice. Being a team therapist was demanding, time-consuming. A normal relationship may struggle because of the schedule and the travel. But someone on the team would totally understand.

"That does make a lot of sense, actually," Jinny said.

Her stomach churned with the revelation, or were those butterflies?

"Don't sound so surprised."

"Well, I think the last time I asked you for advice was when Marta Dribble made fun of that bad haircut I got in fourth grade. You told me to put toenail clippings in her sandwich. I got a semester's worth of detention for that."

"Hey, she had it coming."

Jinny groaned and covered her face with her hands. *What was happening to her?*

She was talking about *liking* Emmett Hall, and getting butterflies while doing so. She felt like she was back in junior high with her first crush.

"Look at you," Dean cooed.

"Please don't." She lifted her gaze to his and wanted to slap the teasing smile right off his fat face.

"I don't know if I've ever seen you fret over a guy before. It's so cute." He laughed as she chucked her straw at him. "You must really like him."

"No," she snapped. "I don't know. Maybe."

"Well, good. I'm happy for you. I mean, you could do worse. He's got a good job, and he's a heck of a lot more mature than the last guy you dated. Maybe it'll work out better than you think."

Jinny bit her lip. This conversation was beyond surreal. "And you're sure you're okay with this?"

"Yeah. Absolutely." He leaned forward and offered her a smile. "The more I think about it, the more I can see it. Go for it."

CHAPTER TWENTY

Emmett

E mmett surveyed the room. It was jam-packed with
people. Nearly every slot machine within sight had
a body in front of it. They had lucked out getting
a spot at the bar. He hadn't even wanted to come out, but at
nine o'clock, Dean had pounded on the door to his room and
all but dragged him out.

As his eyes scanned the crowd, he could tell himself
he wasn't looking for her all he wanted, but he would be

lying. The idea of Jinny going out alone churned in his gut. She'd saunter around with her large brown eyes and heart-shaped mouth, oblivious to her natural beauty and the innocent girl next door vibe that had most guys stumbling over themselves for a chance to talk to her. Every guy within arm's reach would be clamoring at a chance to buy her a drink.

"What's with you, man?" Dean asked, raising a brow.

"Nothing." Emmett shrugged.

"You're not acting like yourself."

"How so?"

"Well, for one," Dean said, tipping his beer toward him, "there is no way the Emmett I know would be sitting here with me when that redhead over there"—his gaze flicked to the other end of the bar, where a woman in a short black dress blatantly stared at him—"is ogling him. Or the blonde, for that matter." He jerked his head across from them at a blonde woman. Her bold gaze held Emmett's as she licked her lips.

Dean was right. Normally, he'd approach the women in a heartbeat, but his heart wasn't in it.

"So, what gives?" Dean asked. "Even if you try to say they aren't your type, which I know they are, you'd at the very least be attempting to use me as your wingman as you picked up the night's du jour."

Emmett shifted in his seat and brought a hand to the

back of his neck. He wasn't *that* bad. So, he enjoyed the company of women. He liked to have fun and flirt and he didn't relish spending every evening alone. But he didn't have to pick up chicks everywhere he went.

"That's not entirely accurate," he muttered.

"It's totally accurate."

"Maybe I'm not in the mood."

Dean's eyes widened. "Now I know something's up."

Emmett stifled a growl of frustration, annoyed with the direction their conversation had taken. "That's not all I'm about."

Dean snickered like he didn't believe him. With a raised brow, Dean stared at him with a penetrating gaze.

Emmett shifted in his seat. He couldn't tell Dean that he was thinking about Jinny. He had no way of knowing—

"I know what it is." Dean's expression clouded, and Emmett stiffened. "It's the tournament. Man, I should've known. Sorry. It'll be rough for you, won't it?" he asked. "Not getting to play and having to ride the bench?"

Emmett stared down at the drink he'd barely touched. Watching his teammates play without him would suck. He should be out on the court, and having to ride the bench would normally be his sole focus if it weren't for Jinny taking center-stage in his thoughts.

Tomorrow would sting. No doubt about it. The desire to pick up a ball, run out on the court, and charge toward the hoop was so deep, nothing could dull it. Physical therapy and time spent with Jinny had been a distraction, something to occupy him during the passing weeks, but nothing could fill the void of missing out on the thing he loved most.

"Yeah…it'll be rough," Emmett said, feeling the slightest bit of guilt that he hadn't been completely honest.

"I don't know how you're doing it, but hang in there. Before you know it, you'll be back in the game, fumbling the ball and giving up shots, and generally stinking up the court and playing crappy ball."

Emmett scoffed. "You wish you had my turnover rate."

"Maybe, but you'd kill for my defensive rebounding percentage."

Emmett laughed, but the sound died on his lips as his thoughts drifted to Jinny.

"You sure that's all that's bothering you?" Dean asked, taking a sip of his drink. "Nothing happened on the way here, did it?"

Emmett's gaze snapped to his. Act casual, he told himself. "Why? Did she say something?"

Dean shrugged. "Not about that, no."

Emmett sensed there was something he wasn't saying. "Have you talked with her since we got here?"

"I had dinner with her."

Emmett stared at Dean, willing him to continue.

After a few moments of silence, it became clear that if Emmett wanted more information, he'd have to get the ball rolling.

"Minus the part where her beater car broke down, the ride actually wasn't half bad," Emmett said, trying to coax him. "We got along for a change." *Especially the part where she wrapped her hands around my bare back and crushed her mouth to mine.*

"I don't believe it."

"No. Seriously."

Dean made a *huh* sound then asked, "What did you two even talk about? I can't imagine you have much in common. I was partly shocked to see you both still in one piece."

"We have more in common than you'd think," Emmett said evasively.

Dean murmured a noncommittal response. "Well, the drive must've given her time to think. When we had dinner, she actually asked me for my advice. Imagine that."

Emmett's ears perked up. He took a sip of his beer and, over the rim of the glass, casually asked, "Really? What about?"

"It took some prodding, but apparently, she has feelings for someone." Before Emmett could say anything, he continued, "And I don't think it's like with the guys she's been dating the last couple of years. Those guys were all losers—"

"Yeah, you're telling me."

"I think it's real this time, like it could be something serious."

"Really?" Emmett's heart thudded so hard in his chest, he wondered if Dean could hear it. "Who is he? Did she say?"

"All she told me was that it's someone she works with," Dean said in a wry voice.

Emmett's lips curled as he struggled to stifle his smile. When he failed, he quickly brought the back of his hand to his mouth. "That's crazy, huh?"

Did Dean know? Was he waiting for Emmett to own up to being that man? Somehow, Emmett couldn't imagine Jinny telling Dean she had a thing for his best friend. Maybe he was just fishing—trying to see if Emmett knew anything.

"She asked me what I thought," Dean said.

"And?"

"I think it could be tricky," he said, swirling the liquid in his glass. "But it could really work."

Hope flooded through Emmett. He exhaled in relief. "Dean, listen I—"

"I'm going to talk to Gabe."

Emmett flinched. "Gabe?" No, Dean couldn't think...

"Yeah. I mean, it's gotta be Gabe, right? They've been having coffee together almost every week, and I've heard from some of the guys that she's all he talks about. I guess he's pretty smitten." Dean's lips flattened into a grimace. "I admit, he wouldn't have been who I pictured her with, but he's a good guy. They share mutual interests. After I thought about it, I realized they could be good together."

"Jinny and Gabe?"

Were they talking about the same people? No. Just *no*. Gabe was the last person Jinny needed. She needed someone who challenged her. Someone to call her on her crap, to push her. Someone who lit a fire under her cool exterior. She needed someone like *him*, not Gabe.

Dean was still talking, but Emmett wasn't listening.

His thoughts drifted to Jinny. There was no way she had feelings for Gabe. How many times had Emmett seen them together? There was nothing there on her end. No fire. No spark. Not like when they were together.

"...so I figured I'd pull Gabe aside sometime this week. Tell him I approve and sorta give him my blessing to pursue her. I imagine he's a little hesitant about what people will think since she's his coworker now and I'm her brother, so —"

"Whoa." Emmett pushed away from the counter, his head spinning. "Why would you do that?"

Dean shrugged. "Why not?"

Before Emmett could formulate a response, a warm body sidled up next to him. He glanced up to see the blonde had made her way over. She not so discreetly brushed her ample bosom over his arm. He pulled away like he'd caught fire, then ignored her and turned back to Dean.

"Uh, maybe you shouldn't intervene. She doesn't need your stamp of approval. I think she's perfectly capable of handling herself."

"I'm not saying she needs my opinion or approval, but she seemed kind of...I don't know...torn up over it or worried or something. I figured I'd just make it a little easier on her. That's all. Relax, dude."

Dean's gaze focused on something behind Emmett before someone tapped him on the shoulder.

Emmett sighed. The blonde chick, again? Couldn't she take a hint?

He turned with a scowl, eyes blazing. "Not interested," he snapped, and she blinked once, twice, as the words registered, then she scurried off.

Dean's brows furrowed. "What's with you?"

"Nothing, but you should know something." He inhaled. *Here goes nothing.* "The truth is I—"

"The truth is, I'd rather have her with Gabe. I've seen the way some of the guys eye her in the fitness room and from across the gym. I don't like it." The muscle in Dean's jaw pulsed.

Emmett straightened, his back stiff.

"I'd rather have her with him than for her to get tangled up with anyone on the team."

"You know we're part of the team too, right?" Emmett said, tone flat.

"Exactly. I'm different, but take you for example. How many girls have you dated in the last year alone? Most of the guys on the team are the same. I don't want her with a player—some guy that's just using her as another fling or something to pass the time. I don't want her with a guy who uses his celebrity to get him what he wants. Jinny acts tough, but she's not unbreakable. She'd get hurt easily if she really liked the guy, which I suspect she does."

He may as well have said, *I don't want her with someone like you.*

Emmett's stomach plunged, and his hopes fell with it. *Message received.*

"The last thing I want," Dean continued, throwing a wad of cash on the table and standing, "is for her to date a teammate. That wouldn't end well for anyone."

Emmett bit the inside of his cheek as Dean murmured something about heading to his room for the night. He had a game to prepare for. While Emmett...well, he had nothing. No game. No girl. No Jinny.

Lifting his hand, he signaled the bartender to bring another round. "Keep 'em coming."

∞∞∞

His fingers hovered over the send button on his phone as his head spun. Lifting his gaze, he surveyed the sterile surroundings of his hotel room. He should go to bed, sleep off his frustration and his…

What exactly *was* he feeling?

He clutched his chest and rubbed the sore spot that seemed to throb below his ribs. The one that wouldn't quit.

He stumbled toward the bed and flopped down, pressing his back against the upholstered headboard. He wasn't drunk, exactly, but he wasn't sober either. Still, he shouldn't text or call her right now, not after he'd had one too many. Besides, she was probably asleep.

He sighed, and the heaviness inside his chest increased as he replayed his conversation with Dean. *The last thing I want is for her to date a teammate. That wouldn't end well for anyone.*

Emmett had a list a mile long of reasons for why he shouldn't pursue Jinny any further. He could go on about why he should just go to sleep, forget about her, and find someone else. But he was sick of playing it safe. Sick of staying away. Sick of what he should or shouldn't do. What about what he wanted? What about Jinny? Didn't she get a say?

Growling, he snatched his phone and typed. "You up?" He hit send.

His stomach flopped in the answering silence, the stillness of the room. If she ignored it, she was either asleep or not interested, but if she answered, well...that meant something.

JINNY: Yeah.

Okay, not exactly the opening he had hoped for, but she'd answered.

EMMETT: I've been thinking. On the trip home, you should fly and face your fears.

JINNY: Thank you for the advice, creeper, but the fact that you are writing this tells me you don't know me at all. That, and whoever you are, you're not in my phone, so...

Emmett threw his head back and laughed. He'd forgotten that she didn't have his cell number. Oops. So much for the theory that she'd responded because she reciprocated his feelings.

EMMETT: I'm the answer to all your prayers.

JINNY: Nope, still no idea.

EMMETT: I'm your dream come true.

JINNY: Now I'm really confused.

EMMETT: Hmmm... You just spent the most amazing three days of your life riding in a car with me.

JINNY: Trapped in the car, was more like it. You know,

TRYING TO HATE THE PLAYER

you really should work on your word choice. Had you opened with, *I'm your worst nightmare*, then I would've known EXACTLY who it was.

EMMETT: Yeah, right. You know you love me.

JINNY: I admit you're not as loathsome as you used to be. Don't push it.

Emmett grinned as the little bubbles appeared, indicating she was typing.

JINNY: How'd you get my number. Was it Dean? I need a new brother.

Emmett scoffed.

EMMETT: Sort of. I stole it from his phone when he went to the bathroom.

JINNY: Sneaky. I like it.

EMMETT: Well, I would've asked you for it myself, but it's been about a million years since I've had to actually ask a woman for her number.

JINNY: Oh, right. Normally they just throw them at you like confetti. Phone numbers. Body parts. Clothes.

EMMETT: Jealous?

JINNY: Not hardly.

EMMETT: You're bluffing, but I'll let it slide. What time's my PT session tomorrow?

JINNY: Eager to see me, Hall? I figured you got enough of me during the car ride here.

I could never get enough of you, he typed, then thought

better of it and deleted it.

EMMETT: Always.

JINNY: I think you just can't wait to annoy me.

EMMETT: You know you love it.

JINNY: Is love the same thing as hate?

EMMETT: Remember that line? Thin. Very, very thin.

JINNY: You wish.

EMMETT: You're right. I do.

Bubbles appeared then disappeared. There was a long pause as he waited for something to pop up on the screen, but nothing came. He tensed and his mouth went dry as he waited. When his phone buzzed and a message appeared, he smiled.

JINNY: Stop that.

EMMETT: Stop what?

JINNY: Flirting. Saying things like that.

EMMETT: You started it.

JINNY: I did not!

EMMETT: Call it what you will, but you were definitely flirting.

She sent him the angry emoji face and he laughed. He took a deep breath and typed.

EMMETT: Is it crazy that we just spent more than 36 hours in a car together, yet I want to see you again. Right now?

He clutched his phone tight, waiting, willing her to

validate his feelings in some way, no matter how small. But Jinny didn't strike him as the type to wear her heart on her sleeve. She seemed to keep her feelings tucked safely away.

JINNY: Not crazy. I'm irresistible like that.

Emmett's lips quirked.

EMMETT: Go out with me tomorrow. After our session, after you finish working, go out with me. There's no game tomorrow night for the Pumas. You have the time.

JINNY: Like a date?

EMMETT: Exactly like a date.

JINNY: What makes you think I want to go out with you?

EMMETT: Please, who doesn't want to go out with me?

JINNY: True. It must be your modesty.

EMMETT: That's only part of my appeal.

He was going to lose her here if he didn't get real for a moment. It was clear Jinny wasn't going to put herself out there and risk getting burned, and could he blame her?

EMMETT: You have to go out with me because I have a problem only you can help me with.

JINNY: You have a lot of problems, but the only one I can help you with is your knee. Your appointment is at ten a.m. Meet me at the Tomas and Mack Center.

EMMETT: You're wrong. There's something else.

JINNY: What are you doing?

Emmett inhaled and took a leap of faith as his fingers

flew over the keys.

EMMETT: See, there's this girl. I can't stop thinking about her. She's constantly on my mind, and I recently realized we could be something special, something more than I ever thought. The only way I can get her off my mind is to see her. So, that's why you need to go out with me. If you don't, I might never be the same again.

JINNY: You're not funny.

EMMETT: I'm not trying to be.

JINNY: You're serious? Like serious-serious?

EMMETT: Dead serious. So, what's it gonna be?

JINNY: I don't know if this is a good idea. You're my patient. We work together.

EMMETT: I always took you for a risk-taker.

JINNY: Some things are riskier than others.

EMMETT: Sometimes there are millions of reasons why you shouldn't do something and only one for why you should. Life is like that. But you have to ask yourself what you want. What has the chance of making you the happiest. Give me one day. If it sucks, if you hate my guts, then we'll go back to how things were between us, no questions asked.

It seemed like an entire lifespan passed as he waited for her reply. He half expected to see the rising sun peeking around his curtains when his phone finally pinged.

JINNY: Okay. One date.

EMMETT: I'll take it.

Emmett snapped his phone shut, victorious. He hadn't imagined their chemistry in the car. It was real and raw and worth pursuing. And he'd prove it.

CHAPTER
TWENTY-ONE
Jinny

Jinny turned to him. "The Neon Boneyard?"

She'd finished Emmett's session earlier that morning, followed by her appointment with Taylor to work on his ankle. Then she went back to her room, where she showered, changed, and prepared for their date. It had been the single most nerve-racking preparation she had ever experienced. A part of her still couldn't believe she was there with him.

Why had she said yes again?

Oh, yeah. Because their kiss on the side of the road had been the hottest experience of her life. Because he's all she could think about. Because somewhere along the line, between hating him and sparring with him, she had grown to like him. He was real and raw, more so than she ever could've imagined. Dean's stamp of approval and Emmett's flirty texts had been the nail in the proverbial coffin. She could pretend she didn't have feelings for him, but she'd be lying.

"I promise you one date, and you take me to a place called the Neon Boneyard?" she repeated.

Truth be told, a part of her wanted this date to be a disaster. It certainly would make things easier on her. Then they could go back to the way things were, BK—before kiss.

"How do you know you won't love it?" Emmett asked with a raised brow.

"It's a gravel lot."

Emmett flashed her one of his knee-weakening smiles and grabbed her hand, tugging her along behind him. "Come on."

Jinny's heart twisted as the warmth of his palm sunk into her bones. The feel of his callused fingers threading through hers did strange things to her insides.

They entered what appeared to be an orderly junkyard of sorts. Their feet crunched on the gravel as they walked, and Jinny took in her surroundings. Everywhere she turned, there were giant signs—the place was a veritable graveyard for neon lights. Some appeared to be antiques, taken from long-closed hotels, shows, and bars. Relics from casinos, wedding chapels, diners, and businesses stood sentry among the heap of metal and broken lights.

Jinny paused in front of the City Center Motel sign, looking on in awe. "What is this place?"

She shifted her gaze to Emmett, but he was already watching her, his gaze intent on her face. A small smile curled his lips. "It's a storage yard. Most of the neon displays from the golden age of Vegas were produced by the Young Electric Sign Company. They keep this plot filled with them."

"It's...amazing." Her voice softened as they picked their way through the yard. "Kind of sad in a way."

"How so?"

"It's kind of like watching the past fade away before your eyes. What once was shiny and new and alive is now old and unused, sitting here unwanted."

Emmett squeezed her hand. "Kind of like the Land of Misfit Toys."

"Exactly."

"If I thought it would make you sad, or you'd start pulling references from *Rudolph*, I wouldn't have brought you. Sorry."

She turned to him. Without thinking, she reached out for his other hand and clasped it in hers. Staring at their joined hands, she slowly lifted her gaze and swallowed. "No, I love it. It's nostalgic. And it's oddly beautiful, isn't it? In a totally unexpected way."

Kind of like him.

"Yeah, it is." His bourbon eyes penetrated her walls. Could he see how hard her heart was pounding in her chest? Could he sense her nerves?

Dropping her gaze, she asked, "Which one is your favorite?"

"That one's easy. The Boneyard sign when you walk in. You?"

"Definitely the Sassy Sally's one." She eyed the large red letters.

Emmett laughed. "Suits you."

Jinny scoffed and smacked him playfully in the arm as they resumed picking their way through the lot, pointing out relics and things they hadn't noticed the first time.

"How'd you know about this place? I've never been anywhere like it."

Emmett shrugged. "I came here once when I was twelve with my dad. He had to come for work, so he pulled me and my brothers from school, and we all went. I think it was more that he didn't have much help and couldn't afford to pay a babysitter to stay with us for a few days than that it was supposed to be a family vacation. Regardless, he made sure we had fun. It's not like we could go into the casinos, so..."

"How many brothers do you have again?"

He held up four fingers.

Jinny whistled. "And you're the...?"

"Middle child."

"Ah, that explains it."

"Explains what?"

"Why you're so needy. You never got the attention you deserved, did you?"

"Are you teasing me, Kimball?"

A ball of warmth settled in her stomach. "Maybe."

"Easy now. Some might call that flirting." He took a step toward her and reached out, running a hand through her hair and resting it at the base of her skull while her heart threatened to explode.

"Definitely not flirting," she said.

"What would you call it?" he murmured, sliding his hands to her chin and tipping her face to his.

Crap. He was going to kiss her again.

Was she ready? She didn't feel ready.

Suddenly the air went thick. Her lungs struggled to keep up and her heart threatened to riot.

Emmett dipped his head, coming closer, moving in...

Dean had told her to go for it, and her heart agreed, and her body all but threatened to disown her if she didn't allow herself this kiss. But her head pumped the brakes.

How long would it be until they turned back into enemies, flinging insults at each other and trying to get under one another's skin? How long until he realized he'd rather have his short-lived flings?

She turned her head and cleared her throat. "Maybe we should just..." Her voice faded as she tried to get her bearings.

"Pretending you don't want to kiss me again?"

"I didn't even kiss you the first time. You kissed me."

Emmett flashed a knowing grin, and she wanted to smack him. "You didn't seem to mind. And maybe I started them, but you definitely kissed me back."

Pah! She tried to speak, she really did, but it seemed her vocal cords had frozen. Words had escaped her, along with all coherent thought the moment he leaned into her again.

His scent enveloped her, playing tricks with her head. "Admit it. You're dying to kiss me again. You're just afraid it'll turn date one into date two."

She shook her head no, but her body said otherwise as she swayed slightly on her feet, involuntarily leaning closer and breathing him in. His lips hovered inches from her own until she could feel the heat from them. Everything inside her yearned to step forward, to close the tiny gap between them.

Then he stepped away, and it was like someone doused her in freezing water. Everything inside her turned cold.

He smirked at her, his dimples winking. Suddenly, her vocal chords worked.

She clenched her hands by her side. "Do you enjoy teasing me?"

Emmett laughed and crossed his arms over his chest. "You're the tease. You're the one looking up at me with those big brown eyes, soft hair, and pink lips. And your perfume is screwing with my equilibrium."

Jinny felt her cheeks flush. "You're my patient, Emmett. Is this really such a good idea?"

No matter what Dean said or how much sense he made, their working relationship persisted. It couldn't just be ignored.

"Is that the reason you're holding back?" he asked.

"Who said I'm holding back?"

He arched a brow.

"Fine. Yes. Maybe?" she said.

"Again, you don't strike me as a rule-follower."

Jinny crossed her arms over her chest in defiance. "Well, maybe I am. I am most definitely a rule follower. The more rules, the better."

Emmett grunted. "So, you're telling me the only thing stopping you from jumping me is the fact that I am, technically, your patient."

"First of all, 'jumping' you is a rather strong depiction of what I'd like to do—"

"Aha! So, you admit you want me to kiss you again."

"No, I—" She groaned in frustration. "There is no 'technically' about it. You *are* my patient."

"So, I'll get a new therapist." He shrugged, as if to say, *ha, problem solved.*

Jinny gaped before her words found their way up through the back of her throat. "That's absurd."

But hadn't that been what she wanted all along? All this time, she hadn't needed to annoy him or goad him into switching therapists. All she had to do was seduce him. But now that she thought of him going elsewhere for treatment, it rubbed her the wrong way. He was *her* patient. Her pain in the butt. Her nuisance to deal with.

"Is it though?" he asked, as he turned and made his way toward the exit, with her in tow. "It would be worth it if it meant I got you," he said over his shoulder.

She stopped, frozen, rooted to her spot on the gravel as she watched him walk away, his voice trailing behind him. When common sense prevailed, she hurried after him. "Who said I wanted *you*?"

"You didn't need to say it. I just know."

She gritted her teeth, struggling to keep up with his stride, wishing her legs were longer. While he walked casually, she had to break into a sprint just to keep up.

"Okay, Yoda, and how is it you know?" she asked.

He came to a dead stop and spun around, and she crashed into him. Her body met with the hard plane of his chest and she bounced back. When he reached his arms out to steady her, it just threw her more off-balance. Her head spun, and her arms scorched at the contact. She swallowed and shook her head, trying to focus, trying to shove away the feeling inside. The one that screamed at her that he was right. The one that wanted to leap into his arms, to hold his hand, to see what it might be like to be more than Emmett's therapist, his enemy, or his best friend's sister.

He stared down at her, the color of his eyes deepening to a fiery amber. "I know because, when we touch, your pulse races."

She opened her mouth to protest, but he beat her to it.

"You argue with everything I say. The slightest thing I do makes you angry, irritates you. Even a smile from me has you clenching your fists."

"That's ridic—" She stopped abruptly as his gaze darted down to her hands, which were clenched at her side. She loosened them, flexing the tight muscles.

"And when I kissed you"—he stepped forward and

placed a hand on the side of her face—"you responded. You're attracted to me. I can see it in your eyes. Everything else is either an act or apprehension."

"No. It's not. I hat—"

He silenced her with his mouth.

Her body hummed, and all thought ceased. Before she knew what was happening, she was kissing him back, turning herself into a complete liar.

Her hands fisted the soft cotton of his t-shirt while she tilted her head, gaining a better angle on his mouth. Her brain turned to mush as he parted her mouth with his and deepened the kiss with a groan, sending her heart into a tailspin.

When he pulled away, his heavy gaze drank her in. "Face it, Jinny. You don't hate me. You never did."

She started to protest, but he placed a finger over her lips, silencing her. "Give me the week to show you how good we could be together."

"And why would I do that?"

"Because I'm different than you thought. Because I surprised you these last few days. And if you'd admit it to yourself, you're as curious as I am to see if we would actually work."

She stared at him. This was her moment of truth. She could rebuff him and pretend like her heart didn't threaten to beat out of her chest every time he was near.

Pretend like a little piece of her didn't fall for him with every second she spent with him. Pretend that she couldn't stand being around him. Or she could admit she felt something toward him. Something more than hate. Something more than attraction. Things had changed during the car ride, leaving her scrambling to catch up, but maybe it was time she did.

He was right. He had surprised her, and she'd be lying if she said she didn't want to see what they might be like together.

"It would never work," she muttered. It was a pathetic attempt at convincing him this was a bad idea.

"Or we might just surprise you," he said, trailing a thumb over her cheek.

"We're nothing alike...we're fire and ice...we're..." She trailed off, out of excuses.

"Where fire and ice meet, the ice melts. Then you get steam."

She stared at him, knowing she wouldn't say no. She couldn't. For some reason, she was incapable. She only hoped for both their sakes that this wasn't a mistake, because if things went sideways, their careers maybe at stake.

Giving Emmett Hall a chance, lending him even a piece of her heart, felt a whole lot like running into gunfire while everything inside her screamed to turn and head the other way.

∞∞∞

What in the ever-loving world did she do?

She swallowed down the ball of nerves that settled in the back of her throat and stared at her reflection. This was her first time in Vegas. She had no idea what kind of clothes one wore when out and about in Sin City, but the silky blue romper was the only thing she had packed, other than jean shorts and work attire. She had planned on hanging out with the team and going out with Dean to the casinos, maybe a decent restaurant or two, but she had not prepared for a date. And even if she had, she would still be ill-prepared for one with Emmett Hall.

How one planned for a date with a man they'd once loathed was beyond her. She should be wearing armor, a hard hat, a musket strapped to her waist. Anything would suit her better than the thin, silky fabric that clung to her petite frame.

She pinched her eyes closed and turned away from the mirror, asking herself what she had been thinking for the millionth time since that afternoon in the Neon Boneyard.

She'd promised him a chance. But a chance at what? Squashing her heart? Making her look like a fool?

She inhaled a cleansing breath and headed for the door, grabbing her purse on the way out.

She could do this.

CHAPTER TWENTY-TWO

Jinny

Jinny stared at Emmett from across the table. He had that look on his face again. The same expression he wore when she appeared in the lobby—equal parts awe and determination, both of which made her uncomfortable. Somewhere along the way, he had clearly decided to win her over, and Jinny hadn't yet acclimated to the change of plan. With Emmett, she couldn't keep up.

"Stop that," she said.

"Stop what?" He grinned. His teeth were so perfectly straight and white they nearly blinded her. Ugh.

"Looking at me like that."

"Like what?"

"Like I'm a giant steak you're determined to devour."

Emmett smirked and played with the straw in his ice water. "Does it make you uncomfortable? My looking at you?"

"Yes."

"Why?"

Jinny sighed. He was as exasperating on a date as he was when they were sparring. Actually, this date felt much like their usual verbal sparring, only more tactful.

"I don't know, but it's making me nervous," she said.

"Nervous is good."

She raised a brow, but kept her mouth closed. He'd turn anything she said around to his favor. If she wanted to win at whatever game he was playing, she'd need to sit through the rest of dinner mute.

Emmett leaned forward and took a sip of his water. Her stomach clenched with the gesture. "Why didn't you order a drink?" she asked, taking a sip of wine.

"Well, you see, I'm on this date with a lady that I really want to impress. She's wearing the most beautiful ice blue silk, and she has the most beautiful features—a sharp jaw, chiseled cheekbones, and a slim, graceful neck that leads to warm eyes and hair so soft it could bring a grown man to his knees. So, if I want to impress her, I need to have all my wits about me. I'll need every tool in my arsenal, which means"— he shook his glass—"strictly water for me."

She flushed and fidgeted with the napkin in her lap. "You almost looked convincing when you said all of that. Did you rehearse it in front of the mirror in your hotel room?"

Emmett smiled and reached out, plucking the napkin out of her fingers and clasping her hand in his own. He leaned closer until she could smell the scent of his body-wash and make out the shadow of stubble coating his jaw. "I meant every word."

The band around her chest constricted. "Do you really want to impress me?"

He nodded soundlessly.

"Maybe you already have." *Maybe that's why I'm resisting so much*, she wanted to say, but the waitress interrupted them.

Turning her attention to the plate the waitress set in front of her, the tension dissipated as Jinny stared at the monstrosity in front of her.

"What in the world is this?" she asked with wide eyes.

"This," Emmett said, grabbing his fork and knife, "is

Hash House a Go Go's famous sage fried chicken and waffles. I dare you to eat it and not think you've died and gone to heaven."

The plate in front of her was stacked with giant waffles and bacon, piled high with huge pieces of fried chicken, and topped with sugary maple syrup. The sweet and savory scents combined to form a mouthwatering combination.

She smirked. "Instead of taking me to some yuppie black-tie restaurant and ordering fancy food I can't pronounce, you bring me here and get me this. It's like you've implanted yourself in my brain and stolen my thoughts. It's disturbing. I would thank you, but it's too humbling."

"So, I did good?"

"Uh, yeah," Jinny said as she retrieved her utensils and made a move toward her plate.

She paused, glancing at Emmett for direction. She had no clue how to go about attacking this thing.

"There's no right way. You just have to go for it."

She nodded and sliced into her tower, toppling over a piece of chicken and cutting off a portion of everything. She shoved it into her mouth. The moan that escaped the back of her throat was just shy of embarrassing.

She chewed, savoring every bite.

Once she swallowed, she stared at him like he'd given her the cure to cancer. She knew he was a ladies' man, but this... "This. Is. Amazing. I take back every bad word I ever said about you. Every single thing."

"Whoever said the path to a man's heart was through his stomach didn't know Jinny Kimball." He winked then returned to his own plate, and she couldn't even be mad. She didn't care. The food was just that good.

They ate their meals with occasional small talk about the area and the things they'd like to do and see before the end of the week. Once their plates were cleared and Jinny's stomach felt like it might explode, she turned to him.

"So, the guys won their game this afternoon. They have one tomorrow, and Dean was asking about us all going out afterwards."

The flash of disappointment on Emmett's face was not lost on her.

"How are you holding up with not being able to play?" she asked.

Emmett sighed and threw his napkin on the table. "I try not to be negative or think about it too much, but it's sort of unavoidable, you know. You can't sit there and watch, when normally you're the one on the court, and not let it eat you alive. But I guess I'd better get used to it since I'm going to be out a while."

Jinny nodded, understanding. "You'll be out there again. You just need to put in your time first and heal. It'll go fast."

"Yeah, especially since I have this hot therapist."

She glared at him, but the blush in her cheeks contradicted her scowl.

Emmett chuckled, then almost instantly sobered. "Growing up, it was always me and my brothers and my dad. He worked a lot. He had to. With three teenage boys in the house and no mother, our grocery bill was huge. Not to mention all the other expenses. He sacrificed a lot. All the basketball camps, the shoes, the equipment and lessons. He did it all and never complained."

"Of course he did. He loved you."

Emmett nodded. "Whenever he wasn't working, he didn't do something for himself or go out with friends. He played ball with us. It was our thing. The six of us. It's what we did to pass the time. Weekends, holidays, birthdays, celebrations, when we needed cheering up. It didn't matter what season it was or how tired he was. If one of us was upset, or we'd just broke up with a girlfriend, we played. All my brothers were good. You can't play basketball every day of your life and not be. But I always had that extra something. My dad always pulled me aside, told me I was special."

He smiled. "I swear the day I told him I had gone pro was the only day I ever saw him cry. He was *that* proud. So, it's not just me I'm playing for. It's him. It's for all those years he came home from work exhausted, but he still dragged his tired butt outside to our makeshift court in the gravel lot and played with me. It's for all the times he could've been doing something else but wasn't. All the things he could've bought himself but didn't. Basketball is a part of me. It always has been and it always will be. But it's not just about me."

Jinny thought back to the Fourth of July, how Emmett hadn't wanted to go home because, as Dean said, playing basketball was "their thing," and he didn't want to sit on the sidelines and watch. She thought he had used it as an excuse to wreck their party. Now she knew he hadn't, and her heart ached for him. Something deep inside her twisted as she thought of how at a time when he had nowhere to go, she'd been rude to him, so uninviting, when he was clearly hurting.

She swallowed over the lump in her throat and stared down at the empty space in front of her. "I'm sorry. That's..." She trailed off. How could words be so inadequate?

She wanted to help him, and she would. In the only way she knew how.

By treating his injury regardless of her feelings for him—negative or otherwise—she had given him her best care up till now, and she'd continue to do so no matter what happened between them. That had to count for something, right?

"It's okay." Emmett smiled. "I know I'll play again. I just need to keep the faith that I won't get traded and that they'll keep in mind my record. It still sucks though. You know?"

"Yeah. It does." She wanted to reach out, to clasp his hand in hers, but it was like she had spent so much time and energy into putting distance between them that she had no idea how. "What about your mom. Do you still see her?"

"She left us. I was four at the time. My brothers were eight, six, two, and one."

One? Jinny stared, agog. She wasn't the most maternal, but she could never imagine leaving children so young.

"I'm sorry. I shouldn't have asked that," she murmured.

"Nah. It's okay. It was a long time ago. I'm lucky. I had a parent that really cared. Not everyone can say that."

While he was right, his attitude was extraordinary. Having no mother couldn't have been easy, and it made her soften to him. The knowledge that he had no female figure in his life growing up made a whole lot of sense; it explained his rough-around-the-edges demeanor. Growing up in a house full of men had to have been dog-eat-dog.

"He sounds like a good man, your dad. I'd like to meet him," she said, and she meant it.

"He'd love you." His easy tone made her feel slightly less foolish for jumping the gun. "And you'd be the first girl

I brought home, so." He shrugged.

Were they really having this conversation? One minute, she was pushing him away, and the next, she was talking about meeting his family. Their relationship had transformed so quickly it made her head spin.

∞∞∞

They left the restaurant, stepping out into the humid Vegas air. Her skin instantly grew sticky with the heat. But she didn't mind. It somehow took the edge off her nerves at the man walking beside her.

He reached out for her hand, and, though she hesitated, she gave it to him, her movements timid.

The zip of heat from his touch sunk into her skin and straight to her bones. She tried to shake it off, to ignore it, but ignoring him was impossible. His light shined too bright.

"I owe you an apology."

Jinny's gaze sharpened on his face as he looked down at her and continued, "At that party last summer, and in your office a few weeks ago, when I said that stuff about your dad and Dean getting you your job, I didn't mean it."

"Emmett, you don't need—"

"No. I do." He shook his head and squeezed her hand.

Coming to a halt on the sidewalk, he turned to her. "I didn't mean any of it. Not at all."

Jinny stared at him, unsure of what to say. Hadn't this been the moment she had been waiting for? An apology. For him to admit he had been wrong. So, why didn't it feel as victorious as she'd thought it would?

"It was a jerk move because, the truth is, I think you're amazing. I've thought it all along, not just since I've worked with you. You deserve this position. You're incredible at your job." He smiled. "I mean, look at this gait," he said, then held his arms out from his body and strutted with an exaggerated swagger.

She laughed, covering her mouth. "That's some walk ya got there."

"Isn't it?" He grinned at her, and she felt something crack open inside her chest, a vulnerability she hated but felt nonetheless.

Her smile faded. "Maybe it's true, though. Maybe they did get me the job," she said, all the laughter gone from her voice.

"It's not. I know it's not." He stepped closer, placing his fingers under her chin and tipping her head up to his. "I need you to know that I never meant it, and I'm not just saying that or telling you what you want to hear."

"It got under my skin," she admitted. "It's like you read my mind. I don't talk about it much, but it's the one thing I was afraid of all along. That I'd get a position like this on account of my family and not because I deserved it or earned it. It's like you slipped into my head and stole the one thing that could hurt me. My one insecurity."

"I regret it." He exhaled and ran a hand over his face. When he turned his gaze back to her, his mouth pressed into a thin line. "I intended it to hurt. That's why I said it."

"But why? We were getting along. We were hitting it off."

He nodded. "I needed to push you away. I had gotten these glimpses of who you were through Dean, through the time I spent with him and the little time I had been around you. Then when we talked at that party, you were so beautiful, and confident, and funny and…light. And I knew I couldn't have you. That I shouldn't, so…" He shoved his hands in his pockets.

"Emmett, are you messing with me?" she blurted. She had to know. How did he go from one extreme to the next? It made her dizzy. It made her question her judgement.

"Why would I do that?"

A spurt of laughter spilled from her throat. "Because it's what we do. Isn't it? Mess with each other, get one up on each other. Compete. Win."

"So, you think I'm, what? Playing with you? Screwing with your head? Pretending to be interested in you as some kind of game? Do you think Dean would let me live if I did that?"

She turned her gaze to the ground at her feet. The truth was that she wasn't sure what to think. A part of her did think he was playing her, but another part of her believed him. Maybe he really did feel something for her. Or maybe it was wishful thinking. And that thought scared her more than anything.

His gaze trailed over her face, and he leaned in closer, likely presuming she wasn't going to respond. "Jinny, I've liked you from the second I met you, and I've wanted to ask you out for just as long."

"So, why didn't you?"

"I wasn't sure you and I were worth the risk, worth the consequences of being together."

"What consequences?"

"Uh, your brother for one. He made it pretty clear the night of the party that you were off-limits to anyone on the team, let alone me. Apparently, my reputation as being a ladies' man preceded me. And it isn't just my friendship to him that was at stake, but my relationship to the team if it caused tension. I didn't know you very well yet. It was early. It made more sense to cut it off." He smiled ruefully. "Then, I got to know you a little better, but by that time you hated my guts. And you became my therapist, so my hands were pretty much tied."

"And now?" Her eyes shifted to his mouth. She

wanted him to kiss her. The desire was so strong and fierce it hit her like an uppercut.

"I can barely remember the reasons for being apart."

She inhaled as he brought his mouth to hers without warning. She breathed him in as he kissed her.

For the first time in as long as she could remember, she let herself go, turned her thoughts off and stopped second guessing his intentions and just let herself feel. Let herself fall.

CHAPTER TWENTY-THREE

Emmett

E mmett watched Gabe's retreating form. Until Gabe showed up during his therapy session at the gym, Emmett had enjoyed three whole days of not having to witness Gabe's blatant attempts to score a date with Jinny. It had been bliss.

"That guy just doesn't know when to quit, does he?"

Emmett asked, watching Gabe's retreating form.

Jinny snatched Emmett's towel up off the floor and flung it into his arms. "Maybe he just recognizes a good thing when he sees it. You know, most men are nice to the women they like. They don't fling insults at them."

"Oh, I see. I humble myself and apologize, and now you're suddenly hilarious."

Jinny cocked a brow and crossed her arms over her chest. "*I* think I'm funny."

"Okay." Emmett nodded, smirking as he glanced back to the exit. "You know, since you like your buddy Gabe so much, I'll just go grab him. Tell him that you'd like to ride home with him instead of me next weekend. More than thirty *long* hours with Mr. Snooze-fest." Emmett hooked a thumb toward the door and started to walk backward toward it. "I mean, you like him better than me, so..."

Jinny's lips twitched. "Go ahead."

Emmett continued toward the exit to the gym and cupped his hands around his mouth. "Hey, Swanson," he hollered out into the hallway.

The sound of footsteps approached, and he watched Jinny's expression—the slight widening of her eyes—as panic set in.

"You wouldn't," she hissed.

"I just want to give you what you want."

Gabe appeared in the doorway, and Emmett put a

hand on his shoulder like they were old pals. "Oh, hey, man. Jinny and I were just talking and she—"

"Saw that you forgot your water bottle," Jinny interrupted.

Gabe frowned and glanced at the blue water bottle next to the exercise ball. "Uh, that's not mine. Wasn't that yours, Emmett?"

Emmett tried to hide his grin but did a miserable job of it. "It is, actually."

"Oh, whoops. Duh. I'm sorry." Jinny scratched her head. "Gosh, all the traveling must be getting to me. My head is in the clouds," she rambled. "Well, we don't want to keep you. We're done here, anyway, so we'll see you this afternoon at the game."

"Okay," Gabe drawled, glancing between Emmett and Jinny like there was something he was missing. "See ya."

"Later, bro," Emmett said, then waited until he was gone before turning his smile on Jinny.

She narrowed her eyes at him and her cheeks flushed.

He sauntered over to her and brushed the back of his knuckles over the hot skin. "You're so cute when you're angry."

She rolled her eyes, which made him laugh. "So, I'm right, then. You like me, while he bores you to tears."

"If you mean that I, apparently, have feelings for an aggressive, overbearing, cocky, ogre. Then, yes, I suppose you're right."

"So, you have feelings for me now?"

"No." Jinny blanched. "I didn't say—I didn't mean... Would you stop looking at me like that?"

"Like what?"

"Like that." She waved toward him. "With that smug smile on your face and those undress-me eyes."

"I like the way you think, Kimball. But I assure you, I have no idea what you're talking about."

He stepped toward her, all the joking gone from his voice. "Maybe I'm looking at you like this because I have feelings for you, too."

Her breath caught as he reached out, running a hand over her hair. It spilled over her shoulders and smelled like vanilla. With a contented sigh, he pressed his forehead to hers, breathing her in. Something tugged on his heart. Some invisible, intangible thing he'd never felt before.

He was falling head-first for Jinny Kimball.

Jinny

The Pumas were down by ten. Jinny watched as her brother took a pass from Taylor, then pivoted and made for the hoop. The ball soared in the air and drilled into the net.

Gabe clapped beside her while Emmett's stony gaze followed his teammates as they played.

She sat, wedged between the two men, wondering how in the world she got there. Talk about awkward.

Then she remembered Emmett's smile as he took the last seat on the bench, next to where the therapists and staff sat. He thought it was funny—sitting next to her, teasing her with every brush of his thigh against hers and the sidelong glances she tried her best to ignore.

Every so often, he'd curl his hand over the edge of his seat, trailing his pinky over the outside of her knee. Meanwhile, on her other side, Gabe seemed oblivious to the gut-clenching heat in the pit of her stomach. Every five seconds, he'd lean in close to her and comment on the game. But she hardly listened. Even the game was having trouble holding her interest. Instead, her gaze continued to flicker to her right, to the hazel-eyed hunk who was watching the game with rapt interest.

She pretended to watch the play on the court but kept peeking over at him. His gaze followed his teammates as he shouted out directions and encouragement. His feet twitched as they moved like he might jump up at any moment and join them. The longing in his eyes was so intense it tugged on her heart.

This had to be difficult for him. She knew how badly

he wanted to play, to feel the ball under his palm, to fly down the court with his opponent on his heels, shouting out plays like he owned the place.

How many games had she watched him, pretending to be oblivious to how amazing he was? Or how sexy he looked when in control of the ball, navigating the court, dominating the game, like he could do it in his sleep?

Simmer down, Jinny.

When Emmett's gaze met hers, she forced herself to glance away. She watched a few more minutes before she risked another quick glance and was rewarded with his dimples.

When Gabe leaned over her shoulder and said something about how their defense needed to tighten up, she fought the urge to roll her eyes. That wasn't why they were losing.

She pressed her lips into a tight line and stared straight ahead at the game, biting her tongue. Their defense wasn't the problem. They just weren't driving the ball into the hoop on offense. They played a solid first two quarters, but in the second half they stopped driving the ball and weren't drilling their outside shots. Defense had nothing to do with it. If you don't score, you don't win. Simple.

He murmured something else to her about setting screens, and she rolled her eyes.

Normally, he didn't bother her this much, so why was

he irritating her so badly now? Maybe it was the way he continued to hover over her shoulder as they watched the game. Or the way he continually encroached on her personal space. Whatever it was, she'd had enough.

Her eyes slid to her right, and Emmett grinned, raising a brow just as Gabe asked her something. Jinny set her jaw then turned her attention to him. "What?"

She shook her head, trying to ignore Emmett mime-sleeping beside her. When he started fake-snoring, she had to mash her lips together to stifle a laugh.

"I asked what you thought of the city so far. If you've had a chance to see much of it." Gabe said.

Jinny hesitated, wiping the palms of her hands over her pants. She knew where this was headed, and she needed to navigate the question carefully. She needed to turn Gabe down, and if he continued his advances without taking the hint, she would have to tell him there was no chance of anything between them. She needed to be blunt because the guy clearly wasn't getting it. But for now, she'd try for tact. The last thing she wanted was any awkwardness between them, considering she still had to work with him.

"Um, I've been to a few of the restaurants and have done a bit of sightseeing—"

An ear-piercing whistle cut her short, and she jumped.

They glanced toward the sound to see Emmett remove his fingers from his mouth, then clap as a slow-spreading grin grew over his face, seemingly unaware of the conversation beside him. But Jinny knew better. He'd been listening to them the whole game.

She gritted her teeth. He was enjoying this, and she'd make him pay.

Any normal man would be annoyed at Gabe's continued pursuit of her, or they'd be jealous, or *something.* But not Emmett. Emmett was too confident, too secure in himself. It was ridiculously attractive but also inconvenient, since he found Gabe's interest in her more amusing than anything.

She took in his playful smile and dimples. Too bad he was so kissable. His proclivity for irritating her was unmatched.

It would serve Emmett right for her to agree to a date with Gabe. And she was a hair's breadth away from doing it, too. Just to prove a point. With her luck though, he'd let her go through with it as punishment; he knew she wanted to go out with Gabe about as much as she wanted a hole in the head.

Gabe stared at her, waiting.

Crap. What had he asked her again?

Oh, right. Had she seen any of Vegas? Her thoughts drifted to her afternoon at the Neon Boneyard, her dinner last night with Emmett, and breakfast that morning before their therapy session. The stolen moments between work and after games. They had taken every opportunity to sneak in some time together. Only two days left before they'd head for home. The week had all but flown by, thanks to him.

"Actually, I—"

"Aw, come on! That was a foul." Emmett jumped to his feet, waving his arms in vain.

Gabe glared. "Can you keep it down, Hall?"

Emmett pretended not to hear him, an amused smile curling the corners of his lips as he sat back down.

She was going to kill him.

Next to her, Gabe shook his head. "Where were we?"

With a mirthless laugh, she placed her head in her hands. What had she gotten herself into?

This last quarter was going to be a long one.

CHAPTER TWENTY-FOUR

Jinny

After the game and post-game interviews, they boarded a bus for the hotel.

Jinny sat alone, thankful for the silence, and more grateful than ever that Gabe had occupied himself chatting with Coach Bannon. It gave her time to think about Emmett and how badly she wanted to see him again tonight. Although they hadn't made any official plans, spending their free time together, when she could skirt Dean, had become a given.

They piled off the bus at the hotel, and Jinny headed toward the elevators, intent on ordering room service then texting Emmett about going out. Maybe they'd catch a show. Then Dean grabbed her elbow and pulled her aside.

"You seem quiet. You okay?" he asked.

"Sure. Fine." *You know, just pining after your teammate. That's all.*

"Well, the guys are going out tonight. You game?"

"I don't know. I was planning on staying in." By staying in, she meant seeing Emmett in private.

"Come on. It's already Wednesday and we only have two days left. Other than the first night, you haven't come out with us at all. You can't spend every night in your room. It's a crime."

"Hey, I was game yesterday morning for brunch, but you had better things to do." Although, she'd wound up being rather grateful for that because she and Emmett had found this amazing little restaurant...

"It's not my fault Callie called me about wedding venues. She said it couldn't wait." Dean pulled a face. "She made me click on, like, a million links to different places. She was so excited. Then she'd ask me questions about which I thought would be more romantic, and all I wanted to do was tell her I'd marry her in my living room for all I care. But she didn't want to hear that. She wanted to hear about the angle of the sunset, and the view, and do I prefer the beach or the mountains, or—"

"I get the picture." Jinny waved him on. At this rate, they'd be there all day. "But that still doesn't mean I need to go out with you guys."

Going out with them meant no alone time with Emmett. The last thing she wanted was to spend time with him while Dean and Gabe breathed down her neck.

"Too bad," he said. "You're going. And when I mentioned it to Emmett, he agreed."

Ugh. Well, that settled that. A night out with the team. Yay.

A little over an hour later, they were huddled around a blackjack table, watching the men lose more money than she'd make in a month.

Emmett nursed a drink, having barely touched it. She knew this because she had been watching him all evening.

He stood across the table from her, watching her with rapt interest as Gabe tried to give her pointers on blackjack —like she cared—and Dean wasted far more money than she thought reasonable. Every time she tried to slip away, Dean stopped her. It was almost like he *wanted* her with Gabe.

She watched as a blonde in a tight black dress made

eyes at Emmett from the bar. Thankfully, he seemed completely unaware. Either that or he didn't care. Both possibilities made her happy. But to Jinny's horror, the woman eventually mustered her courage and made her way toward their table.

When she sidled up next to Emmett, Jinny's stomach sank. Leaning into him, the knockout blonde said something, then tipped her head back and laughed.

Jinny rolled her eyes and stiffly waited on Emmett's response. With a polite smile, he murmured something to the woman that Jinny couldn't hear.

Whatever it was, the woman's smile fell before she scurried away, and when he turned back to the table, their eyes locked. A wave of relief washed through her, to which he shot her a questioning look, his brow furrowed, as if wondering what she'd thought would happen. She offered him a small shrug, and when he moved to her side of the table, a frenzy of butterflies took flight in her chest.

But Gabe hovered over her. "Do you want to get out of here?"

The sound of his voice startled her. She brought a hand to her throat, where her pulse raced.

"Why don't we go somewhere quieter and get a bite to eat?" he asked.

Next to her, Dean paused mid-game, jostling the giant chips in his hands and widened his eyes meaningfully at

Jinny, giving her a subtle nod.

Frowning at her brother, Jinny grabbed Gabe's arm and tugged him aside in an effort to get away from the table and her brother's prying ears. Dean had been acting bizarre all night.

"Gabe, listen. You're a really great guy, but I think maybe you've gotten the wrong impression. I'm sorry. I'm just not interested in anything more than friendship."

Gabe shifted on his feet, his expression unconvinced as he said, "I thought we seemed to have a lot in common and—"

"We do. It's just…I really want to focus on work. I'd like to stay friends and avoid complications. Keep our private lives separate. I hope you understand."

"I hardly think it would complicate things," Gabe argued.

Great. She may as well be talking to a box of rocks for how well he was listening.

Gabe stepped toward her and trailed a hand up her bare arm. She cringed at his touch, wanting to turn and run the other way, but also not wanting to make a scene. Then Dean appeared.

Thank goodness. She almost sighed with relief until he opened his mouth.

"Jinny and I talked the other day. Just for the record, I think the two of you would be…" Dean's voice trailed off as a familiar scent enveloped her.

Emmett drew her to his side and draped an arm over her shoulders. Every nerve ending in her body snapped with tension and hummed with the feel of him so close.

Dean scowled at Emmett while Gabe narrowed his eyes.

Beside her, Emmett tensed. His hand on her shoulder tightened.

"Is there a problem, Hall?" Gabe asked.

Emmett smiled, but there was nothing friendly about the dark glint in his eye. "I don't know. Is there? Seems to me that Jinny shot you down, and you're having a little trouble understanding."

Dean stepped between them before Gabe could act on the murderous glare in his eyes. "What the heck, man? You're wrong and way out of line. Jinny and Gabe have something going. You're the one interrupting."

Jinny's eyes widened, and she gaped at Dean. *He thought... Oh, no.*

It took her a moment to wrap her mind around it. Dean thought the man she liked was Gabe—that he was the one she had been talking about that first night at dinner.

Stunned speechless, she watched as Gabe crossed his arms over his chest, smirking, like he'd been vindicated.

"Dean, can I talk to you for a second?" Jinny asked, finding her voice.

When he didn't immediately respond, she gripped his shirt in her fist and yanked him off to the side while Emmett stared a hole through Gabe. They were like two battering-rams, ready to fight, but she didn't have time to worry about them. She had her own conversation to take care of.

Once they were out of earshot, she turned on him. "You think I have a thing for Gabe?"

Dean blinked. "Don't you?"

"No!"

"What? Then who?"

Jinny hesitated, shifting on her feet, before her gaze involuntarily flickered over to Emmett, who stood nose-to-nose with Gabe, exchanging what she imagined were some very heated words. When her gaze slid back to Dean, she realized her mistake.

His confused expression morphed into one of open-mouthed shock as his head whipped to Emmett.

"Unbelievable." The muscled flickered in his jaw as he turned on his heel and stalked back to Emmett.

"No! Dean." Jinny scrambled after him, tugging on his arm, practically hanging off of it. She may as well have been a leaf blowing in the wind for all the effect she had.

"Gabe, can I have a moment with my best friend?" Dean said, not wasting any time.

"Sure. I'm done here." Gabe shot Jinny one last lingering look then stormed off.

"Dude, tell me you aren't messing around with my sister."

Jinny wrung her hands in front of her, glancing between them, not knowing what she should do. Beg and plead Dean to let it go? Emmett wasn't a toddler. He was perfectly capable of handling himself. So why did this feel so dangerous?

Emmett squared his shoulders as if preparing for a fight, which only made Jinny's heart pound faster. She couldn't take it. Stepping in front of Dean, she said, "It's not like that. We haven't even done anything yet."

"Yet?" His gaze snapped to her.

"You know what I mean." She glared at him. "We like each other."

Dean laughed and waved a hand toward Emmett. "He doesn't even know what that means, Jinny. I thought you, of all people, knew what kind of guy he was."

"He's not like you think he is." Her voice shook, betraying her emotions.

"Jinny, it's okay. Let us talk it out," Emmett said. "Why don't I meet you back at your room in a bit?"

Dean scoffed. "Over my dead body."

"I'm pretty sure your sister is capable of making her own decisions."

"Apparently not."

"Dean—" Jinny started.

He turned his steel-blue gaze to hers, shutting her up. "I thought I made it clear I never wanted her involved with a teammate. Especially not you. But you just take whatever you want. Emmett does what Emmett wants. Do I have it right?"

"No. It's not like that. Not with her."

Dean snorted. "You know, when she told me she had feelings for someone at work, I assumed it was Gabe because that made sense. But this..." He shook his head and placed his hands on his hips. "This doesn't make any sense at all."

"Dean, lower your voice." Jinny glanced around the room. Some of the team members huddled around the blackjack table had begun to stare.

But he wasn't to be deterred. He stepped even closer to Emmett, eyes blazing. "And when I mentioned it to you at the bar, you just smiled and went along with it. The whole time knowing it was you I was talking about. You must've had a pretty good laugh about that, huh?" Dean backed up and looked over at Jinny. "When I gave you my approval, it wasn't for him."

Emmett reached out and gripped Dean's arm. In slow motion, Dean ripped it away, the vein in his forehead pulsing angrily.

Jinny held her breath in the passing silence, unsure of whether she should intervene, but Emmett beat her to it. "I care about her. More than I've ever cared about anyone. This is serious. I'm not just messing around or playing with her head. You have to believe me."

Dean shook his head. "No, I don't." He took another step back and pointed. "You may still be my teammate, but you're not my friend."

With one final icy glare, he stormed out of the casino.

Emmett

Emmett paused in front of Jinny's room and shoved his hands in his pockets. "Well, that could've gone better."

Jinny scoffed and leaned back against the wall. "You could say that. You didn't have to come to my rescue with Gabe, you know."

Emmett grimaced and waved her away. "I was so sick of hearing that idiot refuse to listen to your rejection. It was annoying. I mean, the guy is either totally desperate or clueless. Besides..." He stepped forward and reached out, gently intertwining her fingers with his. "Maybe it's not so bad for people to know about us. Maybe I want everyone to know you're mine."

"Yours, huh? And when was that decided?"

Emmett's pulse thrummed like a drum. Every time he was around her, he felt more alive than ever before. The more time he spent with her, the less time he wanted to be away from her. And it didn't scare him. He welcomed it. Wanted it—this feeling of not wanting to be without.

He gazed down into her soft brown eyes. "You know you want to be mine. You always have."

She laughed. "You're so full of yourself."

He moved his hands, gripping her by the waist and drawing her in. "So, tell me you want to be mine, then."

"I don't know what you're asking." The glimmer in her eyes teased him.

"You're going to make me say it?"

When she nodded, he laughed and swayed with her in his arms, pulling her against his chest. "I feel like I'm in seventh grade again, but here goes." He pulled away from her and slid his hands up her arms, noting the way her skin flushed at his touch. "Jinny Kimball, will you be my girlfriend, so Gabe will keep his grubby paws off you?"

She bit her lip, but there was no hiding her smile—it was bright and brilliant, just like her.

When she nodded and pressed her forehead to his, he contemplated kissing her despite how wrong it was, considering Dean wasn't speaking to him.

"What about my brother?" she asked.

Emmett sighed. "He'll get used to it. He has to," he

murmured against her lips before he pressed them to his.

He parted her lips with his own, taking in the heady scent of her perfume. He fisted a hand in her hair and tugged, the same way she tugged on his heart. Everything about her drew him in, and as he angled her head to the side, he felt himself fall.

Being with Jinny was a renewal, a breath of fresh air. She was everything good that life had to offer. Everything he had waited for. Everything he had been missing—that single piece of his life he had yet to find.

And now that he'd found her, he'd fight tooth and nail to never let her go.

He slowed the kiss, brushing his lips over hers once more, then gently nudged her back as he pulled away. "You better go," he said, nodding toward the door to her room.

Jinny hesitated as if unsure whether to listen or not. Her lips were pink from their kiss, and he knew just how soft they felt on his, so when he nodded again to the door and she moved toward it, he sagged with relief. He didn't think he had the self-restraint to be a gentleman.

She pushed her key card into the lock. "Goodnight."

"I'll see you tomorrow?"

"It's our last day in Vegas," she said, and in her eyes was everything she'd left unspoken.

"When we get back home, nothing changes. If anything, it'll only get better."

"Promise?" Jinny asked.

"Promise."

She nodded and disappeared inside. With a grin, he turned around, trying to decide on the best plan of action for winning Dean's approval, when a figure hovering a few doors down stopped him in his tracks.

Emmett glanced up to meet Gabe's eyes and fought the sigh on his lips.

Gabe grinned. "It's a cozy little relationship you got going there. Isn't it?"

"I don't need to explain myself to you." Emmett pushed him aside and continued toward his room at the end of the hall, but Gabe followed.

"I mean, patient and therapist. How cozy. And only six weeks on the job. Man, she moved fast, huh?"

Emmett whirled on him. He could say whatever he wanted about him, but not Jinny.

He poked a finger in Gabe's slimy chest, trying to keep his temper in check. "Back off, Gabe, before you say something you'll regret."

When Gabe smirked, Emmett forced his fists to his sides before he put them to good use. The punk.

"I wonder what Garrison would say about this? Or Bannon, for that matter? It's not like Jinny's officially on probation or anything, but this year was supposed to be sort of a testing period, to see how she worked out. I'm guessing you'll give her a stellar review at the end of the year. Thorough, too."

Emmett clenched his teeth and cracked his neck. He was *this* close—

"But I wonder what Garrison will have to say when two of his star players"—he glanced down to Emmett's bad knee—"or one of his star players, anyway, is feuding over a girl. And not just any girl, but his therapist. Sleeping with your teammate's sister just seems like poor sportsmanship, don't you think?"

Emmett lunged forward and grabbed Gabe's shirt, ready to cream him. He wanted to cram his fist down his throat and make him eat it. But Gabe's smirk broke through his anger.

Gabe wanted this. He wanted Emmett to lose control. If he assaulted him, Gabe won. With his injury and the Jinny situation, an assault would get him booted from the team. Three strikes, you're out.

Slowly, Emmett peeled his fingers from Gabe's shirt, releasing him. "You don't know the first thing about it. Stay out of it," he warned.

CHAPTER TWENTY-FIVE

Jinny

Jinny glared at Dean for the umpteenth time. "This is ridiculous."

"Don't care."

She scowled and turned her attention to the window. After her final therapy session with Emmett in Vegas and the team's final game, the team had headed home on a private plane, while Jinny was stuck with Dean on some ridiculous train ride back to Pittsburgh.

The clanking of the rails beneath them filled the silence. She crossed her arms over her chest and said, "This changes nothing, you know. I'm going to be with Emmett whether you like it or not."

"Whatever. I may have been a little slow on the uptake, but there is no way I was going to let you two have another thirty-six hours on the road unsupervised."

Her head snapped in his direction. "Unsupervised? We're not ten."

Dean grunted, saying nothing.

"He's not like you think he is," she said for the millionth time.

Dean laughed, which made her see red. He was so irritating. It was a wonder her best friend wanted to marry him.

"Jin, he took two women as his date to the gala. Every time I see him, he has a new one on his arm. He goes through them like chewing gum, popping a new piece every time the old one loses its flavor."

"That's because he wasn't serious about any of them. Sure, he took a lot of women *out*," she said, exaggerating the word. "But that was it. He looks like a total player, I admit, but he's really not. I got to know him. The real him. Most of these women just want money or fame or some kind of publicity to launch a career blogging fashion." She rolled her eyes, thinking of one particular story Emmett told her about a pretty redhead he dated for a couple weeks before he discovered her true intentions. "He just never met anyone worth settling down for. Until now."

"You?" Dean scoffed.

"Is that so hard to believe? Gosh, Dean. Do you even hear yourself? I'm your sister. You don't think I'm worthy of a commitment?"

"Of course I do. Why do you think I'm so angry?"

"I don't know. Because you're a controlling jerk?"

"Guess again."

"If Emmett's so bad, then why are you even friends with him?"

That shut him up. Dean paused, the muscle in his jaw flexing before he finally answered. "I didn't say he was *all* bad."

"Can't you admit there's a chance you're wrong about him?"

Dean sighed as Jinny continued to stare a hole through the side of his face.

"I liked it better when you hated each other," he grumbled.

Jinny tipped her head to the side. "I admit, it seemed less...complicated. But I'm not sure it was ever hate." *More like a slow-simmering attraction.* "So, are you going to let off?

Are you going to make up with him and stop being stupid about this?"

Dean shook his head. "I don't think so."

Jinny threw her hands up in defeat and stared at the passing landscape. She'd almost had him.

"No matter what, he broke the bro-code. You don't date a dude's sister. Ever. You don't kiss her. You don't picture her naked. You don't do…whatever it is you've done."

"We did nothing!"

"And it better stay that way."

Jinny groaned.

"He should've come to me first."

Jinny bit her lip. "Maybe, but our situation is complicated. There was more than his friendship with you to consider, like us working together and what that meant."

"Exactly."

Jinny turned back to the window, so frustrated she wanted to rip her hair out. There was no talking to him right now. She may as well wait until Dean got home and spoke with Callie. She would make him see reason, surely.

For now, she was done discussing it. All her arguing with Dean accomplished was to plant a seed of doubt. She tried to ignore it, but now that she was away from Emmett, it was easy to wonder if this thing between them really was real, if she *was* any different than the women before her. Maybe he'd spend another week with her and realize she wasn't what he wanted. She was too strong-headed, their working relationship too complicated. They'd gone from zero to a hundred this past week. Maybe that wasn't the best foundation for a relationship.

Jinny worried her lip with her teeth, pushing the thoughts aside. Emmett promised her nothing would change once they got home. And she believed him. She had to.

$$\infty\infty\infty$$

Jinny shuffled into the office early Monday morning with a gallon of coffee fueling her step. She and Dean had arrived home late Sunday evening, and she had hardly slept, anxious for her appointment with Emmett this morning. She needed to confirm their connection in Vegas hadn't been a figment of her imagination—hadn't been one big dream—that they'd continue on now that they were back in Pittsburgh.

She unlocked her office door, flicked on the lights, and stepped inside. Setting her coffee down on her desk, she sat and opened her calendar to prep for the week ahead.

She'd need to add James to her schedule after a twisted ankle in Vegas. Other than that, not much had changed in the ten days they'd been away.

She picked up her pen and began to fill him into her schedule when she heard a knock on the door. Gabe forced a smile from the doorway, which she reciprocated. Despite how annoyingly persistent he'd been, she wanted to maintain a solid working relationship. She only hoped he felt the same.

"Hi, Gabe. How are you this morning?"

Gabe motioned toward the hallway. "Uh, we're having a staff meeting this morning in five."

"Oh." Jinny glanced at her wristwatch. "My first appointment is in thirty minutes. Do you think it'll be long?" she asked, praying he said no. Her first appointment was with Emmett and she'd hate to be late.

"It should be fine," he said, but she noted the way he wouldn't meet her eye.

Frowning, she grabbed her coffee and followed him down the hallway, past the gym and the administration offices, and into the boardroom in the back. When she entered, she was surprised to find Coach Garrison and Craig Bannon in attendance. In fact, as she surveyed the room, she realized it was just the four of them. None of the other staff was there.

Her smile faded as she slowly made her way to the table and set her coffee down, a sinking feeling in her gut.

She lowered herself into a chair and glanced to Gabe, hoping for an indication as to what this was about, but he wouldn't meet her eye.

Bannon cleared his throat. "Ms. Kimball," he said in greeting, his tone all business. "I hate to do this, but we wanted to have a little sit-down. Some things were brought to our attention following the Vegas trip, so we thought it best to clear the air."

Jinny's blood ran cold. This was about Emmett. She felt it in her veins.

Would they fire her? *This couldn't be happening.* After only six weeks on the job, she'd either get a slap on the wrist or, worse, canned for an inappropriate work relationship. How completely mortifying.

Jinny folded her hands on the table, trying to suppress the blush rising to her cheeks. Her gaze flickered to Gabe, but he still refused to look at her. The coward. This had to be his doing. He'd ratted her out like they were in Kindergarten and Emmett had stolen his pencil.

"It's been brought to our attention that you are seeing one of the Pumas star players. And that this player happens to be one of your current patients."

Jinny hesitated. What could she say? Deny it? Insist it wouldn't affect her work or the team?

She cleared her throat, mustering her courage to speak. "That is correct."

Bannon sighed, while Garrison looked disappointed and splayed his hands over the table. "Look, I'm going to give it to you straight here. You're great at what you do, and Bannon wants to keep you on staff," he said, nodding toward the team manager. "But the situation concerns us. It presents certain problems. Problems that, being a new team, we don't want to take on."

"I can promise you, my personal relationships will not bleed into my professional life," Jinny said.

Bannon frowned. "I don't see how you can promise that since the two are so intertwined. We've been informed of the tensions building between Emmett and certain teammates due to your relationship."

Dean.

Jinny seethed as Gabe finally turned to her. "I'm sorry, Jinny, but for the sake of the team, I had to tell them about this."

Sure, he did. Never mind the knife twisting in her back. Why couldn't he mind his own business? Was this really over his concern for the team? Or because he'd lost? Maybe she should inform Bannon of his inappropriate advances. But that would just make Jinny seem even more like a liability, like it was all her fault. The blame would surely fall on her lap because she was the woman.

"Dean will be fine. He's just being an overprotective brother," she said. "He's never liked anyone I've dated."

Bannon shook his head. "Regardless, we cannot have the situation persist. Even if tensions with the team fades, we can't have your personal bias or preferences interfere with your ability as a professional. Not to mention, seeing as how Emmett was the one to provide us with a recommendation on your behalf prior to your hire—"

"He what?"

Jinny blinked. Did she hear them right? Emmett had been the one to refer her for the job?

"Yes, and you can see how that might look with the two of you now dating."

Jinny's stomach churned, and her thoughts swirled as she stifled a groan. This looked bad. Why would he not tell her he had provided a reference for her job? Now they probably thought he only did so because they were seeing each other prior to her being hired. It was the furthest thing from the truth, but they'd never believe her now.

"We don't believe in making personal life choices for our staff," Bannon continued. "That's why we're letting you choose. You can either stop seeing Hall, or we can provide you with a great letter of recommendation for whatever alternative career path in physical therapy you choose to pursue."

Jinny's stomach sunk. So, that was it? Either choose Emmett—a brand new, uncertain relationship—or choose her career? It wasn't even a choice. Choosing Emmett was like buying a lottery ticket and then quitting your job because you were so sure you would win. It would be senseless, reckless, even. They had only just begun.

Stupid, stupid, stupid. She knew better than to get involved with him. Set aside the fact that he wasn't the arrogant jerk she had thought, how dumb was she to ignore the fact that he was her patient? Getting involved with him should've been off-limits from the start. And it was. Until something between them shifted. Somewhere on the road from Pittsburgh to Vegas, things had changed between them, and what had been a spark of attraction turned into something deeper.

She hesitated a moment, trying to find her voice and the energy to speak. A monumental effort, considering she felt drained. "I'll speak to him. If it's okay with you, sir, I'd also like to transfer his care to another therapist."

What was she saying? Her heart screamed at her to find another way. But this was her dream. Her livelihood.

"I think that's very wise. And it shows your dedication to the job. Thank you, Miss Kimball. I guess we're done here," Bannon said.

"Um, if it's okay. I might go home for the day."

She clutched her stomach. It roiled, an unexpected nausea bubbling up her throat. She pressed her fingers to her lips then muttered, "I'm not feeling so well."

"No problem." Bannon nodded and flashed her a sympathetic smile.

Jinny sat in the boardroom until they'd left. Silence

surrounded her, providing her little comfort. When she finally mustered the energy to stand, she grabbed her coffee cup with shaking hands and exited, only to have Gabe approach her.

"Jinny, I'm sorr—"

"Save it," she snapped, holding her hand out. She didn't want to hear his lousy excuses. She was done with him. She'd only put up with him before because they were coworkers. She wanted to be professional, but any kindness she'd had to offer before was gone.

She headed straight to the waiting room, where Emmett sat, early for their appointment.

She took in his royal-blue running shorts, the snug, white t-shirt, and the way his thick hair curled around his ears, and her heart squeezed. Call her a coward, but she couldn't face him right now. She needed a moment to herself. She needed to process everything that just happened, the fact that she'd looked like a fool in front of the Pumas team members, the coach, the team manager, Gabe...

Spinning on her heel, she hurried back to her office, where she dialed Gloria, the receptionist, and asked that she cancel her appointments for the day, giving the excuse that she was sick and would be leaving for home.

CHAPTER TWENTY-SIX

Jinny

S he spent the afternoon driving around the city aimlessly and drinking one too many espressos until her hands shook and her heart was in fits.

By the time she arrived back at her apartment, her nerves were raw, and she was more on edge than she had been that morning during the meeting. Soon, her caffeine buzz would fade, and a crash would follow. She couldn't wait.

She swung open the front door, finding no solace in the bright and cheery exterior. Pushing her way inside, she dropped her purse by the door and was greeted by Callie before she even had her shoes off.

"What the heck happened?" she asked, blocking her entry into the kitchen. "You got in late last night. I spoke with Dean. He told me about you and Emmett then I tried to call you all day at your office and on your cell. Gloria said you were sick. I was worried."

"What are you doing home?" Jinny asked.

Callie's expression turned sheepish. "I took the day off. Dean and I are supposed to spend it together."

Jinny nodded, wordlessly. When she said nothing, Callie reached out and touched her arm. "Jinny, you're scaring me. Emmett came—"

"He's here?"

Callie nodded, and Jinny's gaze shifted behind her, focusing on the leather chair, where Emmett sat, leaning forward with his elbows on his thighs. When his eyes met hers, her heart thumped in her chest.

"Great," Jinny mumbled through her tight throat.

"I'll give you guys a minute," Callie said, clearly realizing that whatever was wrong with Jinny had something to do with the man sitting in her living room.

Jinny took a deep breath and headed toward him. The remnants of coffee buzzed in her veins. Whatever expression she wore must've looked ominous, because as she approached, his expression morphed into one of concern.

She stopped in front of him and cleared her throat, then sunk down into the sofa.

"What's going on? Are you sick?" he asked, his gaze traveling over every inch of her, looking for a sign of illness, but she knew he'd find none. All he'd see was her weary, tired eyes.

"I've felt better. But, no, I'm fine." She took a deep breath, wondering why this was so hard. They'd spent ten days together—three trapped in a car, and seven in Vegas. Her chest shouldn't feel hollow or her heart heavy. They had barely begun anything, so ending it shouldn't hurt.

"I had a meeting with some of the staff today. Swanson, Garrison, and Bannon to be exact," she said.

It was better to rip the bandage off fast. It might hurt more initially, but the sting would fade faster in the long run.

Emmett's eyes widened. "And?"

"Why didn't you tell me that you recommended me for the job?"

Out of all the things to address first, this was maybe the most irrelevant, but it was the first thing she could force out. Maybe it was the irony of it all. He had accused her of getting the job due to her familial connections. It was what put a wedge between them in the first place. But all along, *he* had given her a recommendation.

He raked a hand through his hair and winced. "Are you mad? I only put in a good word because I knew you had already applied. I caught wind of it and thought you deserved it—"

"It's fine." She shook her head then sighed. "I'm not mad. I wish you would've told me though. It makes our situation look particularly bad. Like you tried to get me the job just because you had an ulterior motive."

"That's not true."

"I know that," she said, raising her voice. "But Gabe told them about us...that we're dating, seeing each other. Who knows what else. He also filled them in as to how angry Dean was."

Emmett winced. "Okay, and?"

"I didn't deny it. What's the point? I told them it was probably best that someone else take over your therapy."

Emmett nodded, his jaw hardening with the knowledge. "Sure. Yeah, that's probably for the best. I mean, I want to work with you, but if it means we can be together, then..." He shrugged and reached for her hands. "It's a small price to pay."

His fingers clasped hers, causing a painful thumping in her chest. "You don't understand. They don't want us seeing each other."

"They can't tell you what to do with your personal

life."

"Whether or not it's legal, I don't know, but they gave me an ultimatum. I'm six weeks in. I don't have a leg to stand on or a way to fight them. It's my job or us."

She stood, moving away from him, needing the distance. She needed to breathe without inhaling his spicy cologne, without the warmth of his skin on hers.

"There has to be a solution." Emmett shrugged like it was no big deal.

For the first time since her meeting that morning, Jinny felt a well of anger rise inside of her. "There's not."

"So, we sneak around. We hide it. Now that I'm not your patient anymore, it'll be so much easier."

She stared at him, biting her tongue, saying nothing.

"Jinny, I promised you nothing would change, and it hasn't. I still feel the same way about you. I'm not just going to throw this all away because Gabe is a jealous prick that couldn't stand to see you with me."

Jinny chewed the inside of her cheek, thinking about everything Dean said. She thought of the drive down to Vegas, how she saw another side of Emmett. Her thoughts flickered over their week spent together. But one week did not make a solid relationship. One week was nothing.

"Emmett, I care about you, I do. But we had one good week. Ten days when we weren't at each other's throats. We're just fooling ourselves to think this will work. Just two weeks ago, we couldn't stand one another. I was intent on getting you to switch therapists on your own, and you were busy goading me, doing everything to get under my skin. It's just not realistic to risk my career, my dreams, over one week and a change of heart when everything in your past suggests you'll just get tired of me like all the others and move on. And then what? I'll be jobless *and* single?"

Emmett slammed his fist on the coffee table, making her jump. He shot to his feet and stepped toward her. "I thought you trusted me. I thought I had proved to you that I wasn't that kind of man."

"You did, but—"

"But what?"

Jinny's throat closed. He was asking too much of her, too soon. "I can't risk everything for something that may or may not work. You have to understand that."

He nodded, his jaw hard. "Sure. We're not worth it."

"Emmett, I didn't—"

"So, you just give up? Just like that? Maybe it's new, but I'm falling for you." He reached out and grasped her hands. "Jinny, I've never felt this way before about anyone. And if there's even a chance you're feeling the way I am, and I know that you are, we can't just throw this away."

She turned her head. "Don't make this harder than it needs to be," she whispered.

"Tell me you don't feel the same way, and I'll go."

"Emmett..."

"Say it."

"I think you should leave." Her words fell, heavy and leaden between them.

A moment passed before Emmett dropped her hands and stepped away. "What if your job weren't the issue? What if none of that mattered?"

"But it does."

"What if it didn't? What if they told you they knew, but they didn't care?"

"Then everything would be different. We wouldn't be having this conversation. But that's not reality."

Emmett stared at her. She could all but see the wheels spinning, and she had no idea what he was thinking, but she knew there was no way out of this. They couldn't wish away their circumstances, and sneaking around behind the team's back was a weak plan and a very temporary solution that would eventually blow up in their face.

She couldn't risk all the long nights studying for her exams, the years just scraping by at her residency in order to gain experience. All the hard work, her dreams, would be for nothing. And for what? A chance at love? She didn't even know if they could get there. She didn't even know if Emmett was capable.

She needed to end this and end it now. No leading Emmett on. As long as she was the team's physical therapist and he was a Puma, he was off-limits.

She pressed a hand to his forearm, trying to ignore the flex of muscle beneath her hand or the current of electricity coursing between them. "This thing between us, whatever it was, or whatever it could've been, is over. Better for it to end now, rather than later when one of us could get crushed." More specifically, *her.*

∞∞∞

Jinny strode into the kitchen and nearly went straight back to her bedroom when she spotted Dean standing at the breakfast counter, his arms wrapped around *her* best friend. *Double standard much?*

Never mind. She was strong, independent, and unafraid of confrontation.

And angry. Anger helped.

She stormed into the kitchen and grabbed her travel mug from the dishrack, slammed it on the counter, then poured steaming hot coffee into it before tightening the lid. She wondered if it was hot enough to give third-degree burns, because dumping it over her brother's head sounded pretty good right about now.

She took a sip and moved to the refrigerator, where she retrieved a yogurt. When she turned back around, Dean had released Callie from his grubby paws, and all eyes were on her.

Callie, sensing the tension, smiled a little too brightly. "So, how are you this morning?"

Jinny sipped her coffee, eyeing them over the rim of her cup. "Just peachy."

"It's Friday," Callie added.

"I noticed."

Dean cleared his throat. "Hey, uh, Callie and I were going to that new place in Station Square tonight. They've got an awesome band playing. We thought maybe you might want to come."

Jinny turned her eyes on Dean, burning him with her gaze. "Nope."

"Come on," Callie said.

"Why? So I can be the third wheel for the millionth time? Oh, poor Jinny, she doesn't have anyone, so we'll just drag her along with us wherever we please," she mocked. "Are you going to invite me when you consummate your marriage? Conceive your first child? Do I get to go on your honeymoon?"

"Okay, someone's still bitter," Dean muttered.

Jinny stepped forward, eyes narrowed, shoulders back, prepared for a fight.

It had only been four days since she broke things off with Emmett, but it felt like forever. She was lonely. Work sucked without him. She no longer had appointments with him to secretly anticipate.

She missed his eyes, his smile, those dimples. She missed their back-and-forth—the way he always seemed to know what she was thinking, despite whatever act she put on.

"Yeah. You know what? Maybe I am," Jinny said. "Because when I found out you were in love with Callie, *my best friend*, I supported you. Sure, maybe I laughed a little at the craziness of it, but I was okay with it. Heck, I was even okay with it when I discovered your stupid fake-boyfriend thing was all a ruse. I went along with it because I'm your sister. That's what family does for each other."

She shoved him in the chest, but he barely budged, so she shoved harder. "I supported Callie, too, because that's what friends do. Because I wanted to see both of you happy."

"My situation was completely different," he said.

"No. It really wasn't. But it's fine, big bro. No worries. From now on, I'll be married to my job. You don't have to worry about me falling for the wrong guy because I'm done. *Soooo*, done."

She sauntered out of the kitchen to the sound of Callie pleading for her to come back.

She felt bad for storming out on her. It wasn't Callie she was mad at, but if she was engaged to her brother, then they were a package deal.

Slamming the apartment door behind her, she made her way outside to the rental car she got the week they came back from Vegas. Dean had paid for it in an effort, she suspected, to butter her up.

As she sunk inside, she thought maybe she'd keep it another million years. Maybe she'd rack up a bill so huge, the car would be hers at the end of it.

Okay, maybe this wasn't all Dean's fault. It was hers, of course. She knew better than to date someone at work, but he still could've taken her side. Who knew what the team would've said had Dean supported her—went to bat for her —instead of opposing a relationship with Emmett. Maybe they wouldn't have viewed it as a problem and turned a blind eye.

Whatever. It didn't matter.

She didn't have a future with Emmett. They were a fleeting thing. Her feelings had already started to fade, she told herself.

If only she weren't lying.

CHAPTER TWENTY-SEVEN

Emmett

Almost ten days had passed since they returned from Vegas. Ten days without seeing Jinny.

It was killing him.

If he had known how attached he had grown to her in these six weeks of therapy, of seeing her nearly every day, he would've refused to leave her apartment after she broke it off. He would have insisted on making it work.

Of course, he'd immediately called up Bannon and set up a meeting. He pleaded his case. Told them Dean would come around, but in the end, none of it mattered. They said that if it ended poorly, Jinny would be out of a job.

For an athlete like him, any indiscretions were a slap on the wrist. They overlooked things. And he knew it was true. It happened all the time. Pro-football players abused their girlfriends, were found with drugs, got DUIs, you name it, and they got away with it. It wasn't fair. It was a double standard that had always irritated him. Yet there was nothing he could do about it.

Except one thing.

The thing he had debated on the moment he left Bannon's office. It would be a huge sacrifice.

He and Jinny couldn't have a relationship as long as they both worked for the Pumas, which meant one of them couldn't be a Puma. Simple as that.

He couldn't ask her to ditch her dreams. He understood the trust they needed for a commitment to grow between them. But that didn't mean one of them couldn't make a sacrifice. He loved Pittsburgh. The Pumas were the team to hand him his dreams. His father and brothers visited regularly, and he had grown close to Dean and his other teammates. The thought of playing for anyone else slayed him. But sometimes, to get something you wanted, you had to give up something you loved. An eye-for-an-eye.

Emmett opened the lock screen on his phone. His finger hovered over Bannon's number. He hit send and waited as it rang, holding his breath.

When Bannon answered, he exhaled and said, "I want you to trade me."

∞∞∞

Jinny

Jinny stared at the Pumas team picture in her office. The one she had defaced weeks ago with Emmett's devil horns and tail.

She remembered how excited she was her first day, how much she anticipated being a part of the team. And now... The sight of Gabe's face made her want to punch something (particularly him), and she found it more than difficult at the moment to muster her Puma-pride.

To say she had been in a sour mood since Vegas two weeks ago was the understatement of a lifetime. She had been short and snippy with Callie. She worked Taylor harder than she should've in their session yesterday, calling him a baby when he complained it hurt, and she had all but flipped Bannon the bird when she passed him in the hall. She was a loose cannon, ready to snap at the slightest provocation.

With each day, her heart grew heavier.

She longed to see Emmett. How many times in the last week had she picked up her phone and dialed his number? Each time, she'd quickly erase it before she summoned the courage to press send. After all, she would accomplish nothing by calling him. Hearing his voice would be a temporary salve on her wounds when all she wanted to do was fall into his arms.

Emmett had been right. The jerk. He always was. Which made him all the more irritating. Jinny had fallen for him, and there was nothing she could do about it. It had started on the Fourth of July—maybe even before then—but somewhere between PT and Vegas, she had fallen head over heels.

All in all, it had been a monumentally crappy two weeks, and she didn't know how much longer she could hold out. If only she could think of some way for things to work out.

She racked her brain and came up empty.

Dean didn't help matters. Over the course of the last couple days, he seemed to do a 180. One outing with Emmett and a couple beers, and, suddenly, things were hunky-dory. Well, fan-friggin-tastic for them.

He even had the nerve to tell her she might want to

give Emmett a call, like the last two weeks hadn't even happened.

Yeah, he wasn't winning brother of the year any time soon.

Jinny's office phone buzzed. She lifted it to her ear and answered.

Gloria's voice filled the line. "Hi, Jinny."

When she paused, Jinny rolled her eyes and twirled her hand as if to hurry her along.

"Um," she hesitated. "You have someone here to see you."

"Fine. I'll be right out." Jinny slammed the phone down.

Well, no freakin' duh she had someone to see her. Davis was due in five minutes for his appointment.

She shoved away from her desk and straightened her shirt, reminding herself to put on a smile and be pleasant as she left her office and headed for the waiting room.

When she paused in the open doorway, her gaze surveyed the lobby, and she froze.

There, in the shadows, stood Emmett.

Her heart skipped a beat as she drank him in. His dark hair was disheveled, and he wore his typical attire of athletic shorts and a plain t-shirt that he had absolutely no right looking that good in. When he raised his hand in greeting and his dimples popped, her knees nearly gave out.

She opened her mouth to speak, but the words stalled in her throat as his gaze slid over her features, taking her in like it might be his last chance.

He exhaled and smiled, taking a step toward her. One, then another, and another, and before she could even comprehend what he was doing, he was inches away from her, crushing his mouth to hers.

She breathed him in while his lips wreaked havoc on her psyche. He was all soap and freshly laundered clothes, with a hint of aftershave. Nothing had ever smelled so good.

Sliding her hands to his chest, awareness crept in.

She was in the waiting room of her workplace. Kissing Emmett. And he was off-limits.

She pushed against his chest and pulled away through the ache in her chest. "What are you doing here. You can't —"

"I've been traded."

Jinny reeled back. "What?"

Emmett stared into her eyes, the green flecks dancing in the light. "I'm no longer a Puma."

He paused, like he was waiting for her to catch up, but her brain was fried.

She brought her fingers up to her temples and shook her head. "I don't understand."

"Next season, I will be a Philadelphia 76er."

"But how?"

Emmett shrugged, then reached out and intertwined his fingers in hers. "I asked for the trade, and I got it. I just found out this morning. You're the first person I told, but I'd expect it to be all over ESPN by this afternoon."

Her stomach clenched. She wanted to hope. She wanted to believe she knew what this meant, but she needed to hear it. "Why?"

"That's easy. Some things are worth a sacrifice. And sometimes...you just know."

He dipped his head, kissing her as a sob caught in her throat. "And besides, now I can kiss you anytime I want."

He grinned before Jinny gripped his shirt, pulling him back to her.

EPILOGUE

SIX MONTHS LATER

J inny waited outside the Wells Fargo Center, where the
Philadelphia 76ers just played and won against Washington.

She tilted her head up to the clear blue sky and inhaled. There was nothing better than late November, especially fall days like this one, where the air was seasonably warm yet crisp. The scent of leaves and grass and autumn hung in the breeze, and the holidays loomed right around the corner.

And, okay, maybe it was more than the weather or the 76ers amazing game that put the smile on her face. It didn't hurt that she may be blissfully in love with a certain light-haired, whiskey-eyed point guard.

"Here you are." Emmett's father handed Jinny a styrofoam cup, offering her a warm smile.

His dark hair was sprinkled with a bit of gray, and crow's feet hinted at the corners of his eyes, but overall, he was the spitting image of his middle child.

"Thanks." Jinny took a sip of the coffee then smiled. "I wonder how long we'll have to wait. I imagine they'll do another post-game interview."

"Probably. It's good to see him on the court again, isn't it?"

"It is."

"And in his hometown, no less. I suppose I have you to thank for that." He winked.

He was a charmer, just like his son.

"In a very roundabout way, but I don't mind taking the credit." She laughed.

Emmett had spent the remainder of the summer with Jinny in Pittsburgh until pre-season, when he rented a place in Philly. Now, they'd fallen into a familiar rhythm. His weeks were spent traveling back and forth between the two cities, in between Pumas and 76ers games. It wasn't always easy, and sometimes their schedules conflicted, but being in the NBA meant easier access to transportation and having the money at your disposal to travel on a whim.

Jinny had only visited Philly a few times but had already grown to love all the Hall men. Watching Emmett and his brothers when they got together was a bit like being at the circus. It was loud and chaotic and competitive—much like her own family—and she loved every single second of it. She fit right in with her dry wit, sarcasm, and her ability to roll with the punches.

Mr. Hall—Daniel, as he insisted she call him—took a sip from his cup as he eyed her over the rim. "Now, before we show up in Pittsburgh on Thursday, are you sure your family's up to us crashing your Thanksgiving dinner? Six grown men can really put a dent in the turkey."

Jinny pointed a finger at him. "If you don't show up, you'll answer to me because my mom has been planning this meal for weeks. Trust me. She loves nothing more than cooking for a crowd. Besides, I think she likes Emmett more than me." She grimaced. No doubt, her mother would be fawning all over him the second they walked in.

Jinny arched a brow. "But maybe I should be asking you. How do you feel about a little friendly competition?"

Mr. Hall's eyes lit up. "Like?"

"Well, every Thanksgiving, the Kimball's compete in a

little game of football—"

"You and your competitions." Emmett's voice cut her off.

With a yelp of joy, Jinny turned to him and leapt into his arms. He staggered back as she crushed her mouth to his and laughed.

When she pulled away, her eyes twinkled. "Fourteen points and six assists. Not too shabby for your second game back."

"What can I say? Awesome runs in the family." He leaned down and wrapped his arms around her. "That and I had a pretty girl cheering for me in the stands."

"Yeah?" Jinny's pulse raced.

Mr. Hall cleared his throat. "Ah, how about I meet you back at the house for dinner before your flight?"

"Sure," Emmett said without even so much as a glance in his direction.

"We're making him sick, aren't we?" Jinny asked once he was gone.

"Maybe a little. He raised five boys. He's not used to outward displays of affection."

Jinny reached up, straightening the collar of Emmett's crisp white shirt. "I'm proud of you," she whispered.

"I know."

She laughed and swatted at his arm. "I'm serious. You've done amazing." Then, with a sly grin, she added,

"One game might be a fluke, but not two. So, I think it's safe to say I told you so."

"*You* told me so?"

"Well, yeah. I told you from day one that you'd come back and be better than new."

"Ah, but you told me I wouldn't get traded."

"But you *asked* to get traded, so, technically, I was still right. I win."

Emmett shook his head. "Fine. But I was right about us."

"What?"

Emmett chuckled and kissed her softly on top of her head. "Yeah. I knew all along you had the hots for me, and I told you we would work. But you were so intent on pushing me away."

Jinny smirked, placing her hands on her hips. "I don't remember it being like that. I remember you irritating the crap out of me until you finally wore me down."

Emmett tipped his head back and laughed. "Hey, whatever works. I won the girl, didn't I?"

"Barely," Jinny muttered.

Emmett clasped her hands in his as they made their way to his car.

"Fine," Jinny said. "But I give the best back rubs."

"I can't argue with that. But I give better head rubs."

She narrowed her eyes. "That's only because I have

more hair to work with." She paused in front of the car and her eyes glittered. "Fine, I concede to that, but I still have you beat." She stalked toward him, pinning him against the car. "Because I definitely love you more," she whispered.

"Impossible." Emmett leaned in for a kiss and brushed his mouth lightly over hers. "I definitely win the loving-you-more competition."

Jinny scoffed. "Just like you won the game of Scrabble last night?"

Emmett opened Jinny's door and waited until she slid inside before he closed it and rounded the car. Once inside, he turned to her. "Legit is definitely a word."

"It is not. It's slang for legitimate."

"Exactly. A real word."

"How can I be in love with such a sore loser?"

Emmett feigned shock. "You're in love with someone else?"

Jinny glared at him. "You know, it's kind of cute, actually."

"Do you always have to get the last word?"

"Duh."

Emmett grabbed her left hand, brushing his fingers over her palm. She shivered in response and his eyes darkened, all the playfulness gone. "What would you say if I gave you a ring on Thursday?"

Jinny's heart stilled in her chest. She couldn't breathe.

For a moment, she thought she might pass out before her lungs kicked back in, remembering their job. Warmth spread from her fingers to her toes. She swallowed and asked, "You're giving me a ring?"

"I guess you'll just have to wait and find out." Emmett grinned, and Jinny pressed her right hand to her mouth to hide her growing smile.

Her mind raced as she leaned back in the seat in a daze.

She was in love. And she was going to get married.

Great, now she'd be dying until Thursday.

"See, I totally win."

When Jinny blinked over at him, he added, "As for the love-you-more thing, a proposal definitely clinches it."

"Only you would propose so you could win."

He laughed.

A broad smile spread over her face. "But you're forgetting something."

"What?"

"After you ask, I get the last word."

Read Maya's story next in
RESISTING THE BAD BOY
HERE

Or

Not ready to say goodbye? Turn
the page to read an excerpt.

RESISTING THE
BAD BOY

EXCERPT

CHAPTER ONE

Maya

Maya stared at the pathetic cupcake that her cameraman, Ray, had given her early for her birthday. It was a nice gesture; she should be grateful. And she was.

She was.

She stared down at the vanilla cupcake. The lopsided frosting drooped to the side at a sad angle, kind of like her life.

No, she told herself. Today was a good day, and to-morrow would be even better. Well, for her career, anyway. Her personal life may be pathetic, but at least her career was on-point. She'd just received the news that she scored the biggest interview of her career. Tomorrow morning, she would interview *the* Jordan Woods.

She lifted the cupcake and stared at it with renewed determination. Saturday was her birthday. Only two more days. In her twenty-six years on this planet thus far, she had accomplished a great career and had come from an amazing family. While she couldn't take much credit for her parents or her brother, she had clawed her way to the top of her class at Duquesne University and worked her butt off to snag a job in sports journalism for the city paper. At first she merely assisted, but after two years, she had proved her worth, and just look at her now. She was the leading sports journalist in the city. So, naturally, it was time to bring her personal life up to speed.

No men, though. She was swearing off men. In particular, basketball players.

Her thoughts flickered to her last two relationships. Both disasters. She'd spent too much time with Dean Kimball of the Pittsburgh Puma's, hoping he'd come around and stop pining away for his sister's best friend—although she hadn't known at the time the "who," she merely knew there was someone else occupying his heart. Then, she tried to forget him with a short-lived relationship with a man who was Dean's complete opposite, but that ended poorly when she dumped him because she thought Dean still had feelings for her. She made a fool out of herself, compromised her integrity, and left with her tail between her legs, so to speak.

She would not make that mistake again.

No, her personal goals were more wide-ranging. She wanted friends. Yes, friends. Like kindred spirits, cut-from-the-same-cloth type friends. Maybe it was pathetic, but in her twenty-six years of life, she had little to no relationships outside of her family and work.

She grew up a tomboy, in love with sports, hating all things girly. Then her parents had a major *whoops* and found themselves pregnant with an almost-nine-year-old at home. By the time her brother was diagnosed with autism, Maya was twelve, and her parent's lives weren't the only ones that changed. From that moment on, life became all about helping her family, making things easier on them, and assisting with her brother in any way she could. It wasn't until late high school that she found her X-chromosome. By then, she had already formed a group of guy friends and alienated the girls at school. She was one of the "bros," preferring football games on the weekends to getting mani-pedis with "the girls."

In short, she had no girl friends. Never did.

But it was about time she got some. Friends, that is, particularly of the female variety.

As of Saturday, she'd be twenty-seven. She was going to make some girl friends, real friends, true friends like you saw in the movies and read about in books. She'd get a life and do more than watch movies alone and drive her brother to and from his social activities. Even at eighteen, with no license, and a pervasive developmental disorder, the kid had more of a social life than she did, for goodness sake.

With her vow fresh in her mind, she dragged her finger through the thick frosting then plunged the glob in her mouth, licking her finger clean. "Happy early birthday to me.

Jordan

Jordan sighed as he stared out at the view, ignoring the buzzing in his ear—a buzzing also known as his agent, Ron.

The sky was a blanket of cerulean blue above the skyscraper buildings. Huge swaths of flowers bloomed bright pink and red under the warm Californian sun. He knew from the short drive there that the balmy sixty-eight-degree afternoon awaited him when he left the confines of this office.

If only he could leave now.

In a matter of hours, he'd be headed for the East Coast, and he craved one last glimpse of the beach and a stroll down Santa Monica Pier.

The buzzing continued as Ron droned on about erratic behavior and contracts and whatever else. Man, he was worked up today.

Jordan turned his attention back to him. Ron's face bloomed a deep red as he paused in his tirade, taking a deep breath. His cheeks puffed out like a blowfish and Jordan knew from experience he was every bit as prickly. He didn't want an explanation from Jordan. All he wanted was for him to play nice, like a good boy, so he could continue collecting his four percent commission.

Well, better luck next time, bro, because Jordan Woods doesn't change for anyone.

Ron leaned back in his chair and scrubbed a hand over his ruddy face. "I mean, disorderly conduct, I can deal with that. But assault and battery charges? What were you thinking?"

Ron paused, waiting. This was the part where he acted like he wanted Jordan to explain himself, but he really didn't. Jordan was a pain in his butt, even if he did make him good money. All Ron wanted was for Jordan to play basketball, keep his mouth shut, his hands to himself, and make his life easier. And, really, that was fine with Jordan because he and Ron wanted the same thing. Jordan didn't want to get booted from the league any more than Ron wanted to see him gone. Basketball may have been his livelihood, but it was more than that. It was his lifeline, the only thing keeping him sane most days.

"Look, I had a bad weekend." Jordan shrugged.

"A bad weekend? A bad..." Ron scoffed. "A bad weekend is getting a scratch on your car, spilling your coffee, or running into your ex. It's not cracking someone's nose open."

"He deserved it."

Ron gaped, and Jordan fought the urge to roll his eyes. Really, he should be used to this by now.

"Please help me to understand, in a way that I can take to our publicist and garner you some sympathy, why you broke someone's nose."

"It's like this. My mom's dirtbag boyfriend gave her a black eye. So I gave him a fist in the face. End of story. Afterward, I was more than a little upset that she wasn't pressing charges, so I had a few drinks and let loose. Can you really blame me?"

"When you have a few drinks and run through the fountains at a very crowded, very public shopping center practically nude, then yes."

"The ladies seemed to enjoy it." Jordan winked, but by the look on Ron's face, he wasn't amused. Straightening, Jordan forced a sober expression. "Listen, I know you want to spin this to the media to work in my favor, but you're not bringing my mom and her life into this. We're not some daytime soap opera, so you'll have to come up with something else. Say it was self-defense, whatever, but no one in the public is to know she's with a woman-beater. You hear?"

Ron stared at him, blinking. "Why do you make my job so hard, Jordan? Why? Enlighten me."

"Because I can. Because you take my money."

"Not enough," Ron muttered. "You do realize that if you allowed us to go public with your mother's story, the *full story* about your childhood, people would feel sorry for you and all you've been through. It would score you some much needed compassion and sympathy. Everyone already knows you grew up in the projects. Let us tell them—"

"I said, no." A bolt of anger zipped up Jordan's spine.

"Fine." Ron shook his head. "I'm getting too old for this crap."

Whatever. Ron's attitude didn't faze Jordan. He was used to it. He may not be happy, but too bad. He'd have to deal. Jordan wouldn't sully his mother's name or bring her into the spotlight just to ease his burden. It was one thing to be the poor kid from Oakland, California, but it was another thing entirely to be the kid who stood by and witnessed his mother go from one abusive relationship to the next.

No, he wouldn't be that guy. He wasn't a spectacle.

He was the Comeback Kid, and that's the way he liked it. He had risen from his impoverished roots to make something of himself and had a reputation for being a game closer—the guy who could score at the last second, earning his team a win.

His mother's life was no one else's business.

Her current boyfriend, Chris, was her fourth abusive relationship, and this weekend was the third time the low-life had beaten her up in the last six months. But Jordan was so close to convincing her to leave him. If his PR people ousted her now, she'd spook. He couldn't risk that. His move to Pittsburgh could be her new lease on life. He just needed to convince her to go with him, and right now, he was closer than ever. The last thing he needed was this getting out right before she made the big decision to finally turn her life around.

Ron tapped his pen on the desk. "We'll pay Mr...." He consulted the paper in front of him. "We'll offer Mr. Greene a settlement to drop the charges and keep quiet. We can potentially manage to get you off the hook, but—"

Jordan slammed a fist on the desk in front of him, cutting him off. "No. We are *not* paying him a dime."

"We don't have a choice."

"So, let me get this straight." The vein pulsed in Jordan's forehead as he continued, "He beats women, and when he finally gets what he has coming to him, he gets paid for being abusive? Is that right?"

"What exactly do you want me to do, Jordan? Let's take a look at your rap sheet over the last few years, shall we?" He glanced at the paper in front of him. "Public intoxication, drug paraphernalia, DUI—"

"You know I'm clean! The drugs weren't mine." Jordan interrupted. They were left in his mother's car, probably from her latest flame, but Ron waved him off and continued reading.

"—disorderly conduct, assault on multiple occasions, and now these fresh charges, *after* you just finished up a twelve-game suspension in the league. You've been suspended too many times to count in the six years you've been playing ball. One more strike and you're out. Do you understand that? It doesn't matter how good you are."

He held his index finger and thumb a hair apart. "You're this close to getting booted. One more altercation. One more criminal charge, or scandal, and no one else will pick you up. I barely got the Pittsburgh Pumas to take you this time around. No one wants you anymore. You're a liability. It was by the skin of my teeth I got you a new contract. Comeback Kid or not, you're going to make yourself disposable real fast."

Jordan chewed the inside of his cheek, biting off the

things he really wanted to say because they would get him nowhere.

You're a liability. Those words stung.

Maybe Ron was right. But it didn't change anything.

Jordan raked a hand through his short, dark hair. His life was spiraling. He knew it. Ron knew it. Everyone in the league knew it. He felt like he was driving a car with no steering and no breaks, on icy roads—reckless and wild and ready to crash at any moment.

Dealing with his mother's situation and the revolving door of crap-relationships had left him angry at the world. Basketball had been his escape growing up. A way to get off the streets. To forget the drugs that surrounded his childhood home. The gangs, the crime, his mother's latest abuser, and the fact he had no father. But somehow, basketball wasn't enough anymore. Where he once found solace in the exertion of playing ball, over the last few years, he found his frustration and anger spilling out into the game —fighting with players, arguing with coaches, even punching a fan, resulting in a twelve-game suspension last year. His name was constantly in the headlines. His latest antics a source of entertainment. He went from the Comeback Kid to the NBA bad boy in a matter of years.

He needed to find a way to grip the wheel of his life and regain control. Just because his mother had a penchant for abusive men, didn't mean he needed to swoop in and solve her problems. He couldn't protect her forever. Not when it was wrecking his career. He was one step away from being without a job.

He knew this, yet...

He bent forward in his chair, clasped his hands over the back of his head, and exhaled a steady stream of air before he straightened and said, "I get it."

"Good. So, we'll take care of Mr. Greene, but I'm going to tell you what you're going to do. It's time you cleaned up your image. Give the league the Comeback Kid again. That young, raw, talented man they recruited six years ago. You're going to get on a plane to Pittsburgh, join the Puma's, and end the season with a bang. And I don't mean the kind with your fist. I want you on your best behavior. You're going to turn your image around."

"Turn my image around? You think everyone will just forget the last few years?" Jordan arched a brow.

"People love a comeback. You're going to add new meaning to your nickname and go from the rebel without a cause, to a boy scout. There are some fine men on that team that you could learn a thing or two from."

Jordan laughed. "You mean like that loser, Dean Kimball? Please." Jordan rolled his eyes. "I saw the rose stunt he pulled on the news with that chick he liked. I'll never be *that* guy, so you can stop dreaming."

Ron pointed at him, his mouth an angry line. "That's

exactly what I expect. I don't care how you change your image, but you better do it, or you can find a new agent to clean up your mess. And here's a tip. No one would be crazy enough to touch you, not with your salary dropping with each trade like it has, and not with the very real possibility you might not get re-signed after this."

Jordan's grin fell. He fisted his hands in his lap, his expression tight. "Fine. Any idea on how I'm to accomplish this miraculous transformation?"

"Join a club, go to church, do some volunteer work, or meet a nice woman and settle down. Or do all of the above, I don't care, but from now on, I expect you to be the model player, on your best behavior. The next headline I want to see better be an uplifting story. You're going to be freaking Mother Teresa incarnate. Are we clear?"

"Crystal." Jordan stood. He was finished. He'd heard enough and had a flight to catch.

He flashed Ron an exaggerated thumbs-up, then headed for the door.

CHAPTER TWO

Maya

T he set crew bustled about the studio. Maya was
giddy as they prepped her for the camera, affixing
her mic to the inside of her pale gray suit jacket.
Someone brushed the stray hair from her eye and pow-
dered her nose.

She wasn't some high-profile national sports journalist, but this was maybe the biggest interview of her career.
Jordan Woods was practically a legend in the NBA. Not

solely known for his skill on the court, but his attitude on and off as well. He was in perpetual hot water with the league, and often, the law. The media, the press, everyone wanted a piece of him, but he never did interviews of this kind, never answered personal questions. The most you got from Jordan was a couple clipped responses at the end of the game, about the game (if you were lucky). Just this winter, Maya had heard he was offered an exorbitant amount to do a special on BEYOND THE LENS—a major pop culture news program—and turned it down.

And now, Maya was about to get more than lucky because he had agreed to this solo interview upon his arrival in Pittsburgh. For free. According to his PR people, he wanted a fresh start with the Puma's.

More like, he was in trouble again and needed to save face, she mused.

Whatever. His loss was her gain. Whether it was a way to assuage the NBA and clear his name or not, this interview was gold.

After the crew stopped fussing with her, Maya checked her makeup and added an extra dusting of powder to her nose, then skimmed her eyes down her body. She looked good—sharp and professional in her pale gray suit and fitted pink shirt.

She flicked a hand over her jet-black chin-length hair, grown out from the pixie cut she had last year. Then she rubbed her glossed lips together as she heard the producer of *Mornings in the Burgh* give her the signal.

It was go-time.

She walked out onto the makeshift set, took a seat in the chair closest to the camera, and stared straight into the lens. When they gave her the cue to begin, she smiled and started, "Good morning, Pittsburgh sports fans. We have some exciting news in the Burgh. In case you haven't heard, the Puma's took a rather controversial and exciting trade for the rookie team. As of yesterday, it was official. NBA Bad Boy, also known as The Comeback Kid, Jordan Woods, will be joining the Puma ranks as of next week. And we have him here with us this morning, ladies and gentlemen, for an exclusive interview. Let's bring him out."

She grinned and turned in the direction Jordan was to emerge. He sauntered out on cue with his eyes fixed on the camera. And when he paused, then turned his gaze on her before sinking into the chair beside her, Maya's heart skipped a beat. Her breath caught.

He had the most gorgeous brown eyes she had ever seen—dark, like freshly brewed coffee. His tanned skin, notably a product of the California sun, glowed under the lights, and his navy-blue suit fit his trim form to perfection. She had seen him on television many times. She had also seen him on the court before, but not up close. Not like this. Right in her face.

He was striking.

Maya moved her eyes from his, shaking off her reaction and the flutter of nerves, reminding herself she was a professional and not a hormone-riddled teenager.

Once seated, she glanced down at her cue cards for support since forming words suddenly seemed daunting. "Welcome to Pittsburgh, Jordan," she said, noting her slightly off-pitch tone.

She started with the typical questions about his move and how he found his first couple days in the new city, then launched into the heart of things. "So, Jordan, I think what everyone really wants to know is, which Jordan will we get at the game next Tuesday? Will we get The Comeback Kid or the Bad Boy?"

"Which one do you want?" He threw her question back at her, grinning.

She shifted in her seat, a chuckle spilling from her lips. "Well, I think I speak for everyone in the city when I say maybe we want a little of both, but we need The Comeback Kid. We're winding down on a mostly losing season, a first for the Puma's since their blazing start in the league three years ago."

Jordan nodded in understanding. "Losing Emmett Hall this year hurt Pittsburgh. But now that I'm here, we'll bounce back." He winked at her, and though she hated herself for it, she felt the heat of that gesture shoot through her body, straight down to her toes.

She cleared her throat, ready to ask…

Wait…what was her next question?

Her heart rate picked up. She racked her brain for something—anything—to ask him.

She opened her mouth, but nothing came out. *Oh. My. Gosh. Speak!*

Just because he was gorgeous didn't mean she had to get tongue-tied.

Remember. Basketball. Games. Dribble. Ball… Oh, this was bad. Then it clicked.

Her smile faltered for only a moment before she recovered and cleared her throat. "You're coming off a twelve-game suspension. Are you ready?" she asked, mentally patting herself on the back.

"More than ready. My palms are itching for a ball."

"How long until you get another suspension? That seems to be your pattern, does it not?"

The question didn't seem to faze him. His lips curled as he said, "It won't happen this time. I'm going to finish out the season with a bang, and then next year, I'll return better than ever. I'll prove the naysayers wrong."

"The naysayers?" she asked.

He nodded. "The ones who say I won't last, that I'll finally get the boot, that I can't stay out of trouble. I'm not going anywhere." His eyes darkened with his tone.

Yeah, right, Maya thought; he'd become a regular boy scout.

She stifled a snort. "So you're turning a new leaf? Changing your image?"

"Something like that."

"Rumor has it you got in trouble again, just this past weekend. Any truth to that?"

Jordan cranked his neck from side to side.

Was he getting angry? Uncomfortable? It made Maya smile in anticipation; her minor snafu forgotten. She was getting a rise out of him.

"I may have had an incident at a water fountain where my clothes went missing, but anything else is untrue. All rumor."

Maya grinned and tilted her head, watching him as she asked, "So the police weren't called on you for assault and battery?"

Irritation flickered in his gaze. He hadn't been prepared for that. No doubt, he thought his PR people had suppressed that story, but Maya did her homework. And having an old friend with connections didn't hurt.

"Nope." His jaw tightened.

She had expected the denial. She couldn't make him talk. Still, a girl had to try.

"Some people are excited about the trade; some are dreading the moment you set foot on Puma-court. What do you want Pittsburgh to know about you?"

He looked directly at the camera. "I'm here to play ball and win games, nothing more. I think you'll find a completely different Jordan Woods come game-day next week. One that's focused, motivated, and takes his anger out on the court and nowhere else."

Maya's gaze sharpened. "I think what people want to know is, what are you so angry about?"

He hesitated, and she noticed his clenched fist. "Everybody has something that sets them off."

"Some more than most," Maya said. "But why does Jordan Woods have such a short fuse, and how do you plan on combatting it?"

"I've never allowed myself to become rooted in one place. I've never invested myself fully in a team since my first year. But it's time that changed. I plan on getting more involved in the community, planting roots, forming ties in Pittsburgh. I'm making a change, and I think it'll show on the court."

Maya nodded. He only half answered her question, but she'd let it slide. "Forming ties to the community? Anything specific you'd like to share?"

"I'm scoping my options. My agent is helping me find a worthy cause. The right charity to get involved in. And I plan on purchasing a house instead of renting. I plan on staying in Pittsburgh long term. This is my home now."

"You still have family back in California. No plans to get back there?"

Something flickered in his eyes, but he quickly squashed it. He was good at hiding.

He shrugged, his face a mask of indifference. "My mom's all I've got, but I'm working on getting her to move out here. Sometimes we all need a change."

Maya sensed a wall go up. He was done, so she backed off the bad-boy questions and wrapped up the interview, discussing his strategy going into the end of the season, and by the time they winded down, Maya's stomach was tangled in knots.

The cameras faded away, and the crew trickled on and off the set, taking equipment down and shifting things for the regular news segment to follow.

Maya sat in the chair, scolding herself for her semi-crappy interview when she noticed for the first time that Jordan hadn't actually left like she'd thought. Instead, he stood a few feet away, hands in pockets, smirk firmly in place, if not looking a little annoyed.

"So, you're the city sports journalist, huh?" he asked.

She stood, wanting to be on solid ground. Face-to-face. Well, or as close to it as she'd come, considering she was vertically challenged. It felt too vulnerable in her chair.

"Yeah, that's me."

His eyes skimmed up and down her body, assessing.

She should be irritated and appalled at how blatantly he checked her out, but all she felt was fire. A knot tightened her chest, sending a punch of attraction straight through her core.

Crap, Maya, it's not like you've never been in the presence of a hot guy before. Get a grip.

But Jordan was more than easy on the eyes—more than a smooth, sharp jaw with a perfect smile and brawn. He was...*magnetic*, and something inside her was pulled to him, which made Jordan Woods dangerous.

Maya clenched her hands into fists at her side, as if the gesture might somehow root herself further into the ground. To save herself from his dark, brooding eyes.

"So, I'll be seeing more of you, then," he said matter of fact.

He was relaxed. The picture of confidence. The exact opposite of how she felt at the moment, which irked her.

She nodded, saying nothing and telling herself it was because she wanted to keep the conversation short and professional. She didn't need, nor did she want, any sort of social relationship with him.

"Well, Maya Hawkins, I'll see you around." He grinned and turned, walking off the set and leaving her to stare after his retreating form.

CHAPTER THREE

Jordan

J ordan pressed his phone to his ear, unable to shake a certain blue-eyed, raven-haired sports reporter from his head. She had nerve; he'd give her that. Despite his public relations team giving her a list of topics she couldn't touch, she went there. But it didn't matter. A little intrigue was always good, and he traversed the choppy waters of her questions smoothly.

When Ron answered, he gave no lead-in and no preamble. "Hey, I'm taking you up on your idea. Find me a charity STAT."

"Hold on a minute, who is this?" Ron asked.

"Hilarious."

"No, I'm serious, because I think this is Jordan Woods, and I think you are actually saying you're taking my advice."

"I thought it was a demand, not advice."

"Good point," Ron conceded.

"Just do it. Find something easy, something fun that'll garner the press you want."

"Will do," Ron answered. "But, you know, you could do this yourself."

"Why should I do it myself when I have you? That's why you make the big bucks, Ron. Help a brother out."

Ron grumbled under his breath while Jordan laughed and hung up.

In reality, Jordan didn't really care about change. Most of the crap he spieled for the interview was nonsense. While it was true he wanted to stay out of trouble, he had no desire to change who he was. People could take him or leave him. He didn't care either way, but something about Maya's doubtful expression got under his skin. She was so sure he was full of crap, which made him want to prove her wrong. Rub it in her face like she rubbed those personal questions in his.

She might be hot, but she'd soon be wrong and hot.

He'd see her on the court; that much was a given. So he'd spend some time helping a charity, volunteering, whatever, and then he'd rub it in her smug face.

Clicking the lock on his car, he slid onto the buttery leather of his cherry red Ferrari. He bought it two years ago when the Lakers clinched the finals and won the Larry O'Brien NBA Championship Trophy. Right around the time his mother dumped her boyfriend and traded him in for Chris.

Jordan started the car and revved the engine. Having a project—something to whittle away the time—was a good idea. With his mother still in California, he had little to occupy his time or his thoughts outside of basketball. Until she accepted his offer for a fresh start, he'd keep himself busy. Maybe it would help him forget the anvil of worry around his neck, constantly threatening to sink him.

When he arrived back to his temporary home at the Residences in Pittsburgh downtown, he showered and ordered room service. It wasn't until he sunk down onto the bed of his giant penthouse suite that his phone rang.

"Jordan," he answered.

"Hey, I found the perfect gig."

Jordan grinned. Soon Maya Hawkins and all the other reporters out there criticizing him would eat crow. "Shoot."

"The Autism Network of Pittsburgh, a regional charity and support group for people with autism."

"Okay," Jordan drawled. He headed to the giant kitchen, gleaming with miles of marble countertops, a giant island, state-of-the-art range, and professional grade ovens.

What a waste, he mused. He'd never use any of it.

"And what will I be doing there?" he asked.

"It's not what you'll be doing there that matters. It's who you'll be doing it with."

Jordan rolled his eyes and grabbed a tub of peanuts from the pantry, cramming a handful into his mouth. "The suspense is killing me."

"Maya Hawkins."

Jordan choked on a nut, hacking into the phone before he desperately grappled at the fridge and found a beer. Cracking it open, he took a long pull then asked, "You mean, the reporter? The chick from this morning?"

"The exact same chick," Ron said, the word rolling awkwardly off his tongue. "She helps out at functions, attends events and meetings. She's there all the time."

"Why?" Jordan scrunched up his face in revulsion. It wasn't that he hated charity, but he couldn't imagine why someone as put together as she was would spend her spare time doing volunteer work. With her looks, her job, and connections, he couldn't imagine she wanted for attention or companionship. Men probably wet themselves at the idea of dating a sports reporter. But not him.

"Get this," Ron said, dragging the answer out, and Jordan had to squeeze the edge of the marble counter to stop from screaming at him to get on with it already. "She has an autistic brother. He's in the group."

Jordan felt the corners of his mouth pull into a smile.

As if reading his thoughts, Ron continued, "It's the perfect charity for you to attach yourself to because it comes with a mouthpiece to the media. The journalist. And not just any charity, but one that means something personal to her."

"Yeah, it's pretty perfect," Jordan said. Maybe proving the smug Maya Hawkins wrong would be easier than he thought. Not only would she hear about it, but she'd get a front-row seat to his "transformation."

"What else do you know about her? She certainly seemed to know a lot about me, things that were supposed to be handled," he said, referring to the assault and battery charges. If she found out that Ron had paid Chris off, Jordan's reputation would be ruined for good. There'd be no coming back.

"She graduated from Duquesne University. Bright girl. Close to her family, which is why she's so involved with her brother. Not much of a social life, unless you count her dating a Puma almost two years ago."

Jordan scrubbed a hand over the stubble on his jaw. "A Puma? Interesting. Who?"

"Dean Kimball."

Jordan guffawed. "The rose guy." Figured. He should've pegged her for the goody-two-shoes type. How completely boring.

"You seem awfully interested in this girl."

Jordan would have to be an idiot not to hear Ron's warning tone.

"I didn't like the questions she asked. I'm just trying to figure out how she knew to ask them."

"She's a reporter. They have their ways, but no one knows we paid that lowlife. Just do your job out there and show up at the next network meeting. It's tomorrow. Don't be antagonizing to her. We need her on our side, Woods, not against us."

"Yeah, sure," he said, sounding only mildly patronizing.

He had no doubt Maya Hawkins would line up to be his ally. And Chris would drop dead of a heart attack next week. If Jordan were only that lucky.

"Call and set everything up," Jordan said. "Text me the time and place, and I'll be there."

He thought of Maya with her laser-sharp eyes, her heart-shaped mouth, and smug smile. If nothing else, at least he could enjoy the view while he was working.

Continue Resisting the Bad Boy
Click HERE

Made in the USA
Middletown, DE
11 August 2021